Outstanding praise for *Lois Lenz, Lesbian Secretary*!

"Unabashedly campy and titillating, [...] tale of 1950s lesbian career girls loose in [...]
—*Publishers Wee[...]*

"Nolan squeezes her kicky premise [...] the pulp in *Lois Lenz, Lesbian Secretary* [...]
—*Entertainment W[...]*

"Monica Nolan's first novel, *Lois Lenz, Lesbian Secretary*, is a delicious contemporary homage to queer pulp novels . . ."
—*Bay Times*

"In her second book, Monica Nolan gives us what we really want—a campy pulp filled with gratuitous lesbian sex, communism, reefer madness and ruthless dictation . . ."—*Curve* magazine

And praise for *The Big Book of Lesbian Horse Stories*!

"Cleverly merging two genres that are a perfect match, but somehow have never met, *The Big Book of Lesbian Horse Stories* is a hilarious cross-breeding of the lesbian pulp novel and the horse-girl fantasia. Authors Alisa Surkis and Monica Nolan clearly know their stuff, sending up a century of girl-loves-horse and girl-loves-girl stories with pitch-perfect language, pacing and plots."
—*Bitch* magazine

"You know how the old adage goes: You can't judge a book by its cover. Well, *The Big Book of Lesbian Horse Stories* is an exception to the rule. The collection's tawdry tales of equine-loving lesbos are as vibrant, juicy, and pulpy as the sexy cover illustration. The stories are wildly entertaining . . . saddle up for this fun ride."
—*Out*

"The book can be loved for what it is—eight vintage stories of ladies, lust and the pretty ponies they love. It's kind of like *Black Beauty* for big girls."—*Portland Mercury*

"If, like me, you have a section of bookshelf devoted entirely to books you purchased solely for the sake of their glorious titles, you will undoubtedly be delighted to add to it the wonderfully named *The Big Book of Lesbian Horse Stories*. You might, too—as I did—actually enjoy the stories. Part of the fun of picking one's way through this book comes not just from anticipating which particular genre the authors will take on next, but also from discovering how they've worked an equine theme into possibly unlikely settings."
—Sarah Waters, *The Erotic Review*

Books by Monica Nolan

THE BIG BOOK OF LESBIAN HORSE STORIES
(with Alisa Surkis)

LOIS LENZ, LESBIAN SECRETARY

BOBBY BLANCHARD, LESBIAN GYM TEACHER

Published by Kensington Publishing Corporation

Bobby Blanchard, Lesbian Gym Teacher

MONICA NOLAN

KENSINGTON BOOKS
www.kensingtonbooks.com

KENSINGTON BOOKS are published by

Kensington Publishing Corp.
119 West 40th Street
New York, NY 10018

All Kensington titles, imprints, and distributed lines are available at special quantity discounts for bulk purchases for sales promotion, premiums, fund-raising, educational, or institutional use.

Special book excerpts or customized printings can also be created to fit specific needs. For details, write or phone the office of the Kensington Special Sales Manager: Attn. Special Sales Department. Kensington Publishing Corp., 119 West 40th Street, New York, NY 10018. Phone: 1-800-221-2647.

Kensington and the K logo Reg. U.S. Pat. & TM Off.

ISBN-13: 978-0-7582-3206-9
ISBN-10: 0-7582-3206-3

First Kensington Trade Paperback Printing: May 2010
10 9 8 7 6 5 4 3 2 1

Printed in the United States of America

For Julie Ann,
who wanted a nice little love story

Bobby Blanchard, Lesbian Gym Teacher

Chapter One

Welcome to Metamora!

The young co-ed slipped her hand into Bobby's and the quick, simple gesture unleashed an avalanche of desire inside Bobby, nearly rocking the older girl off her feet. "Follow me," her new friend whispered, leading Bobby off the hockey field and into the woods. Her hair, the pale blond of buttermilk, gleamed in the dappled light. Bobby could hear the cries of her teammates as they drove the ball toward the goal. She looked down at her gym tunic. Should she go back and finish the game? But her desire was stronger than her sportsmanship, and she followed the younger student deeper into the dark forest.

What was her name? It bothered Bobby that she couldn't remember. The girl stopped suddenly, and pulled Bobby to her. Bobby's senses were swamped with her softness, her sweet perfume. Even as she kissed her hungrily, she noticed that the girl wasn't blond really—her hair was auburn. *Has she always been a redhead?* Bobby wondered, *and I just never noticed?* Her uneasiness grew. "What position do you play?" she asked, but the girl stepped back saying only, "This way."

It was too dark now to see clearly, and Bobby moved

forward carefully. The girl was far ahead, disappearing behind a tree. Bobby took a step, and suddenly the ground gave way beneath her feet. In a split second of sickened shock, she knew she'd lost her footing and had gone off the edge, and now she was plummeting into the void, falling, falling to her certain death.

"Adena!" called a voice. Bobby Blanchard woke with a start, still dizzy from her vivid dream. The afternoon sun slanted through the train window next to her as the Muskrat River Local glided slowly to a stop in front of a tiny brick station.

"All out for Adena," the conductor called again.

Bobby wiped her clammy palms on her tweed skirt and gathered her purse, jacket, and the issue of *Field Hockey Today* she'd fallen asleep over. Darn those nightmares! Would she ever be able to doze off without that dream rising from her subconscious to pounce on her? The doctor at the hospital had told her such recurring nightmares weren't uncommon after an accident like hers. Of course, she had only told him about the falling part, not the way they always started, with a pretty girl whose face she couldn't see. What on earth did *that* mean?

"Let me get that, ma'am." The conductor hastened down the aisle as he saw Bobby reach up to the luggage rack, but she swung her big plaid suitcase down easily. "Never mind." She smiled. Her shoulder hardly twinged now—at least her body had recovered, if her subconscious hadn't.

"This too?" The conductor took down a long, skinny package, wrapped in layers of brown paper and string, and looked at it quizzically. "Some kind of musical instrument?"

"No, it's a hockey stick." Bobby snatched it from him. "For field hockey."

Her lucky stick, a parting gift from Madge, the assistant coach her freshman year. Why, this very stick had scored the winning goal in the 1962 Women's National Field

Hockey Championship just last fall—a record third straight victory for the Elliott College Spitfires. Would it win her success in her new career?

Holding the stick in one hand and the suitcase in her other, Bobby descended from the train, almost tripping in the unaccustomed confines of her narrow skirt. Recovering her balance, she glanced about her as the two other disembarking passengers hurried away.

Tall and rangy, her wavy chestnut hair trimmed short, her face tanned and windburned from years of playing outdoors, the ex–field hockey player looked older than her twenty-three years. Green-gray eyes above high cheekbones, narrowed thoughtfully as she surveyed Adena's main street. A drugstore, a five-and-dime, a movie theater, and a sporting goods store. Quite a change after Bay City! And she wouldn't even be living in the town, but up on the bluff along the river.

Bobby shrugged her shoulders against the too-tight tweed jacket. The doctor had advised rest and quiet—that was one of the reasons she'd taken this job. But how much quiet could she take?

"Miss Blanchard? Roberta Blanchard?"

Bobby turned. A smiling young woman in blue gingham pedal pushers was getting out of a paneled station wagon.

"That's me—but call me Bobby, Bobby with a 'y.'" Bobby went through life correcting the misguided people who insisted on calling her "Bobbi."

The two women shook hands. "Glad to meet you, Bobby. I'm Mona Gilvang, Metamora's housekeeper. We've corresponded."

Gosh! Bobby couldn't help running her eyes over her attractive chauffeur. She certainly hadn't imagined that the businesslike letters signed "Mrs. Gilvang" had been written by someone so young and good-looking. Wisps of dark red hair escaped from the confines of Mona Gilvang's chignon and curled attractively around a heart-shaped face, fresh as any schoolgirl's. Yet her lush, if petite, figure marked her as mature with a capital *M*. Where was Mr. Gilvang? Bobby wondered.

"I'm sorry I'm late," the housekeeper apologized, picking up Bobby's heavy suitcase before Bobby could stop her. She led the way to the station wagon, already crowded with bags and packages. "These last few days before term starts are always *so* frantic."

"Oh, don't worry, Mrs. Gilvang," said Bobby, taking the bag from her and efficiently tucking it between a box of groceries and a coil of garden hose. She slammed the tailgate closed. "I just got off the train." She paused by the passenger door, which had the words "Metamora Academy for Young Ladies" painted on it in black script. *I'm a gym teacher at a girls' boarding school*, she told herself for the tenth time. It still didn't seem real.

"Call me Mona." The housekeeper was already in the driver's seat, and Bobby hastened to slide into the passenger's side. "Excuse the mess," Mona chattered as she started the engine. "We get most things delivered, but some of the staff act as if they're marooned on a desert island, and anyone going to town is regarded as a sort of rescue party." They were driving along Main Street now. The housekeeper drove expertly, speeding a little. "I had to get cream of tartar for the cook, the new Math Mistress wanted a book they'd ordered for her at the Book Nook—I told her next time she should have me order it—that's Bryce Bowles's tennis racket back there, newly restrung, and a certain someone desperately wanted milk of magnesia—I won't say who!" She laughed gaily.

"Oh, there's a new Math Mistress too?" Out of the bewildering stream of chatter, Bobby seized on this reassuring bit of information. She wouldn't be the only newcomer.

"Yes, she arrived Monday," Mona added, as if sensing

Bobby's nervousness. "I know the both of you will feel right at home at Metamora. The staff is *very* friendly."

"Oh, sure," agreed Bobby dubiously. "And I guess you're used to teachers coming and going."

"What do you mean?" Mona swerved a little as she shot Bobby a sharp glance.

"Well—like Miss Fayne," Bobby pointed out. Her predecessor had left her teaching career behind for a June wedding.

"Oh, her." Mona was dismissive. "She was an exception. Our teachers tend to stay on at the Academy. Miss Froelich, our former Math Mistress, is more typical—she died on the job."

"Oh!" said Bobby, startled.

"She was close to retiring anyway," Mona reassured her. "Miss Butler, her replacement, is just out of college, like you. She arrived yesterday. A very striking girl—quite a change from Miss Froelich!"

With one hand on the wheel, Mona fished a cigarette out of her breast pocket. Automatically, Bobby struck a match, one handed, from the supply she always carried. Mona leaned over a little and cupped Bobby's hand in hers while she drew the smoke into her lungs.

"Thanks—I didn't know you athletic types smoked."

"Oh, I don't smoke, I just—just generally carry matches," Bobby stammered. She changed the subject, asking, "And your husband—does he work at Metamora too?"

Mona exhaled a cloud of smoke before she replied, "I'm a widow. My husband died several years ago."

"Gee, that's tough," Bobby murmured. She wondered if this tragedy had forced Mona into employment at Metamora.

"Oh, I've quite recovered from my loss," Mona said blithely. "The merry widow, that's me."

Or was it possible that the pretty housekeeper had her own reasons for choosing the all-female atmosphere of the exclusive school? Bobby had heard about married women who harbored hankerings for female companionship, although she'd never actually known such a creature.

Until lately, the hockey player reminded herself grimly. This past summer it seemed like wedding invitations or engagement announcements arrived almost weekly from the girls Bobby had gotten especially friendly with at Elliott College. Sometimes she got a panicky feeling that the supply of young, nubile girls, which had seemed inexhaustible during her college days when a fresh batch arrived every fall, was inexplicably drying up.

I latched on to Elaine just in time, Bobby mused. The young candy striper she'd met at the hospital this summer was as nubile as any Elliott College frosh.

"Oh dear, I meant to give you a tour of Adena—have you ever been to Adena?" Mona's voice recalled Bobby to the present. They were driving through the outskirts of town, the gabled Victorian houses and modern ranch-style homes rapidly giving way to farmland, fields of ripening corn, the occasional silo. Mona twisted around and glanced back at the disappearing town. "Well, that was Adena. The Bijou changes movies once a week, and the Flame Inn has what it calls a 'ladies' lounge.' It's a nice respite when you've overdosed on adolescent girls. And Bay City is only an hour away by train."

Mona turned left at a deserted crossroads and the road began to climb into the woods. The fields of corn disappeared, and pine trees took their place.

"What are the students like?" Bobby asked. "Any star athletes I should know about?"

"I guess Miss Craybill didn't mention that Metamora girls aren't a very athletic bunch, although maybe that was Miss Fayne's fault. They mostly think of themselves as artistic or literary, and lately spiritualism's been the fad."

"Spiritualism?" Bobby was puzzled.

"Oh, séances, contacting the spirit world, exorcising ghosts, things like that." Mona maneuvered the station wagon up the twisting road as she spoke. The automobile wove its way through a dense forest of gloomy pines that blocked the afternoon sun. *Like the forest in my dream*, Bobby realized, trying to suppress a prickle of irrational fear.

"... And we even had to remove Madame Blavatsky's works from the school library." Mona was still talking about Metamora's fey fad. "I suppose it's inevitable, given the school's location."

"'An idyllic spot overlooking the wide blue waters of the Muskrat River.'" Bobby quoted the school brochure, which she'd studied thoroughly. "It doesn't sound very otherworldly."

Mona smiled. "You're forgetting the Mesquakie Massacre. The girls prefer to think of the campus as a haunted spot, soaked in the blood of innocent settlers, killed by savage Indians back in 1823. Lately they've become quite obsessed by the idea that the campus is cursed, I suppose because—" She broke off and shrugged. "Well, adolescent girls have morbid imaginations and a tendency toward the dramatic. What can you do? We were probably just as bad when we were their age."

"I guess," murmured Bobby politely.

Thinking back on her own high school years, Bobby couldn't remember any morbid tendencies. Basketball, golf, softball, tennis, badminton, baseball, football, pond hockey, swimming, track, and, of course, field hockey; pursuing those activities had kept her too busy for the hobbies of other girls her age. But now she was faced with a whole school full of "average teens," the kind of girl who pined over the latest crooner and spent her allowance on lipsticks instead of a leather baseball mitt. Bobby knew the rules of every game from archery to tetherball and could recite the five points of perfect posture, but what did she really know about adolescent girls? How did a gym teacher go about "molding young minds," as the professor of her Child Development class had put it?

The woods had begun to thin, and the road to level out. Now there were birch trees, with silvery leaves, scattered among the stately pines. The blue sky was visible again. At a fork in the road, a sign pointing left read MESQUAKIE POINT STATE PARK.

"That's where the settlement was." Mona gestured as she turned right. "And undoubtedly where the massacre happened. But it does no good to tell the girls that. Last term Linda Kerwin brought a ouija board back to school after Christmas vacation, and she and her friends worked themselves into a perfect frenzy, convinced they'd made contact with a pioneer girl their own age. Supposedly she told them she'd been tortured and, er, ravished by the Indians. Some of the staff thought Linda needed a psychiatrist, but *I* was mostly impressed that they'd spelled all the gruesome details out, letter by letter! And Miss Otis said Linda had no ability to concentrate!" Mona laughed so infectiously that Bobby joined in.

"What did happen?" she asked.

"Oh, Miss Craybill confiscated the ouija board and Linda lost town privileges for a week. School life is a series of tempests in a teapot. I hope you won't find it too dull."

"I'm sure I won't," Bobby replied. *I'll be too busy figuring out this teaching business*, she thought to herself.

What had Miss Craybill said during their brief interview? "My Games Mistress needs to demonstrate discretion . . . impeccable behavior . . . responsibility as a role model. . . ." The imposing phrases blurred in Bobby's brain.

A final twist in the road brought them in sight of a pair of massive stone pillars. A wrought-iron gate stood open and a black-painted iron arch between the two pillars spelled out the words "Metamora Academy" in elaborate wrought-iron curlicues. The station wagon jounced through the opening.

"Welcome to Metamora!" said Mona Gilvang.

Chapter Two

Miss Watkins Weighs In

"You're telling me to be a gym teacher? At a girls' high school?" Astonishment had snapped Bobby out of her usual lethargy and she was sitting straight up in her blue cotton hospital robe, eyes wide and jaw hanging open.

It was June, three months before Bobby stepped off the train in Adena. June, when the as-yet-unheard-of Miss Fayne was exchanging vows with her fiancé. June, when Bobby was trapped in Bay City General Hospital, plodding her way hopelessly through the round of doctor's appointments, massages, and physical therapy treatments. June, when the sunny weather, the gay cotton dresses the girls wore, the warm smell of mown grass all mocked Bobby as she contemplated the ruins of the dreams she'd dreamed and the plans she'd made. Her accidental fall had shattered them as surely as it had shattered her right humerus.

"You majored in physical education all through college," Miss Watkins pointed out, in that reasonable, encouraging tone that drove Bobby batty.

The June heat made the hospital vocational counselor's

tiny office unbearably stuffy. A fly buzzed in the corner of the narrow window, blindly searching for a way out. *I'm that fly,* Bobby thought, *just as trapped.* A wave of wretchedness washed over her and she slumped back down, wishing in her misery that a giant fly swatter would splat down on her and end her unhappy life. Miss Watkins was waiting for an answer.

"I don't have any talent for teaching," Bobby said. "I only majored in phys ed because, well, it's what you do when you're good at sports."

Hadn't well-meaning Miss Watkins reviewed her record and seen the mediocre parade of Cs that had trailed her through college? Bobby knew she wasn't bright. But it hadn't mattered, so long as she could play field hockey. She'd planned to go pro. The recruiter for the U.S. National Women's Field Hockey Team had as much as promised her a place on the squad. But who wanted a wing with a compound fracture in the right arm?

Miss Watkins was flipping through Bobby's academic records, a little furrow in her brow. "But just last semester you took a special graduate-level seminar—Coaching: Team versus Player." She looked up at Bobby with a smile meant to be encouraging. "And you 'aced' it, as my students used to say."

Even the usually crisp Miss Watkins looked wilted by the heat, Bobby noticed. Her cheeks were flushed pink, and her brown curls clung damply to her temples. She had shed the lime green jacket that matched her sleeveless linen sheath. "Well, Bobby?" she asked, her voice sharp.

Bobby shrugged. "That was a fluke," she said impatiently. Coaching wasn't the same as teaching, didn't this woman know anything? Bobby's eyes wandered to the fly, which had stopped buzzing and was walking in fruitless circles in the upper corner of the glass pane.

Miss Watkins pushed her chair back. "Listen to me, Bobby, you've got to snap out of this fog of despair!" She stood up and lowered the top half of the window a few inches. Using a green punch card, she gently guided the forlorn fly to the edge of the frame. It hovered uncertainly an instant, and then zoomed off into the world beyond. "Believe me—you're not out of the game yet!" She sat back down and pushed the green punch card toward Bobby. "Do you recognize this?"

"No," said Bobby, tearing her eyes away from the fly's flight to freedom to look at the punch card. "What is it?"

"It's the Spindle-Janska Personality Penchant Assessment I administered last week. It's one of the most respected diagnostic tools a career counselor has at her disposal. Do you want to hear the results?" Without waiting for an answer, the vocational counselor opened a folder and began reading. "Subject has discipline and focus in the highest degree. Reductive communication this subject's strong suit. Charisma combined with a strong sense of command make this subject ideal for high-ranking military office, guru, or high school principal."

"That can't be me!" Bobby gasped in disbelief. "I'm just your typical athlete, all brawn, no brains. Are you sure you haven't mixed my test results with someone else's?"

"Bobby, Bobby," chided Miss Watkins, "you've got to lose this insecurity complex you've built up about your brains. Who captained the Spitfires to victory the past two years? Who was voted 'Most Inspirational' by the Midwest Regional Women's Field Hockey League? You earned those honors with more than muscles! Everything in your records shows that you're exceptionally suited to help girls learn new skills!"

Bobby's mind was whirling. "Help girls learn new skills"—that certainly described her love life, but she'd never made the connection between that impulse and the

pedagogy courses she'd barely passed. "But my grades—
my brains—" Bobby struggled to express herself. "A
teacher has to be smart." How she'd sweated over those
lesson plan assignments in Pedagogy II, how lost she'd
felt when the class discussed the pros and cons of module-
based teaching!

"I won't pretend your grades and test scores aren't a
hurdle you'll have to overcome," Miss Watkins admitted.
"They'll be the first thing your future employers see. But
what we counselors are learning is that they're not always a sound indication of future success in a given field.
Quite frankly, I think the real problem is your lack of
confidence."

Bobby sat still, stunned by the vocational counselor's
uncanny perception. She might have fooled her teachers and
her teammates with her breezy bravado, but Miss Watkins
seemed to see straight through the facade, through to the
Bobby who feared that people would discover the depths
of her dumbness, that without a position in professional
field hockey, she would end up another sports hero has-
been, handing out towels at the YMCA, cooking beans
over a hot plate in some residential hotel.

"As it happens," Miss Watkins was continuing, as she
riffled through the pile of folders on her desk, "I know a
school in need of a physical education instructor, and I
think my recommendation and your Elliott College degree
will counterbalance those Cs you're so concerned about.
Here." She pushed a brochure at Bobby. Bobby picked it
up, reading the words "We Mold Character" over a picture of a green square of lawn surrounded by gothic gray
stone buildings.

"It's called the Metamora Academy," Miss Watkins continued. "It's a small school, rather exclusive. I think you'll
do well there."

Bobby flipped through the brochure, skimming the descriptions of the "highly trained staff" and "unique educational aids." She tried to picture herself leading a bevy of exclusive girls through a module on kinetics. Was she really capable of such a thing?

"Shall I give the Headmistress a call?" Without waiting for Bobby's answer, Miss Watkins picked up the phone and dialed.

Now, three months later, as Bobby leaned on the windowsill of her new home, the picture from the brochure had come to life. Before her lay the quiet green quadrangle, surrounded by gothic gray stone buildings, crisscrossed with flagstone pathways. It was a tranquil scene. The only movement came from a tall, thin girl in a gray skirt and blazer with red piping—the Metamora uniform. She crossed the square of grass, paused a moment by a white column that poked up from a bed of purple flowers at the far end, before turning left and leaving Bobby's view. Then the place was as quiet and still again as a monastery.

Or a nunnery would be more accurate, Bobby reflected, turning back to her bed, piled high with gym tunics and jerseys. She plucked her Spitfires pennant out from under her old Spitfires uniform and, crossing to the sitting room that completed her two-room suite, she carefully tacked it up above the mantelpiece.

Maybe Miss Watkins was right and she had a gift for teaching. Yet as Bobby unpacked, she couldn't help wondering if this pedagogical opportunity had come too late. Ever since the accident, she felt changed, in some fundamental way. Before her fall, she could always count on her body if not her brains. But now . . .

It wasn't just her nightmares, disturbing as they were. The dizziness and the irrational fear of falling had migrated from her dreams to her waking life. Lately, even a steep staircase could leave her gasping and nauseated. She'd managed to conceal her weakness so far, but what if the students saw her in one of her bad spells? How would she maintain her authority?

Closing her eyes she made herself remember the accident—the shadowy pool—the rippling reflections of the water on the wall—the shrieks of tipsy laughter. She felt again the wet grittiness of the diving board under her damp feet, and the slow-motion sensation of her feet slipping out from under her, her calf banging on the diving board's edge as she fell—

Bobby opened her eyes with a gasp, swaying dizzily, and grabbed the mantel for balance. It was hopeless. She'd thought maybe she could harden herself against the fear, exercise her willpower the way she'd exercise a weak muscle. But she only made herself dizzy and sick. She'd just have to avoid heights until this queer feeling went away.

Bobby returned to her unpacking. Fortunately, her suite of rooms in Cornwall, the dormitory for the third form, was safely on the first floor, right by the entrance. This was so she could monitor the girls, Mona had explained. Her new duties included enforcing lights-out, censoring reading material, doling out prescribed medications, and confiscating unauthorized snacks. Mona had given her a handbook, with a daunting list of dormitory dos and donts.

Bobby was already having trouble remembering the odd names for each class. The students weren't called freshman and sophomores, etc, like in most high schools. At Metamora they were third formers, fourth formers, etc. Mona had written it all down for Bobby:

Third Form = Freshmen
Fourth Form = Sophomores
Fifth Form = Juniors
Sixth Form = Seniors

A big part of the job, Mona had emphasized, was "helping the third formers acclimate themselves to boarding school life." Would Bobby be able to buck up a homesick new student, or console a girl who'd gotten the Curse for the first time?

Even if she wasn't the housemother type, she did know games, physiology, kinetics, even some of the more obscure branches of ethnic dance, Bobby reminded herself as she unwrapped her lucky stick and swung it experimentally. For a moment she pretended she was back on the field with the rest of the Spitfires, in the final quarter of the game against the Bayard Blackhawks. Block that pass! Send it to Chick! Run up to position! Swing for the goal!

The heavy clunk of her 1962 Nationals trophy falling on the floor pulled Bobby abruptly from her daydream. Swinging her stick at imaginary balls, she'd only succeeded in knocking the statuette off its perch on her desk.

Bobby started guiltily at a knock on the door. Was it Mona, come to check on her? Or maybe the Headmistress, that Miss Craybill who had interviewed her in Bay City?

But when Bobby opened the door, it was neither. A tall, willowy brunette leaned in the doorway, appraising the young phys ed teacher through half-closed eyes.

Chapter Three

Sherry in the Faculty Lounge

"Hello," she said in a voice that had been polished by whiskey and cigarettes. "I'm Laura Burnham—Metamora's Art Mistress."

"I'm—"

"Bobby Blanchard, our new Games Mistress, I know." Laura uncoiled herself from the doorway and slid sinuously into the room. "Mind if I come in?"

"Please," Bobby said, unable to take her eyes off the brunette bombshell.

It wasn't just her va-va-voom figure that made the Art Mistress look as out of place in the Metamora dorm room as an orchid in an alpine meadow. Her thick brown hair was piled untidily on her head and her eyes outlined with kohl. Heavy gold hoops swung from her ears, and she wore a red-checked dress with tiny puffed sleeves. As she bent over to pick up the field hockey trophy Bobby had knocked to the floor, one sleeve slid off her shoulder, giving Bobby a tantalizing glimpse of the Art Mistress's cleavage.

"I've come to collect you for sherry hour in the faculty lounge. Mona sent me—although I'm not really the welcome-wagon type."

Bobby wasn't complaining. "Sherry hour," she said hopefully. "Does that mean . . . ?"

"Just sherry." Laura dashed Bobby's hopes for an ice-cold beer. The Art Mistress set the trophy on the bureau after reading the plaque and looked around the room at Bobby's belongings with a kind of restless curiosity. "Miss Craybill comes from fine old teetotaling stock. Her aunt smashed bottles with Carrie Nation, or maybe she just opened the old girl's mail. Anyway, what it boils down to is no hard liquor for us. So we lap up our sherry and pretend we like it."

"Well, if that's what they're pouring, lead me to it," Bobby said, trying to be agreeable. "I'm looking forward to meeting the other teachers."

They walked out Cornwall's front door into the sunny quadrangle. Laura pointed out buildings and classrooms in a desultory fashion. "The dorm next to yours is Manchester, where the fourth formers live. Over in Suffolk and Rutland we get the fifth and sixth formers. Essex is classrooms, with faculty quarters on the top floor."

Manchester, Suffolk, thought Bobby. There was something familiar about those names. Aloud she asked, "The building names, are they—" and Laura finished, "Named after the counties of England, yes. Metamora prides itself on carrying out the public-school tradition of the motherland."

Bobby gulped. She'd been about to ask if they were famous Metamora alumnae. Darn her ignorance!

Laura led the way across the quadrangle, following the looping gravel walk. "The faculty lounge is there, in Kent." Laura pointed at a kind of medieval castle covered in ivy that stood at the east end of the quadrangle. "Mona lives in Devon, the little annex to Kent, next to Dorset. The dining hall is in Dorset. Miss Craybill has an apartment on the third floor of Kent. Miss Froelich lived there too—until this spring, of course." She glanced at Bobby. "You've heard about Miss Froelich?"

"The math teacher? Mona told me she died last semester." Bobby was craning her neck back to look up at the round tower, complete with slits for archers and a crenelated battlement, that rose from one corner of Kent. "Can you go up to the top of that tower?" Perhaps she could train herself to overcome her fear, a flight of steps at a time. But when she looked back at Laura, the other woman was staring at Bobby with an expression of shocked disdain.

"Wouldn't that be a tad morbid?" she asked acidly. "Climb it if you want to—I'm going to have my sherry with the others." Before Bobby could reply, she turned on her heel and stalked up the steps to the medieval front doors.

Is that artistic temperament? Bobby wondered. She followed in the footsteps of the moody Art Mistress, pausing to look at the white pedestal she'd seen from her window, which stood to one side of the steps, just below the tower. On closer examination it proved to be an old-fashioned sundial, worn and mossy, planted in a bed of pansies and bleeding hearts. The words *"tempus fugit"* were engraved around the edges.

What's that mean? Bobby puzzled over the foreign phrase before moving on.

She climbed the steps to the double doors, all heavy wood and oversized wrought-iron hinges, and tugged it open. The capricious Art Mistress was nowhere in sight, but Bobby could hear a distant hum of conversation. She followed the sound down the cool, dim corridor to another medieval door, this time with a brass plate that said FACULTY LOUNGE. Pulling it open, she wondered how the sherry was holding out.

The faculty lounge was a spacious room with a vaulted

barrel ceiling, like the dining hall of some ascetic order. The walls were paneled halfway up with dark wood, and a hoop-shaped iron chandelier hung at either end. The windows, thickly covered with ivy, let in a greenish light, giving the people grouped around the cavernous fireplace at the far end of the room the air of fish in an aquarium. Bobby went hesitantly toward them and was relieved when Mona swam forward to greet her.

"There you are! I was afraid you'd gotten lost." Mona had replaced her capris and blouse with a gaily striped dress and a matching bolero jacket. Bobby wondered if she ought to have changed out of her drip-dry short-sleeved blouse and navy slacks.

Darn, I knew I needed more teacher-type clothes, she scolded herself as she told Mona, "I'm sorry if I'm late."

"Where's Laura? I sent her to show you the way."

"She showed me as far as the building," said Bobby diplomatically.

"That Laura! Well, I'm glad you found us. I'll get you a glass of sherry." Mona bustled away leaving Bobby standing next to the teacher Mona had been talking to, a hook-nosed woman, her black hair streaked with silver.

"I'm Bobby Blanchard, the new Games Mistress," Bobby introduced herself.

"Concetta Rasphigi. Chemistry." The older woman studied Bobby for a moment with cold, dark eyes, and then her gaze wandered away to rest on some point of interest above Bobby's head. She wore an unpressed, sacklike dress of some heavy black material.

Unable to think of anything else to say, Bobby stole a glance at the assembled company. As far as she could see, Metamora's teachers were all women, all talking animatedly, most of them wreathed in cigarette smoke. Bits of conversation drifted over from a group of Bobby's new colleagues : "Greece was an extravagance, but as Goethe said, '*Die beste Bildung findet ein gescheiter Mensch auf Reisen!*'" "I got quite an education myself this summer. When the kids talked about a rumble, I thought, 'Well, it's all part of the continuum of experience.'" "What you should have done is sicced Munty on them as their sub-prefect!" The trio of teachers burst into laughter.

It all sounded like gibberish to Bobby, even the parts in English.

"Here you are!" Mona handed her a small glass of sherry with a radiant smile. Bobby took a sip. It tasted like cough medicine.

"I'll introduce you around, shall I?" Mona gave Bobby's arm a little squeeze, whether of encouragement or to assess the gym teacher's biceps, Bobby wasn't sure. "This is Concetta Rasphigi, Chemistry Mistress extraordinaire!"

"We've met." Miss Rasphigi's expression did not change.

"You must have really made an impression on Connie," Mona whispered as she led Bobby toward the three women Bobby had been eavesdropping on. "It usually takes her a while to warm up to strangers. A brilliant woman, really brilliant, but she lives in a world of her own. Ladies, allow me to introduce our new Games Mistress, Bobby Blanchard. Bobby, I'd like you to meet Serena Rapp, our German Mistress, Alice Bjorklund, who teaches English, and Hoppy Fiske, Mistress of Current Events. Watch out Hoppy doesn't draft you for one of her causes!"

"Shame on you, Mona!" The Current Events Mistress was as brisk and bright eyed as a squirrel. She waggled a playful finger at Mona before asking Bobby eagerly, "Are you registered to vote?"

"I—I think so," Bobby stammered.

"Have you signed a petition in support of the Russell-Einstein Manifesto?"

"*Genug!*" interrupted the strapping German Mistress, tapping the ash off her gold-tipped cigarette. "*Willkommen!* Welcome to Metamora, my little Games Mistress!"

"Thank you," murmured Bobby. It was the first time in years she'd been called little, but it was true, the German Mistress topped her by several inches. She was like a . . . What did they call them? Not a Viking, but it started with a *V. Think, Bobby!* Bobby commanded herself. But before the word could come, Miss Rapp was asking her, "Where did you teach before? Wherever it was, I can promise you, Metamora will be a million times better!"

"This is my first teaching position." To her dismay, Bobby felt herself blushing.

"Is Bobby short for Roberta?" asked the English Mistress in a gentle voice. She was rather dowdy and unathletic looking, but Bobby was grateful for a question she could answer.

"Yes, Bobby with a—" but Bobby's explanation was cut short. A thin, older woman with gray hair cropped short poked her head into their circle. "Have any of you seen Madame Melville?" she asked urgently.

"Bunny, this is Bobby Blanchard, our new Games Mistress," Mona said soothingly as she patted the newcomer's arm. "Belinda Otis, our Latin Mistress, and Miss Craybill's right-hand man!" Miss Otis gave Bobby a distracted nod.

"What do you want with Yvette?" boomed the German Mistress. "You know she never comes to these things!"

"But she promised me . . ."

Mona led Bobby away before she could find out what Yvette had promised Bunny. They stopped by a very old woman sitting in an armchair. Her eyes were closed, and her hair, lit by a shaft of light, was snow white.

"That's Gussie Gunderson, our Greek Mistress," whispered Mona. "She graduated from Metamora in 1904.

We won't wake her." The two women stood and looked at the sleeping Greek Mistress respectfully before moving on.

"Bryce, Ole, I'd like you to meet Bobby Blanchard, our new Games Mistress." Bobby was struck by the contrast between the two men who stood up politely from the Victorian love seat. Bryce was a short, plump man who wore his hair rather long and sported a sky blue tie, with white and yellow flowers. Ole's tanned, deeply grooved face and the swelling biceps that strained the fabric of his short-sleeved shirt spoke of an active outdoor life.

"How do you do," the two men chorused.

"Bryce Bowles is our Biology Master—"

"But I prefer botany," the teacher interrupted, beaming.

"—And Olaf Amundsen is Metamora's groundskeeper." Mona added in an undertone, "The Amundsen family has kept the grounds since Metamora was founded."

"Let me know if you want any changes to the athletic field, Miss Blanchard," Olaf told her.

"Thank you," said Bobby gratefully. "Call me Bobby." It was restful to find herself talking about something she knew. "How often do you chalk—"

"Well, if it isn't the other members of Metamora's Men's Club!" Bobby's question was interrupted by a man with horn-rimmed glasses, a pipe clenched between his teeth, and a shock of bushy brown hair. Laura Burnham, the Art Mistress, drifted along in his wake. "Howsa fella?"

"Hello, Ken," said Bryce Bowles politely. Ole Amundsen said nothing.

"Bobby, I'd like you to meet Ken Burnham, our History Master. You've met his wife, Laura, of course. Bad Laura, leaving Bobby to wander the campus all alone! Bobby Blanchard, our new Games Mistress."

It had never occurred to Bobby that the Art Mistress was married—and Ken Burnham made it seem even more unlikely.

"Welcome, Bobbi—may I call you Bobbi?" Ken shook Bobby's hand vigorously. "Welcome to Metamora! Laura and I are back for our fourth year and we just think it's a great old school—don't we, honeybun?"

"Certainly, darling," said Laura with a smile that showed all her teeth. Bobby thought that no one had ever looked less like a honeybun. "It's Bobby with a 'y,'" she corrected the History Master.

"My apologies! Are you interested in mounds, by any chance?" Ken asked her.

"Mounds?" Bobby repeated, her eyes wandering to Laura. The Biology Master and groundskeeper had slipped away.

"Indian burial mounds. This part of the country's full of 'em!"

"Beware, Bobby, Ken has a deep passion for tribal history!" Mona trilled a little laugh. "Oh, Enid!" She pulled a dark-haired woman into the group. "I'd like you to meet our new Games Mistress. Bobby Blanchard, Enid Butler, our new Math Mistress."

"How do you do?" said Enid, turning her head to expel a lungful of smoke. She wore black cat's-eye glasses and her dark hair was the color of polished ebony. Her bangs bisected her pale forehead in a precise line and she wore a severely simple brown dress.

So this was the new Math Mistress! "It's nice to meet another rookie," said Bobby enthusiastically.

"I'm not precisely a 'rookie.' I've taught summer session at the Friendship School in Bay City the past two years," Enid corrected her coolly.

"Oh!" *I'm being too sensitive,* Bobby told herself. *She didn't mean to snub me.* "Well, I'm an absolute beginner, except for some assistant coaching in college. Truthfully, I'm feeling a little nervous about Tuesday." Tuesday was the first day of classes.

"You'll be fine," said Ken heartily, with a wave of his pipe. Did he ever light it? Bobby wondered. Perhaps Miss Craybill frowned on pipe smoking as well as drinking. "Just think of the Iroquois prisoners, forced to run the gauntlet!"

"And when you teach something as basic as gym, you can always tell them to do laps when you run out of material," Enid added. "That's what my high school gym teacher used to do."

"It's not—there's much more involved than laps." Bobby was shaken. *Is this girl deliberately insulting me?* "If you graduated from high school thinking that's all there was to gym, you certainly must have gotten a bum specimen of a physical education instructor!"

"I didn't mind," Enid assured her. "I'd work on proofs for geometry in my head as I jogged."

"You know, the Menominee exported wild rice and must have had some system of mathematical accounting," Ken began, and Enid turned to him politely.

As Ken droned on, Bobby noticed that Laura had disappeared again, and that even Mona's bright smile of interest was becoming fixed. Covertly, she looked around the room. Maybe she didn't need to worry about purchasing more feminine clothing. Miss Rapp was wearing tailored scarlet slacks, which emphasized her generous hips. *Valkyrie*—that was the word. Hoppy Fiske—laughing now with Bryce Bowles—had paired a pale blue sweater set with a wrinkled fiesta skirt. Bryce's golf pants were as flamboyant as his tie, while Miss Otis, Bobby realized, was clad in the Metamora school uniform: charcoal gray skirt with red piping, white blouse with red tie. She was deep in conversation with Miss Craybill, the Headmistress who'd interviewed Bobby in Bay City. When Ken paused for breath, Bobby suggested to Mona, "Maybe I should go say hello to Miss Craybill."

"Excellent idea," Mona cried, coming to life instantly, and they made their escape, leaving only the irritating Enid to the minutiae of Menominee mathematics.

"Isn't Enid stunning?" Was that a knowing nudge the housekeeper gave Bobby? "And she's brilliant, really brilliant! One of the up-and-coming math minds, her advisor told Miss Craybill."

Bobby imagined Mona describing her to other teachers as a brilliant physical education instructor.

"Miss Craybill!" caroled Mona, interrupting the headmistress's conversation with Miss Otis. "Here's Bobby Blanchard, at last!"

Miss Craybill took Bobby's hand in both of hers. "Welcome, Miss Blanchard, welcome." She was a small woman, her pepper-and-salt hair in an old-fashioned bun. When they had first met she had reminded Bobby of one of those plump little birds that cocks its head and looks at you with bright eyes. Now, however, her gaze wandered as she asked, "Your rooms are comfortable? I'm so glad. And the gymnasium? Of course you haven't had time to visit our physical education facilities yet. Not to worry. Mona's given you the keys?"

"Not yet, but I will, Miss Craybill," Mona answered for her. She added to Bobby, "Maybe it will soothe your jitters to look at Miss Fayne's records from last year."

"Jitters?" Miss Craybill's eyes stopped roving the room distractedly and focused fully on the young Games Mistress for the first time. "Now, you're not to feel nervous! Not in the least. I trust Miss Watkins's recommendation implicitly. Implicitly."

"Oh, I'm not really that worried," Bobby was embarrassed. "I've done some work over the summer, and I came up with some lesson plans I think will be real—corkers!" She fished the Anglicism out of her memory triumphantly.

"Excellent, excellent!"

"One is on timekeeping in history." Bobby warmed to her subject. She'd show Miss Craybill she could be as intellectual as the rest of the faculty. "First I'd invite"— That was something she'd learned in her pedagogy class, you were never supposed to tell the student to do something, you were supposed to "invite" him. It seemed silly to Bobby, because if the student was in class and you were the teacher, it wasn't like he could refuse your invitation. But she used the word in her lesson plans religiously—"I'd invite the students to imagine what life was like before stopwatches were invented. How would you time a race? How would you tell when it was halftime? For example, hourglasses. I guess they were accurate, but how would you stop and start them? And then imagine even further back, when people used sundials." Someone gasped, but Bobby was too involved to notice who or wonder why. "Would it even be possible to use a sundial to organize, say, a field hockey game?

"Then I'd move to the practical module." Bobby was full of enthusiasm now. "Maybe this is a little unorthodox, but I noticed you have a sundial out there in the quadrangle, and it might be fun to take the class out there, kind of like a . . ." Bobby noticed suddenly that the chatter in the room had died away and everyone was looking at Miss Craybill and her in consternation. "A little field trip," Bobby wound up lamely.

Miss Otis wore an expression of helpless horror and Miss Craybill—she no longer looked like a little bird, but a sick woman. Her eyes were not quite focused in her bloodless face, and her hand was to her chest, as if she had difficulty breathing. "I feel unwell," she said. The housekeeper sprang to Miss Craybill's side and supported her as she stumbled unsteadily out of the room.

As the flabbergasted gym teacher wondered what was so terrible about timekeeping, Miss Otis yanked her into the shadow of one of the granite gargoyles that flanked the fireplace. "Didn't Mona *explain?*" she hissed.

The murmur of conversation had begun again in the rest of the faculty lounge. "Explain what?" said Bobby, bewildered.

"About Miss Froelich!"

"She said she died, that's all."

"Oh, my dear." Miss Otis blew her breath out in exasperation. "Nerissa Froelich fell from Kent Tower this past June. She landed next to the sundial, and that's where Miss Craybill found her—dead."

Chapter Four

A Picnic with Elaine

The afternoon sun beat down on the still campus as Bobby emerged from Cornwall and walked swiftly down the road to the big stone gates. No one else seemed to be stirring and that suited her fine; she didn't want to answer any questions about where she was going.

At the gate she leaned against the cool gray pillar, shaded by a big pine tree, and ran her fingers through her hair. She glanced at her wristwatch. Elaine had said 3:30.

A cold beer in a dim bar with Elaine looking adoringly across the table at her, that's what Bobby needed. And then later they'd go back to the Ellman mansion—of course, Elaine would drop Bobby off first on a deserted stretch of Glen Valley Road, so she could sneak around the back way and they wouldn't be seen together. But except for the sneaking around part, it would be almost like that poem Elaine had recited when they'd first strolled on the green lawn in front of the hospital, about thou and I and a jug of wine or something. Bobby couldn't remember the exact words. But she remembered Elaine wearing her candy striper uniform and reciting it, looking like a younger Nina Foch, a slender brunette with a husky voice.

The smooth purr of Elaine's little blue Triumph announced her arrival. Bobby slid into the passenger seat. "Hi, honey," she said, leaning over for a kiss. But Elaine was already wrestling the car into a narrow U-turn, pointing it back toward Adena. "Not here," she said instantly.

"Afraid the squirrels will tell?" Bobby couldn't help asking.

"Don't sulk." Elaine glanced over at the disappointed gym teacher and demanded, "What on earth are you wearing a skirt for?"

Bobby looked down at her cotton skirt, then back at Elaine. "Aren't we going to the Flame Inn?"

Elaine shifted gears impatiently. "Bobby, you know I can't afford to be seen with you in a place like that."

"Who's going to notice? Who's going to care if two girlfriends have a quiet drink together?"

It was an argument they'd had before and Bobby knew how it would play out, like a scene in a movie she'd watched too many times.

"A girl in my position gets gossiped about," said Elaine on cue. "And we don't look like we do our nails together."

Elaine was picky about appearances, and it was hard to predict what would please her. Bobby's penchant for pants in public always made Elaine uneasy. But when Bobby was forced to forgo her favorite dungarees for a skirt, Elaine complained she "didn't look like herself."

"That's why I wore the darned skirt," Bobby argued halfheartedly. "And who's going to know you in a hick town like Adena anyway?"

Elaine arched an eyebrow. "Didn't you notice the Ellman Cycle store on the corner of Main and Mesquakie? It's one of the top-selling stores in this part of the state. The manager sat at our table at the annual sales dinner. He's been to our house!"

Bobby was silenced. That was the drawback of being with a girl like Elaine Ellman, daughter of Eddie Ellman, granddaughter of Erwin Ellman, the founder of Ellman's Bicycles. Ellman bicycles were everywhere. And Elaine was convinced every salesman was reporting her activities back to her overprotective father.

"So where are we going?"

"I thought we'd have a picnic at Mesquakie Point."

"A picnic," Bobby repeated.

"Well, where are we supposed to go?" Elaine blew up. "You're the one who had to take this crazy job out in the sticks! Games Mistress!"

Bobby held her tongue as Elaine turned right onto Mesquakie Point Road. Clearly the young candy striper was in one of her irritable moods, when the littlest thing was liable to set her off. Bobby reminded herself of the pressure Elaine was under—her candy-striping duties kept her on the go three afternoons a week, and innumerable social obligations claimed the rest of her time. It was no wonder she was out of sorts.

"Take that left up ahead," Bobby suggested after they'd driven a few minutes in silence.

"Why? The picnic grounds are this way."

"Ole Amundsen, Metamora's groundskeeper, told me this road goes all the way to the point and no one ever uses it. He says there's better spots here than the public picnic grounds. It'll be nice and—private."

"Oh, you! You only have one thing on your mind." But Elaine made the turn and Bobby knew she wasn't really annoyed. At the hospital, Elaine had always been ready to duck into an empty occupational therapy room for some heavy petting.

Several minutes later the Triumph bumped off the road and stopped between two majestic firs. Bobby lifted the picnic basket from the trunk and carried it through a grove of younger trees and brush to the clearing while Elaine followed with a heavy blanket. There was no sound but the wind in the trees and, faint in the distance, the rushing water of the Muskrat River rapids. Bobby set down the picnic basket and helped Elaine spread the blanket. She noticed a faint indentation in the ground, and a ragged line of stones. "Look." She kicked one of the stones, half buried in the earth. "It's an old foundation stone. We're picnicking in someone's front yard."

"Whose? This has been a state park forever."

"One of the massacred settlers, probably. Don't you know the state park is here because of the massacre?"

"I'd forgotten." Elaine shivered. "It gives me the willies. Should we look for someplace else?"

"We're fine here," said Bobby, dropping to the blanket and lying back. She reached up her hand. "I'll chase any ghosts away."

Elaine took her hand and Bobby felt instantly the almost electric charge between them, a current that pulled its power from the sneaking around, their little spats, the famous Ellman name, the innocent candy-striper uniform, even Bobby's new status as a teacher. She drew Elaine down next to her on the striped blanket. Elaine lay back, her eyes half closed as Bobby pulled Elaine's blouse out of the waistband of her skirt so she could slide one hand underneath while she undid the buttons with her other hand. Elaine lay passively, a little smile on her lips, doing nothing except arching her back slightly, so Bobby could reach underneath her and undo the catch of her lacy white brassiere.

"Better?" murmured Bobby in her ear as she began caressing the supine girl.

"Mmm . . ." Elaine was never much for words in situations like this. Or action. But that suited Bobby fine. Like Coach Mabel always used to say, "When you get control of the ball, keep control of the ball. Don't pass it to a player who's unprepared."

Elaine moaned and rocked her hips. She pulled Bobby's head down, and Bobby lost track of her own metaphor in the hot delight that was Elaine's kiss. Was Elaine the ball or the other player? Was she defense or offense? Who had possession of the ball now, at this particular moment in time, when Elaine's thigh was grinding into Bobby's crotch and Bobby had her hand up Elaine's skirt and their lips were fused together? Who was winning?

Later, they both lay on the blanket, Elaine's head pillowed on Bobby's shoulder. They'd consumed the picnic Elaine had brought, as ravenous for the food as they'd been for each other. Bobby had her hand curled around the last beer. Elaine lit a cigarette, and Bobby watched the haze of blue-gray smoke slowly rise and dissipate in the clear country air. "Want one?" Elaine asked.

"I'm in training," Bobby replied automatically.

Elaine turned to look at Bobby, propping her head on her hand. Her large brown eyes, fringed with dark lashes, were extraordinarily beautiful, and Bobby wanted to dive into them and die a delicious death by drowning. She leaned forward, intending to kiss the freckled tip of Elaine's nose, but the other girl blocked her, taking a drag on her cigarette.

"In training for what?" Elaine asked. "You're not on a field hockey team anymore. You're not going pro, like you planned."

The words sounded harsh, issuing from those velvety red lips. Bobby leaned back and looked at the sky. "No, I'm not on a team anymore." Not on a team. Not a right wing. Not going out with the rest of the girls for early-morning sprints and drills. On her own. "But I'm a physical education instructor now—"

"Gym teacher!" Elaine hooted. "I still can't believe Metamora hired you!"

"What do you mean? Why not?"

"Metamora . . . Well, it's just not you, Bobby. It has a reputation. Famous women have gone to Metamora— like Mamie McArdle, the columnist, Harriet Hurd, the diplomat, and Vivian Mercer-Mayer, the socially prominent heiress. Metamora's caviar on toast points, and you, you're more pork and beans." She added hastily, "Don't get me wrong, darling, you know I love pork and beans."

Bobby didn't mind the comparison. She liked pork and beans too. But she was curious about Elaine's sudden expertise. "How do you know so much about Metamora?"

"Elsie Cooper went there," said Elaine as if this explained everything. Sometimes she forgot that she'd never introduced Bobby to anyone in her social circle. "Actually, she almost had a nervous breakdown when she was rejected by Metamora's chapter of the Daughters of the American Pioneers. You know," she said as Bobby looked at her blankly. "That high school society. The chapter at Metamora is supposed to be terribly exclusive."

"Well, the teachers aren't exclusive. They're all nice and friendly." Bobby made a mental reservation in the case of Enid Butler. "Besides, Miss Watkins said—"

"Oh, those silly tests." Elaine dismissed the vocational counselor with a wave of her hand. "Are you honestly going to turn yourself into a gym teacher because a punch card tells you to?"

"Well, what do you think I should do?" Bobby asked weakly.

"I think you should become a golf pro at the Glen Valley Country Club," said Elaine decisively.

"A golf pro," Bobby repeated thoughtfully. In some ways the idea was tempting—at the country club, no one would expect her to be intellectual. And maybe it would be nice to finally meet some of Elaine's social circle. Bobby was tired of her teammates calling her "Back-alley Bobby."

"Of course, we'd have to pretend not to know each other. Do you think you could remember to call me Miss Ellman, just at first?" Elaine dipped her head and kissed Bobby swiftly, flicking her tongue teasingly against Bobby's. "Just think, I could improve my golf game and see you at the same time! Wouldn't that be wonderful?"

"Sure," Bobby murmured as Elaine threw her leg over Bobby's. Bobby slid her hand over the curve of Elaine's hip, and Elaine kissed her with increasing passion

A branch cracked in the stillness and Elaine sat up suddenly, still astride Bobby. "What was that?"

"Nothing," said Bobby, her hands squeezing Elaine's rounded bottom. "A squirrel or a bear or something." As Elaine continued to look around nervously, she couldn't help adding, "I don't think it's your father, or even the manager of Adena's Ellman Cycle shop."

"That's not funny," Elaine bristled. She got to her feet and straightened her skirt. "It's getting late. We should go."

Bobby didn't argue. The golden glow of twilight was dimming, and the cares and worries of her new job flooded back in. The bulk of students would arrive on Monday and her lesson plans were still in a jumble. Elaine's stories about Metamora's caviar-eating girls had done nothing to quiet the butterflies in her stomach.

"You'll think about the golf pro position, won't you?" said Elaine as they packed the picnic things.

"Sure, sure." Bobby didn't want to quarrel with the cycle heiress—or have to admit that her golf game wasn't what it should be.

Elaine carefully backed the roadster onto the rutted side road and they bounced their way back to the paved road.

"Did you see that?" Bobby exclaimed just as they reached the main road.

"What?" The little Triumph picked up speed.

"Nothing," said Bobby. She thought she'd seen a shadowy figure, bicycling through the trees. But that was ridiculous. It must have been some sort of optical illusion. There was no sense in alarming Elaine.

It was probably a deer, she told herself.

Chapter Five
Peasant Dance

Bobby blew her whistle and the fourth formers stopped shambling through the Russian peasant dance she'd been attempting to teach them, sagging collectively in relief. "Straight spines, straight spines!" Bobby called reprovingly as she made her way to the phonograph where Bartók was still spinning around. The bell rang, marking the end of the period, and she lifted the needle off the record. "Class dismissed!"

The young gym teacher felt as relieved as her students at the conclusion of the hour's gyrations. Miss Fayne's lesson plans were as dull as ditchwater, but after the disastrous reception of her timekeeping lesson, Bobby had decided to play it safe and stick to the established curriculum. After all, Miss Fayne had taught at Metamora for three years!

Yet she had to admit that she was as bored by the Russian peasants as her students seemed to be.

"Miss Blanchard, Miss Blanchard!" Karen Woynarowski was hopping up and down with eagerness. "Can I ask you a personal question?"

At least the students had warmed to her as a woman, if not as a teacher. As usual, a crowd of them in their scarlet gym tunics were hanging around her desk, thrusting out excuse slips for Bobby to sign, asking for advice, or just peppering her with questions on every subject under the sun.

"Go ahead, Karen." Bobby smiled.

"What kind of beauty routine do you follow at night, Miss Blanchard?" blurted the blushing fourth former. There were self-conscious giggles from the group of girls as each one pictured the gym teacher, at night, in her bedroom.

"Beauty routine?" What did that mean? "Well, I wash up with soap and water every night before I go to bed, and I brush my teeth, of course," Bobby admitted.

"What do you think of going steady with a boy?" Gwen Norton quickly followed up.

"Steady with a boy?" Bobby was puzzled. "How are you going to go steady with a boy at a girls' school?"

"Miss Fayne said we shouldn't kiss on the first date," another girl broke in.

"But kissing is the point of a date!" said Bobby, astounded at such advice. When she saw the girls exchanging surprised, pleased glances, she wondered if she'd made a mistake. "Probably Miss Fayne was worried that kissing would lead to heavy petting, intercourse, and then pregnancy," she offered, not wanting to contradict her predecessor. The little stir of excitement told her she'd blundered, yet again, onto a forbidden topic.

"I heard you can't get pregnant the first time," said Gwen eagerly.

Bobby's indignation overcame her caution. "Girls who believe that find themselves on a plane to Mexico!" she scolded. "Now, we'll talk about all this more thoroughly next semester in hygiene. Get along and change before you're late for lunch!"

She watched the sophomores—that is, fourth formers— head to the locker room, an indulgent smile on her lips.

These kids kept her on her toes, no question! She didn't always know if she was saying the right thing, but she enjoyed the give-and-take. She had discovered how to manage the freshman—that is, the third form—problems in her dorm. Maybe her methods weren't by the book, but they worked!

Take the other evening, when she'd poked her head into the Cornwall common room. A group of third formers had ganged up on Debby Geissler, and were teasing her about her sleepwalking.

"Girls who sleepwalk aren't right in the head," one girl had declared.

"That's not true!" cried Debby, a plump girl with rosy cheeks. "My doctor said it's just a phase—a hormonal imbalance I'll grow out of—"

"Her hormones are out of joint!"

"Where do you go, Debby?"

"What do you do? I bet you do things you wouldn't do when you're awake!"

Debby was on the brink of tears when Bobby came to her rescue. "Let me tell you something about Debby's sleepwalking," she addressed the gang of girls. "Even asleep, Debby's a model of perfect posture! She's a sleepwalking illustration of all five points!"

The jeering stopped and the third formers looked at Debby respectfully.

"Now, poor posture," Bobby continued. "*That's* a sign of deep-seated problems. Who wants to play a little game?"

"We do, we do!" Even Sandy Milston, Debby's roommate, looked up from the corner of the couch where she was deep in a book.

"Tell me the first point of perfect posture," Bobby asked her rapt audience.

"Firm feet!" the girls chorused with flattering alacrity.

"Patty, why don't you demonstrate."

Patty Suarez obeyed, and Bobby gave her a gentle shove. The girl swayed, but did not topple. "Excellent! You all see how well balanced she is?"

Soon all the girls were testing their balance and attempting to push each other over. Sandy had put her book aside and joined the fun. Teasing Debby was forgotten as the girls giggled and grunted, grappling with each other like wrestlers while Bobby watched with a satisfied smile. The best way to keep the third formers happy was to make sure they had a physical outlet for their youthful energy!

Yes, Bobby thought now, as she picked up her satchel, Miss Watkins had been right about this: Bobby basked in the swarms of young girls surrounding her, at least outside of class. She enjoyed their lively chatter, their eager curiosity, their funny notions. She was more intrigued than annoyed by bookworm Sandy Milston, who was forever acquiring and hiding copies of the books on the forbidden literature list—everything from *Forever Amber* to obscure anthropological texts. Ferreting them out was fun, and the confiscated books had certainly provided Bobby with some interesting bedtime reading!

Bobby headed to Dorset and lunch, taking her usual shortcut through the locker room and out the side entrance, which led to the path that climbed the hill to the quadrangle. "Don't be late for lunch, now," she called to Gwen Norton and Joyce Vandemar, who were still frolicking in the showers.

Life at Metamora agreed with her. Bobby enjoyed the familiar school routine, rising early, going for a run around the athletic field, greeting Bryce and Ole as they strolled to breakfast from the old Amundsen homestead in the woods, Bryce's flowered tie always coordinated with the seasons. She relished the tasty meals Mona and the cook concocted, the eggs Benedict, the Salisbury steak, the macaroni and cheese, the boiled cabbage. Her mouth watered as she anticipated today's lunch menu—liver and onions, mmm!

Bobby joined the growing throng of scarlet-trimmed gray uniforms streaming toward Dorset. A girl in front of her shifted her books, and a folded piece of paper fell to the ground. "Wait—you dropped something." Bobby stopped her. Out of habit she opened the note and read:

> *I think you're divine. I watch you in Art Class all the time. If I could paint anyone's picture, it would be yours, but I could never do you justice. Do you think you could ever like me?*

"Here now, what's the matter with you?" Bobby scolded the blushing girl. "You forgot to sign it! How's your friend going to answer you if you don't sign it?"

Brushing aside the teenager's thanks, Bobby continued up the path, musing on life at Metamora. That was another thing she liked—the atmosphere of warmth and affection that permeated the place. This girl's note was just one example. Half the student body had fervent "pashes," as they called them, on the other half. The faculty, too, fostered close friendships; Bryce and Ole were devoted to each other, as were Alice Bjorklund and Serena Rapp. Elaine had been dead wrong with that caviar on toast business.

If only she didn't feel so overmatched, intellectually speaking, in this new milieu. Bobby passed the sundial, automatically speeding up a little. She might be able to beat Serena at tennis, but she certainly couldn't keep up with her or Hoppy Fiske when they got into one of their arguments about classical versus progressive education.

Noticing Gussie Gunderson standing at the foot of the step up to Dorset, Bobby hurried forward to take her arm and escort her into the dining hall.

πάντα χρόα γῆρας ἤδη
λεῦκαι δ᾽ἐγένοντο τρίχες ἐκ μελαίναν*

murmured the Ancient Greek Mistress as Bobby pulled out a chair for her at the table where the senior faculty sat. Gussie often communicated in unintelligible fragments of Greek, but somehow this didn't bother Bobby. None of the other teachers understood her either.

Except Enid Butler, Bobby thought wryly as she took her seat at a half-filled table. "Good afternoon, Miss Blanchard!" chorused the students, turning beaming faces in her direction.

It was usual at Metamora for the junior faculty to mix with the students for meals. Bobby was pleasantly aware of how the seats at whatever table she chose would fill up as quickly as the seats in a game of musical chairs when the music stops. Today was no exception, and she had to settle a dispute over the last chair, promising to save the disappointed loser a seat at her table at dinner.

All was orderly at the neighboring table, where Enid sat—Enid, who seemed mistress of so much more than mathematics. She debated nuclear disarmament with Hoppy, and even Hoppy had to back down on points of fission she didn't understand. She spoke French with Madame Melville, Greek with Gussie Gunderson, and had even gotten Miss Rasphigi to support her in proposing a physics seminar for Metamora's advanced science and math students. At any rate, Miss Rasphigi's indiffer-

* "Age seizes my skin and turns my hair from black to white."
—Sappho

ent "Why not?" at that particular staff meeting was as enthusiastic as the solitary Chemistry Mistress had gotten about anything thus far.

But it was on educational issues that Bobby felt truly inferior to the attractive young Math Mistress, who had held forth last night about experiential-based learning and modules versus units until Bobby felt like her brain was being pelted by badminton birdies. That night, for the first time at Metamora, she had had one of her nightmares. In this one, Miss Butler chased her through the Mesquakie woods until Bobby tumbled over the bluff into the Muskrat River, which in her dream was as deep and wild as Niagara Falls.

It was hard to believe that the precocious Enid Butler was only just out of college, and that she'd only minored in education, Bobby thought now, looking enviously at Enid's cool profile.

Miss Craybill had taken her place at the senior staff table, next to the Greek Mistress, with sharp-featured Bunny Otis on her other side. Miss Rasphigi, Madame Melville, and Mona made up the rest of the table. The noise of chatter died down, and Miss Craybill bowed her head.

"Let us pray," she said.

After the ragged chorus of thanks for their liver and onions had died away, Miss Craybill picked up a sheet of paper and stood up to make the announcements. "The Young Integrationists are holding their annual elections tonight at seven-thirty in the Kent Common Room, followed by a discussion, 'Hierarchical versus Cooperative Organizational Strategies.' I encourage all interested students to attend. The Metamora Literary Society is also having its first meeting. Anyone interested in helping to produce *The Tower Chimes* is required to attend, but Miss Bjorklund requests that you *please* save your summer poetry for another meeting. This is to be an organizational meeting only. The Problem Solvers . . ."

Miss Craybill was having a good day, Bobby was relieved to observe. It had become clear to the young physical education instructor as well as the rest of the faculty that Miss Craybill was not quite herself. Even in a community that tolerated a wide range of behavior, some of the habits the Headmistress had lately developed might be termed eccentric.

For example, the distraction Bobby had noticed at that first sherry hour had become more pronounced. The other day at lunch Miss Craybill had simply stopped mid-announcement, her attention drawn to a bird outside the window. Exclaiming excitedly, "A short-billed marsh wren!" she had abruptly exited Dorset in pursuit, leaving the students buzzing as Miss Otis finished the announcements. Alice Bjorklund told Bobby that the late Miss Froelich had been an avid bird-watcher—it was surmised she had fallen from the tower while observing the white-breasted nuthatch. "I think Agnes has taken up the hobby as a way of feeling closer to her departed friend," the gentle English Mistress confided, tears filling her eyes. "She's even taken over Nerissa's Life List!"

And then there was the Headmistress's sudden mania for cleaning out the school's dusty storeroom and attics. "Fall cleaning won't hurt anything," said Mona philosophically as she patiently helped Miss Craybill sort through trunks of mildewed academic gowns or boxes of discarded etiquette textbooks. Bryce Bowles, the generally cheery Biology Master, had sternly refused, however, when Miss Craybill suggested she give a good going-over to his and Ole's woodsy retreat. "There's such a thing as privacy!" he exclaimed indignantly.

But on the whole, the staff tried to accommodate their beloved Headmistress, still shaken by the unexpected death of her dear friend, Miss Froelich. It was no wonder she was a little "fragile," said the older teachers diplomatically; "odd," the younger teachers told each other more bluntly.

". . . and lastly, Patty Tompkins is missing her collection of the works of Ayn Rand. No questions asked if it is returned before Study Hall tonight."

Miss Craybill sat down, and conversation broke out immediately. "Have you seen the first issue of *The Metamora Musings*, Miss Blanchard?" asked Peggy Cotler eagerly as the waitresses set down steaming plates of liver and onions in front of each student. "It has the interview I did with you."

"It's out already?" Bobby said. "And you printed my announcement?"

"I sure did," Peggy assured her.

Bobby half rose and then sank back down. "Well, I guess I'll have to wait until after lunch," she complained jokingly. "Seeing as I have to set an example for you girls that doesn't include leaping up in search of reading material."

"Here's my copy, Miss Blanchard!" A half dozen copies were held out to her in an instant. Bobby took a copy from third former Patty Suarez, who sat on her right.

"Remember, kids, we're supposed to be conversing on topical events, cover for me," she instructed as she leafed hastily through the paper. The giggling girls conversed in artificial tones about a recent plane crash and the uproar in Alabama as Bobby turned past stories about club meetings, Prefecture elections (Metamora's name for student government), and an editorial on changing school rules to permit unsupervised strolls in the woods between Metamora and Mesquakie Point ("Why Is Mother Nature Forbidden Territory?"). Her attention was caught briefly by the interview Peggy had written, headlined New Games

MISTRESS WOWS CAMPUS, and she wondered to herself if her hair really was "a cap of iridescent red-gold" and if she really "radiated warmth, wisdom, and wit."

Ah—there was the announcement she was looking for, boxed and placed prominently next to the picture of her sitting in the bleachers. "Metamora Field Hockey Team to be Re-formed," it read. "Tryouts Thursday Afternoon, 4 P.M., Louth Athletic Field."

Chapter Six

Tryouts at the Athletic Field

The notion of a field hockey team at Metamora had started the week after the term began, when Miss Craybill joined her to clean out the equipment room. Rolling aside the heavy archery targets from the back wall, for Miss Craybill was nothing if not thorough, they had uncovered a bundle of ancient shin guards and field hockey sticks, the old-fashioned kind with the long toe.

"Yes, of course," said Miss Craybill when Bobby exclaimed over the discovery. "The Metamora Savages. Miss Dennis, our Games Mistress back in 1929, was swept up by the field hockey craze. I believe she had studied under a well-known player, Constance Apley, I think the name was." The Headmistress poked carefully at the rotted stuffing of the shin guards while Bobby stared at her, agog.

"You don't mean a disciple of Constance Applebee? What a wonderful connection to field hockey history!" the Games Mistress exclaimed. "Do you think we could revive the team? It would be a great thing for the phys ed program! The cost would be minimal, since we already have the most expensive items of equipment, although we'll certainly have to replace those shin guards. I believe I have the expertise to make a success of it—and I think some experience with competitive sports would be healthy for the girls here!"

Miss Craybill looked up from the pile of shin guards. "The girls already participate in the state association of track and field sports," she objected. "And there's archery and tennis as well."

Bobby decided not to remind the Headmistress of Metamora's abysmal record at track and field events. "But don't you see, none of those are truly *team* sports," she argued instead. "There's nothing like field hockey for teaching girls the valuable skill of getting along with the group!"

"Well, if you're willing to . . ." Miss Craybill trailed off as she began to carefully unfurl a stash of table tennis nets, as if hoping to find diamonds wrapped in them. Bobby decided she would take that as consent.

Later that afternoon, after she'd used the third form's body mechanics class to restore the equipment room to order, she went to see Mona in the little office the housekeeper occupied next to the kitchen in Dorset. Mona, Bobby had quickly discovered, was the one to see when you wanted to get things done at Metamora; especially now, when the faculty followed an unspoken rule: Don't bother Miss Craybill unless strictly necessary.

Mona immediately recalled hearing that Metamora had once had a field hockey team back in the thirties.

"You were a big wheel in field hockey, weren't you? What fun for the girls, if you reinstated the team." Mona's face was alight with enthusiasm as she sat at her old-fashioned roll top desk. "All you'll need is Miss Craybill's signature on an equipment disbursement form—or Miss Otis will do. Here." She'd turned from the housekeeping bills she was paying to pluck a blank form from a pigeonhole. "And then there's the paperwork to join the Midwest Regional Secondary School Girls' Field Hockey League—I can help you with that."

Mona's evident delight in the revival of field hockey at Metamora had carried Bobby through the bureaucratic side of the equation, but now she faced the daunting task of forming a squad from scratch. What if not enough girls tried out? Mona had said the students weren't athletically minded.

Now that the fateful Thursday had arrived, Bobby felt nervous. She glanced at the clock. Five minutes to four. The young gym teacher gathered up her blank squad rosters and playbook, walked across the empty gymnasium and out the big double doors that led to Louth Athletic Field. She'd worked late into the evening the night before, helping Ole Amundsen chalk out a regulation hockey field in the center of the track's oval.

Outside the double doors Bobby blinked, briefly blinded by the late-afternoon sun. It was a golden September day, warm with just a hint of fall's coolness. Perfect field hockey weather, she thought. Then she saw that the new hockey field was aflame with scarlet gym tunics. It looked like practically the entire school had turned out for tryouts. Bobby's heart swelled with emotion.

Why, these poor kids have been just craving a field hockey team! she thought. They had simply been waiting for someone to teach them how to satisfy the hunger for physical activity that had been building inside them. *And I'm the one to do it!* thought Bobby as she walked toward the sea of girls.

"How do you feel about the turnout for tryouts, Coach Bobby?" Peggy Cotler approached her, flipping open her reporter's notebook in a businesslike way that couldn't hide her excitement.

"It's terrific." Bobby instinctively raised her voice so that more of the girls could hear. "If the Metamora girls show half as much skill as they do school spirit, why, we've got the makings of a great team!"

"What do you consider to be the qualities—" began Peggy, but Bobby interrupted her. "Interview later—I've got a lot of potential players to put through their paces!" She blew a sharp blast on her whistle. "Everyone to the end line! Count off in groups of ten, and we'll start with some sprints!"

Of course the large turnout meant Bobby spent extra time weeding through the mass of field hockey hopefuls. She started by eliminating the weakest applicants—like precocious Lotta Reiniger, who had skipped a grade and was in the fourth form, although she wouldn't turn thirteen until November. She was followed by eighteen-year-old Munty Blaine, who was as stocky as a stevedore, with a voice as hoarse from her years of illicit smoking. "Your wind's no good," Bobby had to tell her. She'd seen Munty panting asthmatically five minutes into a game of ring toss.

"I'm quitting cigarettes, really I am," rasped Munty pleadingly.

"I'm sorry," said Bobby, really meaning it. To the younger students she could offer the opportunity to try again next year, but this was Munty's last year at Metamora. The disconsolate sixth former threw herself down on the sidelines in despair.

Lotta didn't give up so easily. "If I can't play, can I be your assistant?" she begged. "I can write down everyone's names and help you keep track." And so the pint-sized student followed the rangy gym teacher, busily writing down names as Bobby put each group of girls through basic drills in dribbling, passing, and tackling.

Bobby had to admit that they weren't an inspiring sight.

Most of the girls had never played before. Bobby had passed out copies of the field hockey rules and regulations in all her classes, but learning field hockey from a rule book was like learning the tango by reading step diagrams!

Bobby patiently sifted through the lunging, panting girls, rejecting, suspending final judgment, or marking a particularly promising player's name with a star. Meanwhile, Munty was joined on the sidelines by curious spectators as well as fellow field hockey hopefuls as tryouts continued. Blowing her whistle to signal to the current players attempting to bat the ball around that it was time to surrender their sticks to the next group of eager girls, Bobby realized that her audience had grown to a sizeable number of students, and even included some faculty.

"Why, Mona," Bobby exclaimed. "What are you doing here?" Mona was moving about the crowd, pouring cups of cocoa from a keg she'd strapped to her back and handing out apples from a basket on her arm.

"If the girls won't come to snack hour in the common room, their snacks had better come to them!" Mona replied cheerfully. "I'm terribly excited about this terrific turnout, aren't you? The Midwest Regional Secondary School Girls' Field Hockey League won't know what hit them!"

Bobby was touched. "Gee, Mona, that's awful swell of you." She was working her way through the throng to take the apple Mona was holding out when she almost tripped over Hoppy Fiske. Hoppy was sitting in the midst of a group of girls wearing serious expressions. "Sorry, Hoppy, I didn't see you." She hadn't suspected Hoppy was a field hockey enthusiast. "Why so down?"

"We came to support Misako," she said, glumly.

Misako "Mimi" Nakagawa was a fourth form transfer from Japan. The Young Integrationists Club had taken her under their collective wing, and Bobby had heard that she'd been elected vice president of the group the other night, although her English was still pretty rudimentary.

Now Misako sat with her YI friends with a downcast air.

"Why, Misako did quite well," Bobby said. "I haven't made my final decisions yet—there's every chance you'll make the practice team."

Misako brightened at the news. "I work very hard," she promised.

"It would be a wonderful thing for the league if Misako played," Hoppy said earnestly. "It would certainly show where Metamora stood on the integration question!"

"Well, the practice team and the varsity team are very different things," Bobby tried to explain, dismayed by Hoppy's assumption that a field hockey team was a means of sending political messages. "After all, we want to win, don't we?"

"Integration *will* win," Hoppy said firmly. "It's the only possible way to resolve the current state of affairs."

Bobby gave up trying to explain her field hockey philosophy to the Current Events Mistress. Applause and calls of "Way to go, Kayo!" drew her attention back to the field. Two girls were dribbling, push passing, flicking, and dodging as if they'd been playing field hockey all their lives. The other girls had stopped their attempts to play and backed away, as dancers do when mambo experts take to the floor.

Bobby blew her whistle and the two girls stopped, turning toward her with smiling faces.

"Well, well, what have we here?" Bobby recognized the older girl as Carole "Kayo" Kerwin, an attractive sixth former. Her pale blond hair frothed from a high ponytail, and her long thin nose gave her a patrician air. She exuded confidence and authority. As she wiped the sweat off her forehead with the sleeve of her tunic, an eager fourth former ran up to hand her a towel. Kayo was popular, Bobby knew, likely to be elected Head Prefect in the Prefecture elections next week.

More to the point, Bobby had also noticed her ease and agility in the sixth form's stunts and tumbling class. This display, however, was more than agility. This was experience.

"Our mother taught us how to play," explained Kayo. Bobby looked at the other girl, who had Kayo's coloring but a round impish face. "You must be Linda Kerwin," she realized. This was the girl Mona had told her about, who had caused a scandal with her ouija board the previous year.

"That's right," said Linda cheerfully, twirling her stick.

"Mom played field hockey here, back in the thirties, when Miss Dennis was Games Mistress," Kayo continued. "We'd have scrimmages whenever the Old Girls visited. She's going to be over the moon when she finds out you've reinstated the Savages!"

"Old Girls?" Bobby was puzzled.

"You know, old Metamora girls. They're called Old Girls," Linda explained helpfully.

"She means alumnae," piped up Lotta.

"I know you'll want to see the other Metamorians who also play with us," Kayo told the Games Mistress chummily. "Edie, Beryl, Penny, Sue—"

Bobby interrupted her. "I'm sure if they have your abilities I'll spot them," she said with a smile. She wanted to make it clear to this self-assured senior—that is, sixth former—that she, Coach Bobby, was picking the team—not Metamora's future Head Prefect.

The self-assured sixth former blinked, but kept her poise. "Of course," she said.

Bobby blew two blasts on her whistle. "Next group!" she shouted. Taking the list from Lotta, she starred the names of the Kerwin sisters. Her glance traveled to Kayo, surrounded now by her friends and admirers. Two girls offered her paper cups of water, and Kayo chose one, tilting her head back to drink. Bobby couldn't help noticing the way the sun glinted on the drops of liquid on the girl's full upper lip and silhouetted her figure, which made a mockery of the juvenile gym tunic. Irrelevantly, she wondered what Elaine was up to. *I should give her a call*, she thought as she turned to the next group of players.

The sun was even lower on the horizon by the time Bobby read out the list of girls who'd made the squad. "Penny Gordon, Edith Gunther, Beryl Houck, Susan Howard, Ilsa Jespersen, Dodie Jessup, Kayo Kerwin, Linda Kerwin"—Kayo had been right, of course, about the other Metamorians who had been practicing with the squad of Old Girls;—"Annette Melville, Misako Nakagawa..." Bobby hoped Hoppy would be happy. "Shirley Sarvis, Patty Suarez..." Thirty-five would be the right number, she'd decided. Varsity, Junior Varsity, and a practice squad, plus a couple extras. "Joyce Vandemar, Helen Wechsler, Nancy Yost."

For a while it was pandemonium on the field. Some of the chosen ones squealed and hugged each other, while others simply beamed or tried to act nonchalant. Applause broke out at Kayo's name. A few of the unchosen wept.

"Girls will be girls, won't they?" Mona observed with an indulgent smile as she stood by Bobby surveying the scene. "What an exciting afternoon! My cocoa keg is empty." With a wave, she hurried off to dinner prep at Dorset and the rest of the crowd began to disperse as well. Bobby was deciding she would squeeze in a little scrimmage when she noticed a student on the sidelines, a tall, rawboned girl, her knobby knees showing beneath her gray skirt, the sleeves of her gray blazer too short for her long arms, her regulation scarlet tie missing. She had picked up one of the hockey sticks, and with one hand she was using it to juggle a hockey ball on the end, bouncing it up and down as easy as a mother burping a baby.

Bobby hurried over to the unknown student, excitement catching in her throat. "Who are you?" she demanded. "Where did you learn to do that?"

"Sorry," said the teen, letting the ball drop to the ground and holding out the hockey stick.

"No, that's quite good!" Bobby told her. "What's your name?"

"Angela Cohen O'Shea." There was defiance in the girl's voice and stance.

Bobby tried to place her. "I don't remember seeing you in gym class," she admitted. "What year are you?"

"I'm a junior—or fifth former, I s'pose." The girl shrugged as if Metamorian terms were not only unfamiliar, but also a little ridiculous. "I have a doctor's note excusing me from gym. Allergies," she added laconically.

"You've played field hockey before, haven't you?" Bobby tried to reach the taciturn girl.

"Some."

"Why didn't you try out today?"

"I'm not a joiner." The girl turned away.

"Don't you want to help your school win?" Bobby called after her, although with little hope. She'd seen this type of girl before. A loner. A rebel. No school spirit.

But the girl turned back suddenly. "Against who?"

"Why . . . why, the other teams in the Midwest Regional Secondary School Girls' Field Hockey League," said Bobby, bewildered.

"Does that include St. Margaret Mary's?"

Bobby tried to remember the list of schools she'd glanced through. "I think so," she said cautiously.

"Okay. Count me in."

Bobby decided to wonder later what had motivated the girl's abrupt change of heart. Right now, she wanted to see what else this Angela could do.

A little murmur arose among the newly anointed Savages as Bobby returned to the playing field with Angela in tow. "What's Angle doing here?" she heard Beryl Houck mutter. Beryl was a red-faced, boisterous sixth former with a sharp tongue for students outside her own circle of friends. Ignoring her, Bobby blew her whistle twice and shouted, "All right, Savages, let's try a little scrimmage!" She began assigning positions, explaining, "I'll rotate players on and off so everyone gets a fair shake."

The game, when she cried "Ball in play," was chaotic, only roughly resembling field hockey as the Spitfires played it. Too many of the girls were unfamiliar with the rules. Kayo and Linda and their friends did what they could, shouting, "No obstruction, Annette! You can't get between Beryl and the ball!" or "Offsides, Anna, offsides! Wait for Shirley to get ahead of you."

Still Bobby was pleased. Kayo was a really excellent player, feinting, dodging, and dribbling up the field with ease. And it was amazing how quickly the ignorant girls picked up the game. Her spirits rose. It was just possible the Savages would make a respectable showing, their first season out after so many years.

She turned to Angela, who was watching the game with a bored air. "Sub in for Linda," she told her. She saw the gangly girl tap Linda on the shoulder and take her stick, and then her attention shifted to Edie Gunther in goal, who was positioning herself nicely for a roll-in near the ten-yard line. So she didn't see how Angela stole the ball from Kayo and left her sprawled on the ground while the rest of the squad howled "Foul!" But she did see Angela dribble the ball up the field in under five seconds and whack it into the goal so hard that Dodie Jessup, the other goalie, shrank to one side, not even trying to block. Bobby blew her whistle as Beryl and Penny helped Kayo pick herself up.

"Go, Angle!" shouted Lotta shrilly into the startled silence.

Chapter Seven
The Problem Student

Bobby burst into the faculty lounge at sherry hour in search of Mona. She was just itching to tell someone about her newly discovered athletic phenomenon. To think she had found a girl like Angle at Metamora! The coach of the newly re-formed Savages had discovered that for all her truculent air, the gangly girl was quick to grasp the tips Bobby offered on grip and dodges. And her drive, her passion! She had that elusive quality that turned a basic aptitude for athletics into something more. Bobby had played her discovery as center against Kayo, Beryl, and Linda in succession, and Angle could beat them all on the bully.

True, she'd racked up fouls almost as fast as goals. Shirley, Helen, Anna, and Edie were all bruised and limping after attempts to tackle her. But Bobby felt sure she could tame her prodigy's unbridled aggression. Properly channeled, it would be an asset to the team.

"Mona, you ought to have stayed for the scrimmage . . ." she began, hurrying over to the housekeeper, who was sipping sherry in a corner by the fireplace. Too late, she noticed Miss Otis sitting next to her.

The young gym teacher tended to avoid the humorless Latin Mistress, whose overriding concern for Metamora and its traditions made her an obstacle to any innovation. Faculty gossip said she'd expected Miss Craybill to make her Vice Mistress now that Miss Froelich was dead, and hoped to one day succeed Miss Craybill and become mistress of all Metamora. But Miss Craybill had as yet named no new Vice Mistress, and Miss Otis had to content herself with seniority in the faculty lounge.

Today she swiveled around in her chair to address Bobby. "Is this newfangled sport a proper activity for our Metamora girls?" she asked earnestly. "*Cui bono?*"

Mona stepped in, earning Bobby's silent gratitude. "Field hockey is no newfangled sport, Bunny! The Savages existed *ab aeterno,* or at any rate since 1932. Bobby is simply restoring a lost Metamora tradition."

Miss Otis considered. "That may be, but even a lost tradition must be restored cautiously, with good care."

"I don't know what you mean." Bobby was bewildered. "I got Miss Craybill's go-ahead."

"I think what Bunny means is that the turnout for the field hockey tryouts rather drained the talent from the other clubs that had meetings scheduled this afternoon," Alice Bjorklund interpreted.

"Only four girls showed up for the Latin Club meeting," Miss Otis elaborated. "Even last year's president didn't attend!"

Mr. Burnham took his pipe out of his mouth. "You got me beat, Bunny," he called from the other side of the room. "Only three came to the Diggers' meeting—"

"Metamora's archaeology club," Mona murmured to Bobby.

"—and the girls seemed so genuinely interested when I announced it in class," the History Master concluded wistfully.

Bobby recalled now the notices of extracurricular activities sprinkled through *The Metamora Musings,* or posted on the bulletin board outside the dining room, or announced by Miss Craybill at lunch. In addition to the school newspaper, the literary magazine, and the Young Integrationists Club, there were the Daughters of the American Pioneers Society, the Non-Objectivist Society, study groups, the Prefecture, choruses, a drama troupe— Bobby couldn't remember them all. Somehow the gym teacher hadn't thought of the Savages as competing against the more established staff-sponsored activities, but there was a definite feeling of competition in the faculty room, with memberships the objective, instead of goals.

Even Laura Burnham, who'd draped herself languidly on a window seat and was leafing through a fashion magazine, drawled, "I s'pose I'm lucky I scheduled the Young Abstract Expressionists for Friday afternoon instead of Thursday."

"The Young Integrationists and I joined the throng on the hockey field," Hoppy Fiske told her, with a touch of complacency. "In a cooperative club like ours, one learns to move *with* the current, instead of fight against it."

"Come, come, none of this is Bobby's fault!" Mona chided the miffed teachers. "Girls will be girls. Field hockey is a novelty to them—as is Bobby—and so they flock to her—I mean it."

"I myself do not see the point of all these *cloobs*," said Madame Melville, the French Mistress. She sat a little apart from the other teachers, wreathed in blue smoke as she corrected French exercises. While the other teachers drank the sherry Mona provided, Madame Melville's glass mysteriously held a pale green liquid.

"We are paid to teach them, no?" Her cigarette described a question mark. "Let the girls entertain themselves, or give them more schoolwork if you are afraid of what they might do in their leisure."

Hoppy and Miss Otis rose to Madame's bait, as they

always did, and under cover of their argument over proper enrichment activities, Mona asked Bobby, "What was the big excitement at the scrimmage?"

Bobby forgot about academic rivalries and her squashed enthusiasm rebounded. "That girl! She's a natural! A real athletic whiz kid! She picks up plays like she's picking up loose change! I bet she could play any position I put her in! And drive! She's a tank! The other players give way or get mowed down! I've never seen anything like it!"

Bobby's voice had risen with her excitement and Hoppy broke off her defense of extracurricular activities to ask curiously, "Who is this prodigy?"

"The other girls called her Angle," Bobby looked down at her roster. "Her full name is—"

"Angela Cohen O'Shea!" chorused the other teachers, the expressions on their faces ranging from amusement to sympathy.

"You've got the tiger by the tail with that one, I'm afraid," said Mr. Burnham, nodding his head and sucking his pipe with a trace of smugness.

"Why, what's the matter with her?"

"She's a troublemaker," said Miss Otis succinctly. "She's been late to chapel almost every Sunday, and when I gave her a demerit and a warning the last time, she had the audacity to tell me she's an atheist and shouldn't have to attend at all!"

"Smoking in her bedroom, never observes lights-out. We had to move her to a single after she worked poor Shirley Sarvis into a state of hysterics with her lurid description of the miseries of the migrant farm workers," put in Mr. Burnham.

"Her accent is 'orreeble," observed Madame Melville impartially.

"She's very bright," put in Miss Bjorklund timidly. "But she won't do the work. I'm afraid she'll fail English."

Ken Burnham took the pipe out of his mouth. "Oh, she's bright enough, but she only puts her mind to work making trouble. She told my American history class that it was the pioneers that massacred the Indians at Mesquakie Point, not the reverse. Completely disrupted my lesson plan. A couple of the DAP girls were in tears! I thought Beryl Houck might hit her."

"Why is she such a problem?" Bobby wondered.

"Well, she's a transfer student, and most of our girls have been here since third form," Mona explained. "She came to Metamora last semester, after her enrollment at St. Margaret Mary's, er, didn't work out. She's a high-spirited girl, with very definite opinions. Girls will be girls, after all."

"And there are problems at home," added Ken Burnham solemnly.

"D-I-V-O-R-C-E." Miss Otis spelled it out. "These mixed marriages often run into trouble. Young couples think that love will conquer all, but what happens when they're attending different churches every Sunday? Or in this case," she lowered her voice, "a temple?"

"Those of the Jewish faith worship on Saturday," instructed Hoppy.

"I don't think either of the O'Sheas worships at all," Mona said practically. "Mr. O'Shea is a labor organizer and Mrs. O'Shea is active in the theater. Perhaps we shouldn't speculate about Angela's home life."

"Miss Rasphigi thinks well of her." Enid spoke up for the first time. She was sitting in the armchair opposite Madame Melville, correcting homework papers with mechanical efficiency, her glass of sherry untouched on the table beside her. "She's very quick to learn when the subject interests her, as our Games Mistress observed."

Bobby sat up. Here was an unexpected ally. Perhaps Angle would be the bridge between her and the attrac-

tive, yet distant algebra teacher. Perhaps after dinner she
would suggest to young Miss Butler that the two of them
could put their heads together over the unhappy adolescent. With her teaching knowledge, Enid Butler would
surely have some ideas—she probably knew *Adolescent
Development Patterns* by heart, a textbook Bobby had
only skimmed.

"However, to return to Miss Otis's earlier point, I do
think we ought to consider the disruptive potential of this
addition to Metamora's sports program. We must be certain it doesn't threaten Metamora's academic priorities."

Bobby's nascent hopes died a sudden death. She wasn't
positive, but it sounded like the Math Mistress was against
field hockey!

"Group processes can be a valuable way of teaching
life skills, when properly done. However, it's essential to
be up to date on methodology." Enid rounded on the
young coach suddenly. "You've seen 'Effective Grouping
and the Lone Teacher' in the last issue of *Secondary Pedagogy*, haven't you?"

Bobby gulped and lied. "Of course!"

"'Group processes are not without danger, and only
the naïve teacher will fail to carefully consider class dynamics and antisocial currents, which have the potential
to turn the group into a mob.' Quite a provocative state-
ment, isn't it?"

Bobby looked around the room. Many of the teachers
had a thoughtful air, as if they were considering their
group processes in a new, critical light. Bobby wished
desperately that Bryce and Ole were there—Bryce had a
joking way that lightened serious discussions, and although Ole never said much, Bobby felt sure of his silent
support for Metamora's increased activity in sports. However, the two friends seldom came to sherry hour, preferring to take long nature walks together.

"I think we should guard against the fundamental imbalance at the extracurricular level, not to mention the academic curricula, that occurs in so many schools where team sports are high-status activities." Enid continued remorselessly.

Bobby's head had fogged up again. "She means . . . ?" she whispered to Alice.

"Most schools are too sports crazy," Alice whispered back.

Bobby opened and shut her mouth, trying to think of a way to fight back against this determined attack on her new team. Fortunately, the German Mistress came to her rescue. "*Sans mensa in corpus santus,*" she argued. "And let us remember the Amazons!"

"'Αμαζόνες ἀντιάνειραι,* Gussie Gunderson said suddenly.

There was a knock on the door. A sub-prefect poked her head into the room. "Miss Butler, Mr. Rackham's waiting for you in Manchester."

"I'll be right there." Enid shuffled her corrected papers neatly together and put them in her briefcase. With a "Good night, all," she was gone.

"Gallivanting again!" snorted the German Mistress.

Rod Rackham drove out from Bay City one or two nights a week to take the young algebra instructor out on dates. Bobby had seen him once as he helped Enid into his sedan, a tall, muscular young man, with a handsome, if strong-featured face—all jutting jaw, chiseled cheekbones, and brooding brow. Bobby had noted enviously the perfect fit of his gray flannel suit.

Bobby was grateful for the timely interruption. Another ten minutes of Enid's fluent argument, and the anti-sport teacher might have reduced the Savages to an

---

* "The Amazons, the peers of men."—*The Iliad*

intramural club! It was time to mend fences in the faculty lounge, and she could do that best in the Math Mistress's absence.

"Let's think about what Gussie said before we decide anything," she said, in the certainty that no one else understood Greek either. "After all, she's got the most experience here at Metamora!" She stole a glance at Gussie, who had dozed off again, then turned to the French Mistress. "Madame Melville, did Annette tell you she's playing left wing?"

"Oh? She is becoming such an American girl." The French Mistress attempted her usual blasé tone but could not conceal her pride in her daughter's accomplishment.

If only the rest of the staff had daughters on the team! It was time for drastic measures.

"How about if I cut a practice, or even two?" Bobby suggested. "Would that be less disruptive to the other clubs?" Privately she decided she would study the bulletin board and squeeze in extra practices when she could.

The atmosphere in the faculty lounge lightened considerably. "After all, school spirit is important too," reflected Miss Otis. "Some of the other schools with winning sports teams have done very well when it comes to alumnae donations from former team members."

The conversation turned to the ever-present Old Girls fund-raising efforts, and Bobby decided to make her escape while staff sentiment was still on her side. Besides, now she needed to redo her practice schedules.

Mona pulled her aside before she left, under pretense of taking her sherry glass. "Don't let Enid get you down," the housekeeper whispered. "She's just a little miffed because no one showed up for the first meeting of the Problem Solvers."

Is that all there was behind the Math Mistress's hockey hostility? Bobby wondered as she closed the faculty lounge

door behind her. If so, Bobby prayed a boatload of Metamorians would attend the next math club meeting. The
brainy young Math Mistress often expounded on adolescent psychology, and Bobby would need her advice if she
was going to mold Metamora's problem student into the
Savages' star player!

Bobby had stopped on the steps of Kent, deep in thought,
observing without really seeing a figure bent over the
flower bed that surrounded the sundial. Suddenly she realized that it wasn't Ole, as she'd automatically assumed.
Ole didn't wear tweed suits, with the skirts slightly longer
than was fashionable. It was Miss Craybill—Miss Craybill digging with a hand trowel, tossing uprooted flowers
behind her with feverish energy. Something about her posture, the determination with which she dug, made Bobby
hesitate, the polite greeting dying on her lips. It was as if
the Headmistress was on the track of something far more
sinister than weeds. Bobby turned quietly down the narrow path that led away from the quadrangle, to the gymnasium.

Chapter Eight
A Talk with Angle

Bobby stood studying the sundial the next morning as students streamed past her on their way to breakfast. The purple pansies bobbed in the breeze as if they had never been uprooted.

"You know it's haunted, don't you?" said a conversational voice at her elbow. Bobby turned to find Linda Kerwin next to her, staring respectfully at the sundial.

"Haunted? By whom?" Bobby waited with a half-smile for the stories about pioneer victims for which Linda was famous.

Linda looked both ways as if the spirit world might have corporeal spies. "By the unhappy spirit of Miss Froelich!" she said. "She loved this sundial. It was her class's gift to the school in 1919."

Bobby felt a visceral shock and frowned to conceal her own superstitious shudder. "I'm surprised at you, Linda. I wouldn't have thought a girl as smart as you would still believe in such childish nonsense."

"There are more things in heaven and earth, Coach Blanchard, if you know what I mean."

Bobby knew this was a quotation although she couldn't place it. She took refuge in severity. "At any rate, you should realize that telling everyone that Miss Froelich is haunting the campus could be very painful to Miss—to her friends on the faculty. It's very sad, Miss Froelich's accidental fall from the tower while bird-watching, but not supernatural!"

Linda looked wise. "Sure, that's the *official* story. Anyway, I'm not telling everyone she's haunting the sundial, just you." As an afterthought she added, "Most of the kids know already," before skipping off toward the dining hall.

Bobby followed her, feeling inadequate as a teacher. Enid, no doubt, would have been able to quash this disturbing rumor more effectively.

The big dining hall was filled with chattering students and the waitresses were hurrying to and fro among the long tables with platters of poached eggs on toast.

Bobby saw Angle at one end of a table of fifth and sixth formers, and made a beeline toward the empty chair at its head. Too late she realized the Math Mistress was also heading toward the chair.

"Oh—were you going to . . ."

"Not at all, go ahead," Enid replied with a polite, wintry smile. Bobby sat down, dismayed, and bowed her head for the prayer. Once again, she had managed to offend the enigmatic algebra teacher!

"We're all looking forward to practice this afternoon, Coach," said the girl on her left as soon as the prayer had concluded.

Bobby looked up. She hadn't even noticed Kayo Kerwin sitting at the table, accompanied as usual by her friends Edie Gunther and Beryl Houck. The blond teenager smiled at Bobby with the poise that made her seem so much older than a high school girl.

"Sorry to disappoint you, girls, but practice has been

changed," Bobby replied, accepting a slab of bacon from a passing waitress. Mona had reported that Enid had scheduled another Problem Solvers meeting that afternoon.

The chorus of groans was flattering to the young coach. "Why?" asked Edie from her seat next to Kayo.

"We want to avoid conflicts with other school activities," Bobby explained.

"Like those stupid DIPs, pardon me, DAPs, I suppose," muttered Angle. Kayo said instantly, "The DAPs meet on Tuesdays—it's not *our* fault."

"Whatever you say." Angle rolled her eyes.

Beryl turned on the tall transfer student. "You're just jealous because you don't qualify for membership."

"Like I'd want to be part of you reactionary snobs and your secret Scandinavian rituals!" retorted Angle. "I know what you do—you sing Norwegian songs and drink Swedish *glögg!* Pah!"

"You don't know what you're talking about. We raise money for charity with our living picture pageants," Edie defended the exclusive society.

"Maybe we'll get lucky and you'll all just freeze into one of your quilting-bee or cornhusking poses!" sneered Angle.

"I, for one, am glad to have another day to prepare," Bobby intervened. Exchanging insults definitely did not fit into Miss Craybill's definition of civilized mealtime conversation. "And I'd encourage you girls to use the time to study the field hockey regulations I distributed. Now, who's going to go see *Cleopatra* at the Bijou this Saturday? That Elizabeth Taylor's a looker, isn't she?"

With conversation steered to safer subjects, Bobby covertly studied Metamora's problem student as she sat at the far end of the table, moodily tucking away her breakfast. There was an empty seat beside her, and none

of the other girls addressed a word to her after the exchange with Edie. The only time she spoke was to refuse
another serving of Toad in the Hole, rudely demanding,
"Do you want to make me ill?" before adding, "A couple
slices of plain toast would be good." Little Lotta Reiniger,
sitting across from her, giggled adoringly, but even the evident "pash" the precocious fourth former had on the lanky
fifth former couldn't diminish the chip Angle carried on
her shoulder.

Oddly enough, Angle seemed to be watching Bobby,
even as Bobby watched her. Bobby would discover the
girl's gray eyes turned on her, but Angle hastily looked
down at her plate every time the coach met her glance. As
breakfast ended, amid the clatter of chairs being pulled
out and pushed back in, Angle made her way to Bobby's
side. "Do you drive a blue Triumph?" she asked almost
furtively.

"I don't own a car," said Bobby, confused. "Do you
need a ride somewhere?"

"No," muttered Angle. She walked alongside Bobby in
silence as the gym teacher exited the dining hall and
headed down the path to the gymnasium.

"Are you coming to archery?" asked the Games Mistress in surprise. "What about your leaf mold allergy?"

"It's better," said the taciturn teen. Bobby decided not to
point out that the dead leaves were thick on the ground.

"I guess so long as you avoid walks in the woods you'll
be okay."

"No one can stop me from going to the woods," said
Angle angrily. "It's the only place I can get any privacy!"

"They're your nasal passages," said Bobby mildly. "I'm
just suggesting . . . Don't you like it here at Metamora?"

"I hate it." Angle ground her teeth. "The girls here are
even dumber than the ones at my old school. Always

writing poetry and talking about ghosts, and pashes! And that Miss Otis saying I have to go on one of old Bowling Ball's nature walks if I want to visit the woods, and then she gives me demerits for not wearing knee socks when it's hot enough to fry an egg! 'Young ladies should always have their calves covered.'" Angle made her voice prissy in imitation of the Latin Mistress.

"Miss Otis is a little old-fashioned." Bobby tried to soothe the irate girl.

"I wish we didn't have to wear any stupid uniform," said Angle. "I wish I could dress like you."

Bobby looked down at her Metamora sweatshirt and corduroy slacks.

"It's nice to be comfortable," she admitted without thinking.

That was enough to launch Angle on another harangue. "So why can't we students be comfortable? If I could find even a couple girls who weren't ninnies, I'd organize a walkout in two minutes! My dad says organizing is the only way to force change on the bosses. We'd strike for the right to wear pants! Miss Otis can bring on her knee sock–wearing goons and strikebreakers, but the will of the people will prevail!"

Bobby searched desperately for an argument to stop the tidal wave. "But—but skirts and dresses are part of the fun of being female," she tried, calling to mind a recent issue of *Teenaged* she'd read, in an effort to familiarize herself with her students' concerns. "I mean, girls are lucky because they get to wear, um, kilts and . . . sheaths . . . and crinolines," she concluded uncertainly.

"You can keep your crinolines," Angle retorted. "What I'd like is a sharp gray suit, like Miss Butler's boyfriend wears."

Bobby found herself nodding in agreement. It had been

a nice suit. "But wasn't Miss Butler attractive in that black dress with the scoop neck?" she argued. She wanted to point out to Angle how the knit wool clung to Enid's figure, and how the skirt flared out to reveal her attractive legs when Rod twirled her into his vehicle.

"She was okay," said Angle, in a bored voice. Bobby felt a twinge of resentment on the behalf of the Math Mistress.

"Well, the fact is the Metamora uniform is here to stay," said Bobby, abandoning her perfunctory argument for feminine frills. "It wouldn't be fair to the other girls to have you parading around in a gray flannel suit." She forestalled the argument that she knew was on Angle's lips. "And don't tell me they could wear whatever they wanted. The thing about a uniform is it levels the playing field, d'you see? No student is dressed any better than the next one."

"I guess so," grumbled Angle.

"And just remember, after you graduate next year, you can wear whatever you want," Bobby promised her.

Angle brightened. "I think I'll send away for Gruneman's men's catalog today," she decided.

They'd reached the gymnasium. "For now, just change into your gym tunic," Bobby instructed her. "You know, I think archery is going to be great cross-training for field hockey. It will build your hand-eye coordination, as well as strength in your arms and shoulders."

Angle flashed a sudden smile. "Maybe I'll get more muscular, like you," she said as she hurried to the gym.

Bobby watched her go, wondering if she'd mishandled the encounter. What was the proper response to the teen's irascible temper? Should she have reprimanded Angle for mocking Miss Otis and calling Bryce Bowles by that disrespectful nickname? Should she have made a better case for crinolines? Had she raised false hopes in Angle? The

knobby-kneed girl probably didn't realize that a good
gray suit was going to cost more than a few weeks' allowance!

I've got to swallow my pride and ask Enid for help,
Bobby decided.

Chapter Nine

A Visit to Enid

As twilight fell that evening, Bobby left her dorm, crossed under the narrow stone archway that separated Cornwall from Manchester, and entered the fourth form's dormitory. She wished she were still in the Cornwall common room, playing Parcheesi with her third formers, rather than calling on the brainy Miss Butler!

Passing the doorway of Manchester's common room, she glimpsed Linda Kerwin. The first-string forward was poring over a heavy book with her friends Penny and Sue. Bobby hesitated in the hallway, wondering what mischief they were planning.

No procrastinating, she told herself sternly. After all, this wasn't her dorm to discipline. She continued down the corridor to Enid's suite.

When she knocked, the door swung open instantly.

"Hello, you're—" Enid stopped abruptly at the sight of Bobby, her dark brows arched in surprise. "Oh, hello, Bobby."

The Math Mistress was unexpectedly casual in faded plaid pedal pushers and a dark red blouse. Her smooth cap of hair gleamed like polished ebony and her black-framed glasses emphasized her square features. "What can I do for you?"

"I wondered if you had a minute to talk about Angle." Bobby gulped.

"Angela—surely. Come in."

Enid's suite of rooms mirrored Bobby's in Cornwall, but aside from the layout, the sitting room had nothing in common with the gym teacher's. The walls were lined with books, and more books were piled on Enid's desk and the floor. There were no pennants or photographs on her wall, just an odd painting of colored squares over the fireplace. Bobby's eyes instinctively scanned Enid's desk, looking for a photo of Rod, but there was only a framed picture of a grim-faced pair, undoubtedly her parents.

"Sit down." Enid took a pile of mathematical magazines off the armchair. Bobby sat and Enid turned her desk chair around to face her.

Bobby couldn't help feeling like a pupil in the principal's office as she began, "Well, I'm worried about Angle. She's so—so liable to fly off the handle at the least little thing. And she doesn't seem to have any friends here at Metamora. I thought maybe we could put our heads together and . . ." Bobby trailed off.

Enid leaned back. "Angle is an interesting phenomenon at Metamora. So many factors have combined to make her integration into her peer group unusually difficult."

"Yes, that's what I mean," Bobby said eagerly. She relaxed. Enid would be able to unravel Angle's behavior problems. The brainy teacher would tell the Games Mistress what buttons to push to make the Savages' potential star keep her temper and stop racking up fouls.

Enid counted items off on her fingers. "First, her cultural background separates her from most of the girls here. Second, she entered as a transfer. Third, she should be a sixth former, but because of her abrupt withdrawal from St. Margaret Mary's, she's only a fifth former."

"I didn't know that," Bobby interjected.

"Fourth, her familial crisis has created strong emotions for which she must find an outlet."

"I think field hockey will be a great outlet," Bobby put in eagerly. "I was hoping you could give me some tips on integrating her with the rest of the Savages. . . ." She stopped. Enid was shaking her head, a superior smile on her lips.

"I'm afraid I must disagree with you there. Angela is already chafing against the regimentation of school life. The last thing she needs is additional rules and regulations to follow. I think the dull drills, the insistence on physical discomfort for no good reason, the mind-numbing notion of 'team spirit' may well combine to drive her over the edge into out-and-out rebellion."

Bobby felt like she'd been punched in the stomach. "But—but—I think being on the team will show Angle the importance of working with the group instead of against it! And anyway, what you said isn't true! The drills we do aren't dull, and the physical discomfort has plenty of point. As for team spirit—"

"Let's leave that aside for the moment," said Enid smoothly. "Have you considered the complication of the group dynamics on your team? Angela has singled out the DAP Society members for her special disdain, and the DAPs have responded in kind. Putting her on a DAP-dominated team is like putting a match to a—"

"The Savages aren't DAP dominated," Bobby interrupted heatedly. "Every one of those girls was picked on the basis of her abilities on the field!"

"Of course, I know next to nothing about field hockey." Enid shrugged as if she were admitting ignorance of the native customs of Fiji islanders. "But didn't the team elect Kayo, who's president of the DAPs, as its captain? And isn't it true that Kayo's closest friends—also DAP members—are all on the Varsity squad?"

"Team," corrected Bobby. "And that's just a coincidence."

"I think it would make much more sense to encourage Angela's participation in one of the clubs *not* dominated by those DAP girls. The Problem Solvers, for example. There her abilities will win her the approval and recognition she secretly craves."

"But that's just what field hockey will do for her," expostulated Bobby. "I mean, sure, she can join the math club too, if she wants, but—"

"Very gracious of you, I'm sure!" Anger crackled in Enid's voice.

Bobby felt her temper rise in response to Enid's sarcasm. "But I think you're dead wrong about field hockey! In the first place, there's nothing an adolescent girl needs so much as a physical outlet, something to do with all the hormones and teenaged energy she's got zinging around inside her—"

"You make these girls sound like nothing more than a collection of biological impulses," Enid interrupted with heat. "They've got brains too, you know!"

"In the second place," Bobby continued doggedly, "everyone, sooner or later, has got to learn to get along with society—I mean, isn't that why we have institutions like the United Nations? So people can learn how to get along?" Bobby thought of the many adjustments she'd made to fit into society.

"Are you proposing the Savages as a miniature UN?" Enid's voice dripped with sarcasm. "What you say applies to any number of extracurricular activities. The point is, today's educators agree that we must develop the brains of America's youth, not their brawn! Our country needs leaders who can calculate the curve of a ball mathematically, not empty-headed athletes who merely know how to hit one!"

At that, Bobby lost her temper. "I for one would rather have a hockey player leading me than some cold-blooded mathematician with formaldehyde in her veins!"

The look Enid gave her was pure poison, and Bobby realized she'd gone too far. At that moment there was a rat-a-tat-tat on Enid's door.

It was Laura Burnham, wearing a paint-stained smock. "Are you ready?" she asked Enid in her throaty voice. "Oh, hello!" she added as she caught sight of Bobby. "If it isn't everybody's favorite new teacher."

Bobby's path rarely crossed that of the Art Mistress, to the gym teacher's regret. She'd always wanted to erase the bad impression she'd made at their first meeting. Something about Laura Burnham drew Bobby to the artistic teacher.

But just then she was too hot under the collar to gaze at the appetizing Art Mistress with her usual enjoyment. And in any case, Enid was ushering her out, with an icy apology. "I'm sorry, Bobby, I promised to pose for Laura. Perhaps we can continue this most interesting discussion another time."

Bobby stormed out of Manchester, too agitated to return to Cornwall. She headed to the athletic field. Calisthenics, a session with the barbells she kept in her office, and then some wind sprints would be the perfect outlet for her irritation, whatever Enid might think!

An hour later, after the twelfth lap around the athletic field, Bobby had cooled down enough to regret her hasty remark to Enid about cold-blooded mathematicians. She supposed she'd cooked her goose permanently with the Math Mistress. If Enid had resented her before, their argument had undoubtedly firmed up her enmity, like a pudding left too long on the stove. Bobby could forget about getting help from the brainy teacher!

The stars were out when she climbed the path back to the quadrangle, calmer, if sweaty, and thinking so hard about Angle that she almost bumped into Mona. The housekeeper was wheeling a bicycle to the shed behind Essex.

"Careful, Bobby! I already barked my shin on this bicycle. Those girls! They just abandon them anywhere!" Metamora's usually cheerful housekeeper seemed out of temper.

"Sorry, Mona," Bobby apologized. She knew the old bicycles were the bane of Mona's and Ole's existence. They were kept in the utility shed, and the students were supposed to ask for permission before using them. However, unauthorized bicycle borrowing was rampant.

"Oh, never mind." The housekeeper gave a little laugh. "Girls will be girls! I just wish Munty Blaine hadn't taught so many Metamorians how to jimmy the shed's padlock. Have you been working out? You look awfully invigorated. How about a cup of cocoa with me in Devon?" She put a caressing hand on Bobby's bicep.

"Sorry, not tonight." A daring idea had come to the young teacher—she would study those psychology and education texts herself! After all, Miss Watkins had said she wasn't dumb. Maybe she could figure out Angle all on her own! "I need to hit the books," she explained to the disappointed housekeeper. She was itching to get back to the dorm and delve into *Problems in Adolescent Development*.

"Well, another time." Mona trailed her hand along Bobby's arm as she released her with evident reluctance. Bobby had turned toward Cornwall when Mona recalled her.

"Oh! Before I forget." Bobby turned back. "I thought you should know, Enid went to Miss Craybill with her concerns about the athletic program. She's a brilliant teacher but perhaps a little too serious about government-mandated educational goals. Of course she didn't get very far—Miss Craybill had a date with a crested kingfisher—but you might want to make sure the Savages operate strictly by Metamora's rule book. I'd hate to see the team dissolved before it even plays a game!"

"Thanks," said Bobby automatically as Mona wheeled the bicycle away. The soothing effects of her exercise were done away with in a moment by this new evidence of Enid's implacable hatred for hockey. Well, now the hostility was two-sided!

Bobby swirled the dregs of beer in her glass absent-mindedly as she said, "Could it be something as simple as a growth spurt? I was rereading *Problems in Adolescent Development* from that psych class I had to take, and the author—who's a doctor!—says parents and teachers should never underestimate the profound effects a sudden growth spurt can have on an adolescent. Inadequate sleep—grouchiness—dissociation from a stable peer group—and the next thing you know you have a juvenile delinquent on your hands!"

Elaine shifted restlessly in her seat across the table from Bobby. "When you said you wanted to go someplace quiet and talk about hormonal urges, I didn't picture this," she said, irritable as any sleep-deprived adolescent.

The two girls were sitting in the Ladies' Lounge of the Flame Inn, a cozy room off the bar done up in Late American Rustic. Small cocktail tables in knotty pine filled the room; candles in red-pebbled glass and a moose head on the wall provided ambience.

"Do you want another gin and tonic?" Bobby asked. She looked around for the waitress and pointed at Elaine's empty glass when she caught her eye.

Maybe it had been a mistake, meeting here instead of the Ellmans' deserted pool house, as Elaine had suggested. But Bobby had been learning more from her studies of the adolescent psyche than the importance of integration in the peer group. Chapter 23, "Sex and the Adolescent," had certainly given her pause. "Sex is a natural part of the adolescent's development," the author had written. "It is important not to relegate it to the back alleys and dark corners of the adolescent's world where he will learn to associate it solely with shameful physical urges."

The chapter went on to discuss the many ways young couples could interact with each other in the light of day. While the book's emphasis had been on group roller-skating and church clubs, Bobby felt that meeting Elaine at the Flame Inn was a pretty good start at integrating her special friendship with her peer group.

Now she took a gulp of beer and searched for another topic. It was important to find interests in common besides the physical urges, the book said. "How's candy striping?" she asked.

"My candy striping days are over," said Elaine moodily. "I never liked being around all those sick people anyway. It was just a good excuse to go into Bay City."

Mentally Bobby erased that topic from her list.

"I'm so bored with life I could scream." Elaine was continuing her usual complaint. "Daddy's gotten stricter than ever since I changed my mind about college. If I'd known he was going to cut my allowance, I'd have gone. If only he'd let me get an apartment of my own. . . ."

Bobby had heard this sob story before and her thoughts drifted back to the Savages. The team was shaping up amazingly well after its three official practices and the two unofficial sessions she'd squeezed in. Once she'd given the squad passes from Study Hall, and once she'd taken advantage of the warm September evenings with a post-dinner practice—although she'd held her breath when Miss Craybill wandered by. However, Miss Craybill was gazing up into the trees, looking for a white-breasted nuthatch, and passed without noticing the girls vigorously pursuing the hockey ball across the field.

Yes, the team was making tremendous advances in skill and technique. When the girls elected Kayo captain, they'd given Bobby an active assistant coach. Kayo taught Misako the Indian dribble, corrected Annette's grip, and had the team running drills when Bobby arrived at practice. Tuesday night's practice wouldn't have occurred if Kayo hadn't rescheduled the DAPs meeting. Kayo seemed willing to do anything to make the Savages a success.

Bobby wished she could say the same of Angle, who stubbornly resisted Bobby's efforts to make her a team player. Indignant cries of "Ball hog!" and "Grandstander!" followed her up the field whenever she got hold of the ball.

Yet the coach couldn't blame Angle alone for the lack of teamwork. Much as she hated to admit it, Bobby couldn't deny that there was some truth in Enid's accusation that the DAP girls dominated the Savages. It was natural, Bobby supposed, that after playing together for so long the DAPs tended to pass to the teammate they knew rather than the teammate in the best position. Natural, but unfortunate. What would happen at Friday's game? Would the team forget their factionalism and pull together or would—

"You're not listening!"

Bobby started guiltily. Elaine was looking at her with accusing brown eyes.

"Sure I am," Bobby alibied. "You were talking about your apartment—and your allowance—and how your dad should realize that if you lived in Bay City and got involved in charity events, you'd add to the prestige of Ellman Cycles."

"That was ten minutes ago, Bobby! I was describing a Danish modern tea cart I might purchase. But clearly you're not interested." Elaine stabbed out her cigarette in the knotty pine ashtray.

"Sure I am," Bobby soothed the petulant debutante, secretly wondering if modern furniture could be a bond between them. Then she sat up straight. "Why, there's Mona!"

The Metamora housekeeper was at a corner booth with a svelte blond woman whose back was to Bobby. Bobby couldn't help admiring the delicate ankles peeking out from her crisply creased capris.

"Who's that, another of your college conquests?" inquired Elaine caustically.

"No, I've told you about her, she's the housekeeper at Metamora. She's awfully nice."

Elaine's eyes were like angry brown coals. "First you ignore me, and now you're cruising other girls!" She glanced across the room at Mona's table and stiffened. "Oh, no!"

"What's the matter?"

"That's Mrs. Driscoll—from my mother's bridge club! I can't let her see me here with you! Oh, I knew this was a terrible idea!"

"Look at it this way," Bobby tried to comfort the distraught girl. "We're two friends having a drink together, just like them." A happy thought struck her. "Or what if they're just like us? Maybe your mother's friend is secretly playing on our team!"

"The only thing Dot Driscoll plays is high-stakes bridge!" snapped Elaine.

"Well, keep your shirt on, she's leaving," reported Bobby. She watched as the two women stood up from their table, laughing. She wanted to get a better look at the blonde, and half wished this Mrs. Driscoll would spot Elaine and come over. But Mona's mysterious friend threw a camel's hair coat over her shoulders and exited.

"Why, Bobby, what a pleasure." Bobby's head snapped around. Mona was standing at their table beaming. The young gym teacher had been so busy watching the other woman depart, she hadn't noticed Metamora's housekeeper approach.

"Hello, Mona," Bobby said lamely. She could practically see the smoke coming out of Elaine's ears as the girl fumed inwardly. "This is—this is my friend Elaine Ellman. She was my candy striper at Bay City General."

"Elaine Ellman . . ." Mona held on to the hand Elaine reluctantly extended. "Now, I know I know that name from somewhere."

Bobby knew Mona was going to bring up Ellman bicycles, and that Elaine would be more furious than ever.

"Didn't I read in *The Glen Valley Crier* that you're engaged to Ted Driscoll, son of the dry-cleaning Driscolls?"

Bobby felt as if the ball had been stolen from her just as she was lifting her stick for a shot on goal. She looked at Elaine, waiting for her denial. But Elaine only flushed a little as she answered, "Oh, do you know Ted?"

"I was just chatting with his aunt-by-marriage, Dorothy Driscoll," Mona explained. "I finally forced her to give me her cook's famous coconut cream pie recipe. I'm hoping to tempt Miss Craybill's appetite with a special treat," she told Bobby in an aside.

Bobby was too stunned to respond coherently. "Oh, ah? I mean, that's terrific. Pie, I mean."

"Well, I should be going. Bobby, do you have a way back to Metamora?"

"Bryce and Ole," replied Bobby automatically. "They're picking me up after the show at the Bijou gets out."

"Oh, that's right, they're seeing *The Music Man* again. Well, I'll say good night, then. Nice to have met you, Elaine."

When they were alone again, there was an awkward silence. "You're engaged?" Bobby said at last.

"What of it?" Elaine tossed her head defiantly. "It doesn't make any difference to us."

"But . . . but it does!" Bobby protested. She wished the author of *Adolescent Development Patterns* had dealt with a similar dating problem in his textbook.

"We can still have fun. We can still park at the far end of Glen Mountain Road, and meet in the pool house, and do all the things we like. Look, all my engagement to Ted means is that Daddy will stop bothering me about college and raise my allowance so I can buy a trousseau. I'm not 'off the team,' or however you would put it."

"You may not be off the team, but your team loyalty is certainly in question!" Bobby responded hotly.

Elaine's temper, never placid, began to fray. "Maybe I need a more competent coach," she shot back. "One who understands the point of the game!"

"What are you saying?" demanded Bobby indignantly. "Are you implying my ball-handling skills are slipping? Why, I taught you everything you know! Your technique, your wide knowledge of plays . . . Where do you think you'd be without me?"

Elaine stood up. "Don't be beastly, Bobby Blanchard," she said coldly. "I'm leaving, and I never want to see you or hear another ghastly sports metaphor from you again!" She stalked away, leaving Bobby open-mouthed. Halfway to the door, she turned around and added, "And I'll have you know, I was considered quite a good player at Shady Lane Summer Camp, long before I met you!" She slammed the door of the Flame Inn Ladies' Lounge behind her.

Bobby bent her head over her beer, both angry and astonished. Shady Lane Summer Camp! Hadn't Elaine always said she was the first? Had she ever really known Elaine? Had their romance been no more substantial than a shadow that had disappeared when she'd tried to drag it out of the dark corners into daylight? *Well, good riddance!* she told herself defiantly. The engagement to this dry-cleaning Driscoll boy was the last straw. What had she and Elaine ever had in common besides the brief moments of wordless passion they shared? Bobby was a field hockey fan, and Elaine was an aficionado of modern furniture. It was probably better this way.

As anger faded, melancholy stole in and settled on Bobby's heart like a thick winter fog. What was the matter with her? Why was it she could never hold on to a girl for longer than a semester or a summer break?

And now that she was marooned in Metamora, where would she find a girl, period?

Who needs 'em? Bobby blustered mentally. *To heck with these girls and their engagements! I'll just concentrate on my students.*

Chapter Eleven

Home Game

There was a nervous quiver in Bobby's stomach as she watched the bleachers begin to fill with students, teachers, and even a sprinkling of parents. The big yellow bus from St. Margaret Mary's had arrived and was disgorging their field hockey team, the Holy Martyrs.

"Here come the Holy Virgins," muttered one of the Savages. They were an impressive bunch, Bobby had to admit as she watched the squad of hulking, freckled girls descend and heard them shouting at each other in deep, hoarse voices. Their coach was a stern-faced, square-jawed woman wearing a kilt of black watch plaid that matched the team's uniforms. Next to the Martyrs, the Metamora girls in their brand-new crimson and white pinnies looked a little . . . frivolous.

Bobby wished the Savages' first game wasn't against the top-ranked Martyrs. Her players might talk boldly, calling the team by its unsanctioned nickname, but Bobby knew they were intimidated. However, the schedule set by the Midwest Regional Secondary School Girls' Field Hockey League couldn't be helped.

"Miss Blanchard! Miss Blanchard!" It was Miss Craybill calling to her. Bobby hurried to join the Headmistress, who stood with a little cluster of visitors. "Miss Blanchard, I'd like you to meet some of our family and alumnae," Miss Craybill twittered. "Mrs. O'Shea, Angela's grandmother."

The stout white-haired woman in her shapeless black coat bore no resemblance to her granddaughter, save for the shrewd gray eyes. "Pleased to meet you, I'm sure," she said, pursing up her mouth.

"Your granddaughter is a wonderful athlete—a real natural," Bobby told the old woman. "You must be very proud of her."

"It was God that gave her the gift, not I," Mrs. O'Shea responded sourly. "And the devil may yet put it to his own use. I don't mind telling you, I'd rather Angela were still with that lot." She nodded at the Holy Martyrs as she rattled a string of beads through her hand.

Bobby wondered again why Angie had left St. Margaret Mary's so abruptly, but Miss Craybill's hand was on her arm. "I must steal Miss Blanchard away from you, I'm afraid." As she walked Bobby a few steps away, she murmured, "She pays Angela's tuition, you know," then aloud, "and this is the Kerwins' aunt, Dottie Grimes—pardon me, I often forget my Metamorians' married names! Mrs. Driscoll, I should say."

Bobby hardly heard the introduction. She was face-to-face with the beautiful blonde she'd glimpsed drinking with Mona at the Flame Inn. The unexpected sight of Dot Driscoll was like a blow to her solar plexus. Dorothy Driscoll's face belonged on the cover of *Vogue*, while her figure would be at home on a stage in Vegas. Her ash blond hair made a halo around her face, and she wore a red mohair sweater over double-knit jersey pants that showed the generous flare of her hips. A wide black belt emphasized her hourglass figure. Bobby's head swam.

"Did—did you play hockey like your sister?" she managed to ask.

"No, but I've always been an avid onlooker!" Mrs. Driscoll smiled.

"Dot had a career in insurance before her marriage," Miss Craybill told Bobby.

"I'm just a happy housewife now," laughed Dot.

Bobby searched for small talk but she was too dizzy with desire to do anything but stare at this beautiful apparition, which had appeared on Louth Athletic field like a religious vision.

Celibacy had never suited the ex-hockey player. Ever since she and Elaine had broken it off, Bobby had been prone to these storms of desire, which swept over her with the speed of a forest fire after a dry spell. Anything could spark the flame; and living as she did in a remote girls' boarding school, surrounded at every turn by tempting female flesh, there was no shortage of sparks. One day it would be Mona, bending over the refreshment table to pour out some cocoa. Another time it might be squeezing past Laura Burnham at a faculty meeting. Even Miss Rasphigi, glimpsed one twilight walking toward the chemistry lab, had taken on a certain enigmatic allure. Worst of all, Bobby had discovered that her archenemy, Enid Butler, had the power to attract her!

Then there was Bobby's heightened awareness of the hormonal heat surrounding her in peasant dance, stunts and tumbling, and even tetherball classes. After a particularly vigorous kinetics class, Bobby would often retreat to her office and try to calm herself by studying diagrams of hockey plays while wrapping her overheated head in a cold, wet towel.

Field hockey practice was no better. Why did the girls have to run giggling around the showers snapping damp towels at each other? Why was it that Kayo always seemed to be taking off her blouse when the coach visited the locker room to hustle the players along? Sometimes Bobby even suspected the Savages' captain was deliberately flaunting her charms! Then she pushed the thought away, ashamed of her overheated imagination, and did some pull-ups on the bar across her office doorway.

But Kayo's aunt was of age, and right now all Bobby could think about was pulling Dot Driscoll under the bleachers and exploring at close range the generous curves her attire advertised. She wanted to spirit the blond beauty into the woods nearby, push her up against a tree and—

Why, that's like my dream, Bobby realized with a prickle of horror. *That dream I had on the train.*

Like a swimmer coming up for air, she shook her head, trying to clear away the miasma of lust and fear.

"Coach Bobby! Coach Bobby!" The piping voice of Lotta Reiniger, who had attached herself to the Savages as water girl, pulled Bobby out of her reverie. "They're looking for you on the field!"

Bobby hurried out to the center line, taking one last look over her shoulder at the divine Dot, who was now chatting with Mona. Funny, Mona hadn't mentioned Mrs. Driscoll's relationship to the Kerwins when she'd seen the two of them at the Flame Inn.

The Holy Martyrs' coach and the league umpires were conferring. The official score table was set up, with teen-aged assistants crouched by each scorer. Both teams were on the field now, the Metamora girls practicing their recently learned dodges and tackles more tentatively than usual next to the Holy Martyrs' swagger and skill. Angle stood off to one side, glowering at the Catholic schoolgirls. Bobby paused a moment to ask the sullen teen why she wasn't warming up.

"You're not going to play me, are you?" Angle demanded.

"Your job is to be ready, no matter whether you play or not," Bobby reproved before hurrying on.

In truth, Bobby couldn't decide whether or not to play Angle this game. Although Angle looked up to her, asking her opinion about movies and books, imitating the way she walked ("Like an Indian brave," she'd told Bobby admiringly), the coach couldn't convince the girl to drop her grudge against the DAPs. She had an idea that if she benched the recalcitrant loner, Angle would see that she needed the team as much as the team needed her.

A firm handshake with the Holy Martyrs' coach, a welcome to the ref, a toot on her whistle to round up the Metamorians, and the game began. The starting lineup took the field—Ilsa "Iggy" Jespersen and Kayo as inner forwards, Annette and Beryl as wings. Linda's friends, Penny and Sue, were halfbacks, and Shirley, Helen, and Anna were fullbacks, with Edie in goal. Bobby had tapped Linda for center. The young girl had an ability to anticipate and surprise her opponent, and could win a bully purely through psychological skill.

But something was wrong with Linda today—she seemed intimidated by the big freckled girl with the squinty eyes who crouched opposite her. The ball went to the Holy Martyrs and they drove it into Metamora territory with embarrassing quickness.

"God bless Edie," Bobby thought as the padded girl stopped a shot on goal. The goalie seemed to be the only member of the team who wasn't frightened of the Holy Martyrs. The rest of the Savages stumbled and fumbled until Bobby's cheeks were crimson with embarrassment. It was as if her players had forgotten everything she'd painstakingly drilled into them the past week. At the end of the first half, even Edie had not been able to prevent five goals for the visiting team.

Home 1, visitors 5. The Savages' lone goal was the result of a penalty shot—the ball had scarcely left Metamora territory. Lotta ran to and fro with water for the thirsty Savages. Bobby glanced across the field at the Holy Martyrs, who were barely winded, laughing as they stood around their coach. The hatchet-faced coach was pulling new players off the bench. This, to Bobby, was the final humiliation. The coach was sending in her second string—treating the game like a practice for her team.

Bobby tried to rally her girls. "Penny, what happened to your lunge? You were doing so well last scrimmage!"

Penny looked down. "I don't know, Coach."

"And Beryl, remember how we talked about running parallel and a few steps ahead of Kayo when she has the ball?"

"These players are pulling some dirty tricks," Beryl muttered.

Bobby knit her brows. The Holy Martyrs had been playing a clean game as far as she could tell. Was there something else happening out on the field, something she couldn't see? The whistle blew before she could ask the right wing what she meant. As the girls got to their feet and ran back on to the field, Bobby watched, feeling helpless. So this was life on the sidelines—trying to win the game with your head, making decisions that the players executed!

"Coach Bobby, Coach Bobby!" Lotta was jumping up and down as she frantically sought Bobby's attention. "I can tell you why we're getting beat—that Holy Virgin girl spooked Linda at the bully—she said something terrible about the ghost of Miss Froelich!"

"Lotta, you know there's no ghost—" Bobby began automatically, and then stopped. "What did she say, exactly?"

Lotta looked down at her shoes. "She said Miss Froelich's ghost will always haunt Metamora, that she can never find rest, because—because she—because she jumped from the tower on purpose!"

Bobby smacked her head in despair. Of course—her girls weren't used to the kind of heckling a competitive team like the Holy Martyrs could bring on. And superstitious Linda would be the most vulnerable target for this attack on the Savages' morale!

Angle was suddenly at her other side. "Put me in, Coach, please, put me in!"

Bobby was watching the game. Kayo had won the center bully, and for the first time that day the ball was in Holy Martyr territory. Kayo sped toward the goal, taking the Holy Martyr halfbacks by surprise, but as she lifted her stick for the drive that would score, the umpire's whistle blew. "Offsides!" she called as the Savages' captain looked around in bewilderment. In her inexperience, Annette had run past the Holy Martyrs' two fullbacks and goalie.

"That idiot!" Angle ground her teeth in frustration.

"She's your teammate," Bobby reminded her benched player. If nothing else went right this game, at least she could say her strategy with Angle was beginning to work. The girl was so tormented by her desire to rush out on the field she couldn't sit still.

Edie blocked the penalty shot.

"Put me in, Coach, you've got to put me in!" Angle was pleading now. "I'll be a team player and all that baloney you've been jawing about, I swear!"

"Get ready, then," said Bobby. Angle hadn't phrased her capitulation quite as Bobby wanted to hear it, but she'd made a beginning, and coach and player were united in their desire to see Metamora score at least once. The young coach waved for a time-out. "Number twelve going in for number four," she called to the umpire. Linda trotted off the field, and sat on the bench, looking half

ashamed, half relieved. Angle ran out to take her place at
the bully.

Bobby shaded her eyes and watched anxiously as the
Holy Martyrs' center said something that evoked mocking laughter from her teammates, but Angle only adjusted
her stance, crouching a little more. When the whistle blew,
Angle tapped her stick against her opponent's three times
and then neatly rolled the ball over the other girl's stick,
simultaneously stepping forward and dribbling the ball
upfield before the Holy Martyrs had recovered. Bobby
saw Kayo running parallel on the right, shouting to Angle
to pass, but Angle ignored her. It was like that first scrimmage the day of tryouts. Angle simply boiled upfield and
scored.

There were vociferous cheers from the Metamora supporters in the stands and mutters from the Holy Martyrs.
The ref caught the ball and placed it on the center line.
The two centers took up their positions, in dead silence
this time. Bobby sensed rather than saw the way the Holy
Martyr lifted her stick a trifle higher, bracing for the same
technique Angle had used the first time. But Angle, with a
flick of her wrist, sent the ball through her opponent's legs,
and Kayo scooped it up. Angle ran forward calling, "Back
to me, back to me!" Kayo paused, looking for Beryl, but
Beryl was well guarded. "Back to me, for crissake!"
shouted Angle. Kayo obliged at last, with a smart left pass.

The whistle blew. "Home three, visitors five," shouted
the umpire.

Angle lost the ball on the next bully, but Kayo picked it
up, quick as a wink, and took it upfield, keeping so close
to the alley, Bobby held her breath. "Pass!" shouted Bobby
as she watched the hulking Holy Martyr halfbacks descend on the slender girl. "Pass!"

Kayo passed, but she passed too forcefully—the ball
whizzed past Angle and went to Annette on the left.

Annette lunged to stop it too late, and the ball rolled out of bounds.

As the teams arranged themselves for the roll-in, Bobby saw Angle say something to Kayo, one hand on her hip, the other hand gesticulating. Bobby half rose to intervene, but the whistle blew, and Angle hastily took up position. However, it was Helen who got the ball and flicked it over her opponent's stick as if she'd been doing it all her life. Angle called for the ball, but Helen dribbled on. Bobby frowned. It was as if her whole team had forgotten the passing drills they'd been practicing the last month! But what was Angle doing? Instead of waiting for the pass, she'd run after Helen and stolen the ball from her own astonished teammate. Bobby's jaw dropped. She'd never seen such a thing. Angle scored. It was 4 to 5.

Kayo took the next bully. She just managed to send the ball to Annette with a tricky left pass, but a hulking halfback on the Holy Martyrs tackled Annette, knocking her down. The umpire's whistle blew. "Penalty shot to the Savages!" she shouted.

Bobby and the Savages on the bench held their breath as Annette limped up to the ball and carefully took aim. Cheers erupted as the left forward flicked the ball into the very corner of the Holy Martyr goal and the Holy Martyr goalie made a futile dive to stop it. "Home five, visitors five!" trumpeted the umpire through cupped hands.

Bobby looked at the time. Five minutes left on the clock. Her hands trembled as she shaded her eyes again. Could the Savages actually win, their first time out in twenty years? "Hustle, hustle, you can do it!" she cried to her revived team, even as she reminded herself the odds were against them.

Her team hustled, but the Holy Martyrs were equally determined and their pride was at stake. The Holy Martyrs center knocked the ball halfway down the field on the bully and the determined forward line caught up with it just as the Savage halfbacks grabbed the ball and sent it back to their own forward line. But the Holy Martyrs were all over them like fruit flies on an overripe peach. This would be their strategy, Bobby knew, keep the ball in Metamora's territory, keep the Savages on the defensive.

Yet somehow Shirley managed to send the ball to Annette, and limping Annette was not as heavily guarded as Angle and Kayo. She broke away from the pack, dribbling rapidly up the alley, dangerously close to the sideline. The Savage forward line was at her heels. "Here!" Bobby heard Angle's raucous cry. "Over here!" The Holy Martyr halfbacks were closing in on Annette as she passed off her back foot to Angle, who only managed to dribble a few yards before she too found herself surrounded.

"Angle, here!" screamed Kayo.

Angle feinted left, and then instead of passing, she shot on goal, from just inside the shooting circle. It was a strong, clean shot, straight up the center, but the goalie was prepared, knees together, hands raised, ready to block and kick the ball back downfield.

And then a miracle happened. The ball bounced sideways—on a tuft of grass, a gopher hole, it didn't matter. The goalie made a futile dive, and as the stands erupted in pandemonium, the ball rolled across the end line. The buzzer blew.

The Savages were besides themselves with glee, jumping up and down and embracing each other in an excess of excitement. Their faces were still wreathed in astonished grins as Bobby lined them up to shake hands with the defeated Martyrs. The Holy Martyrs' coach gripped Bobby's hand for a moment and said, "You got a lucky break there, but I guess you earned it." Bobby's heart warmed at this terse praise from the unsmiling veteran of the Midwest

Regional Secondary School Girls' Field Hockey League.
"Next time, we'll be ready," the iron-jawed woman added
with a grim smile.

The girls ran toward the gymnasium, chattering excitedly, and Bobby followed them, passing clusters of Metamora supporters who had descended from the stands.
Mona was the first to congratulate the young field hockey
coach. "Quite an upset!" she said with a wide smile. "Not
many of us expected *that*."

"I certainly didn't!" Bobby responded exuberantly.

"Well done, Coach!" Dot Driscoll made a *V* for victory as she climbed down from the stands. "What a terrific break on that last goal! Once their passing catches
up to their scoring—"

Bobby felt a twinge of guilt. Angle had played like a
prima donna and Bobby should have taken her out the
minute she stole the ball from Helen. And Kayo—had she
overshot that pass to Angle accidentally or on purpose?
"They're still a little rough," she admitted. "And they
haven't quite jelled as a team—"

Kayo's aunt Dot put her hand on Bobby's arm. "Oh,
don't think I'm complaining! It was a smashing game—
just like seeing the long shot win the Derby, with a ticket
in your hand and the odds twenty to one!"

Out of the corner of her eye, Bobby saw Enid exiting
the door to the locker room. Had she missed the winning
goal? Bobby couldn't help hoping the Math Mistress had
witnessed the Savages' triumph. That would teach her to
meddle with Metamora's sports program!

Dot stepped closer, pushing any further thought of
Enid out of the field hockey coach's head. "Besides," she
murmured, "I'm sure you'll whip them into a froth of
perfection in no time! I saw you play the Bayard Blackhawks for the championship last fall." Dot's admiring
eyes played over Bobby's face, flushed with excitement,

and traveled down her lean, lithe frame. Bobby felt like Dot was stripping off the coach's crimson Metamora sweatshirt with her eyes alone. "What do you think of Metamora's chances against Rockford?" Dot asked in a confidential tone. "I don't think that any of their players are as strong as number twelve—do you think you can take them?"

"In field hockey you can never say for sure, but if the Savages continue to make progress . . ." Bobby hardly knew what she was saying as her head spun under an on-slaught of different sensations, the swell of Aunt Dot's breast pressing against her arm, Aunt Dot's expensive scent filling her nose, the heat radiating through Aunt Dot's clothes. Again, the urge to pull Aunt Dot under the bleach-ers and quell her questions about Metamora's odds with a hail of fevered kisses was almost overwhelming.

An automatic glance toward the bleachers told Bobby this would be impossible. Miss Craybill was emerging from their shadow, climbing over the steel struts and poles of the support structure, her eyes on the ground as she scuffed at the dirt with one lace-up shoe. She looked like a Victorian hobo, scrounging for loose change. Tear-ing herself away from the mesmerizing suburban matron with a muttered excuse, Bobby took the distracted Head-mistress's arm.

"Did you drop something, Miss Craybill?"

Miss Craybill looked up, focusing on Bobby with diffi-culty. "Oh no, I just . . . How goes the hockey match? Shouldn't you be out on the field, with your team?"

Bobby's jaw dropped. "The game is over, Miss Cray-bill. Metamora won." She was relieved when Miss Otis swooped down and carried the Headmistress away. She felt deeply troubled by Miss Craybill's latest eccentricity. The Headmistress had wandered off in the middle of the game!

To Bobby's disappointment, Dot had disappeared. As she peered about, searching for the voluptuous blonde, she heard a threatening voice.

"You think you showed us, huh, *Angela?* You think you're a hotshot now at your hotshot new school, with your hotshot new coach? Wait until we come back and beat the pants off you, then see how hotshot you are!"

Bobby turned around and saw Angle standing toe to toe with the freckled forward from the Holy Martyrs, who was flanked by two teammates. Except for their black watch plaid kilts, they looked like a girl gang from the docks of Bay City.

"I'd like to see you Holy Virgins try," taunted Angle. "I thought God was supposed to be on your side—how come he didn't send his only son to help you out at the bully, Duffy?"

Duffy was so pale every freckle stood out. "You're going straight to hell, O'Shea. Even if you weren't half kike, you'd be going straight to hell for what you just said!" She clenched her fists, but one of her teammates tugged at her elbow.

"Leave her be, Kathy, she's right where she belongs at this queer school—everyone knows there's something unnatural about that teacher's death! It's cursed—and so are you!"

Bobby surprised them, stepping from the shadow of the bleachers. "That's enough, all of you! Where's your sportsmanship?" She addressed the Holy Martyrs sternly. "Your bus is leaving soon."

As the three Holy Martyrs hurried away, Bobby reproved Angle. "I'm ashamed of you, Angle! No matter what they said, it's poor sportsmanship to insult the losing team! Remember—you won!"

"That's right!" Angle's face was lit by a grin so dazzling Bobby felt momentarily blinded. "I sure showed them!" Then she was gone. Bobby bit her lip. She wasn't sure Angle had gotten her message about sportsmanship.

Inside the locker room, Kayo and Beryl were in a huddle with Edie.

"She'd better not try that stuff again," Beryl was saying angrily to her friends, and Bobby couldn't help wondering if the boisterous girl was referring to Angle. What was the matter with these kids? Couldn't they set aside their petty jealousies and enjoy the victory?

"What's the problem, Beryl? You sound like your team lost instead of won," said the young coach heartily.

Beryl was flustered by Bobby's sudden appearance, and scrambled for an explanation. "It's Kayo—she can't find her heirloom third-generation Daughters of American Pioneers locket."

"That's too bad," Bobby sympathized, trying to look Kayo in the eye and not let her glance drop to the swelling bosom barely concealed by the teen's skimpy towel. Kayo's pale blond hair, the color of buttermilk, was still damp from her shower. Her skin had the opalescence of a pearl, flushed faintly with pink. "I'm sure it will turn up." Bobby gulped as she backed away. "Don't let it spoil your victory!"

"Did you hear, Mrs. Gilvang's throwing us a party." Kayo stepped forward eagerly. "She said she'd serve cocoa and cookies in Dorset's common room."

"Gosh, girls, I wish I'd known," said Bobby with genuine regret. "But tonight I have an appointment in Bay City."

Chapter Twelve

Bay City

L ooking out the window of the cab as it rolled toward Metamora's front gate, Bobby glimpsed the girls streaming toward Dorset for the impromptu party. She leaned back in her seat, a faint sense of regret tugging at her as she thought of the gay celebration, the rich cups of cocoa, the buttery cookies, and most importantly, the opportunity to foster a sense of team unity. If only she could be in two places at once!

But by the time the driver had passed the stone gateposts and was speeding toward Adena, any second thoughts about her trip to Bay City had fallen away like dried mud flaking off a tennis shoe.

Bobby had been looking forward to this trip to Bay City all day. She was meeting her old teammates for dinner, an informal reunion of the Elliott College Spitfires in honor of Chick, her best friend. Chick had gotten the spot on the National Women's Field Hockey Team after Bobby's accident. She was making a brief visit to the city following a summer at the Swans' lavish training camp on Lake Cranston, just before the renowned team flew to Glasgow for the first leg of their European tour.

Gee, it would be fun to see the old gang! Fond as Bobby had grown of Metamora and her students, it would be a relief to escape the hothouse atmosphere of the school for an evening. It would be a relief to carry on a conversation in English, without those foreign phrases buzzing around her like incomprehensible bees. It would be a relief to talk about calisthenics, field hockey plays, or cross-training with girls who really understood the importance of physical fitness.

At the train station in Adena, Bobby bought a Coke, drinking it in noisy gulps as she waited impatiently for the 5:40 train. She'd been in such a hurry to leave that she hadn't even stopped for a drink of water. Once on the train, she stared unseeingly out the window. In her bowling bag was a paperback novel she'd confiscated from Sandy Milston that morning, but she hadn't had time to put a brown paper wrapper over the picture of the two girls in their lingerie. Instead of reading it, she let her mind wander.

She thought what a good idea it was, bringing the bowling bag as an excuse for dressing in pants, saddle shoes, and a button-up shirt instead of the pumps and skirt a city excursion required. She wondered how her ex-teammates were adjusting to life after college. She was particularly curious about the ones now living in Bay City. Had any of them visited one of those attractive-sounding bars, like the one in the book, where desirable women congregated?

Maybe Pat, she mused. Pat Pressler, former fullback, had a reputation for sophistication. She'd majored in psychology and was full of theories applying what she'd learned in the classroom to her favorite sport. She loved to explain why goalies were more likely than forwards to become alcoholics, or to speculate that players who set up shots but never scored often had domineering mothers. Now she was working for the Bay City Parks and Recreation Department, sharing an apartment with two other Elliott graduates.

In her eagerness to see her old friends, Bobby was the first at the rendezvous. They had agreed to meet at Luigi's, an unpretentious Italian restaurant on the edge of Bay City's bohemian Riverside district. Bobby was sitting in the corner booth sipping a Cinzano when Pat walked in.

"Gee whiz," Bobby exclaimed, "I hardly recognized you!"

At Elliott College the fullback had lived in a sweatshirt and jeans, but today she was wearing pumps, hose, and a skirt.

"I look a sight, don't I?" Pat peeled off her gloves and tossed a battered hat on the seat next to Bobby. "Some of the old biddies at Park and Rec are real sticklers for what they call proper office attire. I think they subconsciously long to put on pants themselves, and thwarting me is the way they suppress their own desires. Give me two seconds in the john and I'll look more human."

Pat had hardly vanished into the restaurant's bathroom when Bobby felt a whack on her shoulder. "Bobby! How's the Games Mistress?"

"Chick!" Bobby jumped up to greet her best chum. "You're looking grand, Chick!"

The two friends thumped each other's shoulders affectionately. Pat returned from the powder room, presentable again, amid a flurry of arrivals. Fran and Bennie (Frances and Bonnie), the inseparable halfbacks nicknamed "the twins" because they always dressed alike—tonight they wore sharply creased plaid Bermuda shorts and knee socks, topped with Elliott College sweaters. Mash (Marcia) Manning, ex-goalie and now social worker trainee came next. She exclaimed over Bobby's bowling bag trick, while Lon (Yolanda) who walked in with her, merely smiled. Lon had never cared what people thought about the way she dressed. Tiny (Elise) and Glen (Glenda) completed the party.

A buzz of greetings filled the air. "Hi, Bennie—or is it Fran?" "Glen! How are the Spitfires doing without us?" "Hello, Mash, didja help the indigent today?" "When are you moving to the city, Tiny?" "Bobby, let's see your shoulder!"

Bobby obligingly lifted her right arm and rotated it in a circle. Chick clapped her hands. "Full range of motion! Bobby, that's terrific!"

"About ninety percent, really, but I'm working on it," Bobby said modestly.

Chick leaned across the table. "I told Sal, one of the trainers at Lake Cranston, about your injury, and she said you should try this exercise . . ."

Unexpectedly, Bobby's mind rocketed off on an odd tangent. *Why, that might have been me,* she thought in wonderment. Only a few months ago the Swans had been the only goal she could imagine. Now she couldn't picture life without Metamora, her students, her team, her new psychological studies.

". . . keeping the shoulders level and the back straight," finished Chick. "You should try it."

"Thanks, I will," Bobby promised her former teammate.

Chick lowered her voice. "And those other—symptoms—they still bothering you?"

Chick was one of the few people who knew about Bobby's dizziness and the queer nightmares.

"I think they're getting better."

Bobby pushed from her mind the remembrance of the incident just the other day when she'd climbed to the top of the bleachers to retrieve an errant hockey ball. She'd made the mistake of glancing over the edge and had found herself on all fours, crawling back to the safety of low ground.

"The odd thing is the dreams. Lately, the girl—remember how I told you there's always a girl? Lately, this girl is another teacher—"

Tiny interrupted them. "Enough with the top-secret confab. Let's eat!"

Everyone was hungry, and as the orders for veal piccata, lasagna, spaghetti and meatballs, plus a couple bottles of chianti flew at the harried waiter, Bobby mused a moment longer on the frequent appearance of Enid Butler in her dreams. Was her subconscious trying to warn her about the duplicitous Math Mistress? Were they clairvoyant dreams?

The night before the game, she'd dreamed that she and Enid were at Mesquakie Point. It was like the picnic with Elaine, only this time she was kissing Enid on the striped blanket. The kisses were dream kisses, impossibly tender and delicious. Then Enid got up, saying, "I need my slippers and bathrobe." Bobby followed her as she entered a stone tower and in her dream she'd somehow known it was a lighthouse on the Muskrat River. At the top of the tower, Enid told her, "My slippers are in the closet." But when Bobby opened the door to get them, there was nothing but thin air, and she tumbled off the tower, down, down to the roaring river rapids below.

Thinking about her theories now, during this boisterous get-together, Bobby scoffed at her own superstition. She was becoming as credulous as some of her students.

The hearty food arrived, and the ex-hockey players ate with gusto. Pat and Bobby compared notes on teenaged athletics. When Pat told her ruefully of the competition for gym time at the neighborhood recreation center, Bobby felt glad anew that she'd ended up at Metamora. At Miss Craybill's school there was no boys' basketball crowding the sports-minded girls out of the gym and into a small room to learn social dance!

Bobby told the whole table about the new field hockey team and the Savages' triumph that afternoon. She demonstrated the winning play, using the salt and pepper shakers as stand-ins for Angle and her opponent, with the bowl of grated cheese and Pat's wineglass marking the goal end. She basked in the keen interest of the other girls. No need to explain the sixteen-yard hit-out to this crowd!

"Great strategy," approved Chick. "You'll be heading toward the finals!"

Bobby shook her head modestly. "I'll just be happy to win a few more games."

Pat put in, "With adolescent girls, at such a volatile stage, anything can happen. Often the psychology of the team is as important as its skill—"

A universal groan went up. "My mother does *not* dominate me," muttered Bennie.

But Bobby's recent readings had made her more receptive. "What do you mean, Pat? Do you think the social adjustment of the girls to each other can really make a difference in the dynamic patterns associated with winning and losing?"

"Get a load of the intellectual!" Tiny nudged Mash so hard she nearly knocked her off her chair. For the first time Bobby felt impatient with their joking. She wanted to hear what Pat had to say.

"I was thinking more about the concept of self-fulfilling prophecies," Pat told her. "Generally it's applied negatively, but—"

"If I could manage to instill in the girls a belief in their team as invincible, you mean?" Bobby jumped on Pat's idea eagerly.

"Yes, a kind of *folie-à-deux,* or in this case, *folie-à-squad,*" Pat agreed.

The other Spitfires rolled their eyes and the discussion drifted to the Swans and their training methods, their top-secret playbook, and the chances at the International Tournament in Orkney. Bobby would ordinarily have been as interested as the rest, but now she turned to Pat and said sotto voce, "I've been worrying a bit about the factions the team is developing. I'm not sure how to handle this—this rivalry."

Pat chewed an olive thoughtfully. "You first have to identify the root of the division. Factions often form as a result of mistrust, which stems from a basic insecurity, a lack of confidence."

"That's true of one player, maybe," Bobby said, thinking of Angle. "But this other girl has it all—a terrific player, pretty, and popular to boot. Her teammates elected her captain."

"Even with all those outward markings of success, she may be plagued by questions about her own identity that cause a deep-seated unease," Pat told her firmly.

"Hey, Bobby, speaking of cross-training," Mash's jolly voice interrupted Pat's pithy analysis, "how's Elaine 'hubba hubba' Ellman?"

"She's . . . well, she's engaged." Bobby broke the news bluntly, and the whole group sobered up.

"Another good kid gone wrong," mourned Mash.

"Is this what we have to look forward to?" asked Fran, now a senior at Elliott.

"Yes," added Bennie anxiously. "What do you do when all your best chums from school start getting married?"

It was a problem they'd all secretly pondered, and now it was out in the open.

"You kids are making a mountain out of a molehill," said Pat with her usual assurance. "Those fly-by-night girls we knew in college aren't the only fish in the sea."

"That's right," said Lon, surprising them all. Lon rarely spoke.

"What do you mean, Lon?" queried Glen.

"You just have to know where to look." Lon seemed to think she'd explained everything.

"You mean—" began Mash.

"I've heard—" muttered Chick.

"In Bay City, is there—" asked Tiny timidly.

"A bar for gay girls?" responded Pat smoothly. "There certainly is! More than one, in fact. It's quite a fascinating study, the different clientele of each bar, and its socio-economic-psychological profile."

"Well, let's go study 'em!" said Mash enthusiastically. "Let's find our captain a new girl!"

"Now?"

"Why not?"

"Sure, now's the time!"

"Is this an individual practice or do we make it a scrimmage?"

Somehow the check was paid and the tipsy teammates rolled out of Luigi's and into the street. The autumn twilight had turned into night, and the Spitfires still at Elliott College looked at their watches and reluctantly bade the graduates farewell. Tiny, Mash, Chick, and Bobby, however, eagerly followed Pat and Lon, the self-appointed experts.

"Where are we going?" Bobby laughed with excited anticipation.

"Francine's, I think, don't you?" Pat consulted Lon, who nodded. "The gang there is mostly career girls, college graduates, like ourselves," Pat explained. "Primarily drawn from the upper-middle, middle-middle, and lower-middle economic strata of society . . ."

Bobby scarcely heard Pat's profiling. She was wondering if there'd be dancing—if she'd meet someone who'd invite her home—if she'd be blond or brunette. Desire fizzed up in her like the head on a pint of beer, welling over the glass rim.

". . . and there's less risk of raids," concluded Pat as they rounded a corner. Bobby and Chick had linked arms and begun to hum the Spitfires' old fight song.

"Fight, fight, fight with all your might!"

"There it is," pointed Pat. Halfway down the block was a small neon sign spelling out the word "Francine's" in blue cursive. Below the name, a pink arrow pointed down a short flight of steps to a door below street level. Light streamed from the porthole in the door and embraced a young couple descending the stairs.

"Hey, that's a fellow," said Tiny in disappointment.

"He'll be in the minority," Pat assured her. "Those two are what's known as 'tourists'—likely a straight couple with a yen for novelty."

The man held open the swinging door for the girl, bathing his companion in light.

"She's a cute little number," said Chick admiringly. "Hey, Bobby, what's with the dodge?"

Bobby had stopped abruptly, and Chick had stumbled. "I know that girl!" she exclaimed. "That's Metamora's Math Mistress, and her boyfriend Rod!"

She gaped at Francine's in a rage of thwarted desire, like a girl stranded on a desert isle who sees a passing ship moving away from her. She couldn't go in now— that went without saying. How would she explain her presence to Enid? Hope flared briefly as she glanced at Lon. Lon was often mistaken for one of the boys—perhaps she would pose as Bobby's date. Then the hope winked out. What would be the point? How could she find a girl for herself if she was supposed to be Lon's steady?

"You said there was more than one gay bar—what about one of the other places?" Mash suggested.

"There's the Knock Knock Lounge in Riverside," Lon said.

"Gee, I don't know." Pat's sophistication slipped a little. "Doesn't it get raided? And I've heard they're friendlier if you're wearing fly fronts and grease your hair." She looked down at her side zipper slacks and ran her fingers through her curly bob uneasily. "It's important to fit in with the group, especially on a first visit."

Bobby had seen the look Mash and Chick exchanged when Pat mentioned raids. Chick was flying to Glasgow in the morning.

"You kids go ahead," the Games Mistress told the group, swallowing her disappointment like an indigestible lump of gristle. "It's late and I ought to be heading back to Metamora anyway." After all, just because a handicap kept her off the field was no reason to spoil the other players' game! She pushed them toward Francine's. "Next time, teammates! It was grand seeing you."

"Next time!" "Good seeing you, Bobby!" "Keep up your guard with those Metamora girls!" the gang called after her. Turning the corner, she saw them clambering down the steps to Francine's and her bitterness increased. *That Enid! It's all her fault*, she thought fiercely as she walked toward Lake Street Station. She bought a *Field and Sport* to distract herself from the stew of lust and frustration bubbling inside her.

With a sigh, she sat down on one of the benches, near an attractive woman whose shapely legs were crossed in front of her. It was only after she looked from the legs to the face that Bobby realized the brunette engrossed in a drugstore paperback was Laura Burnham.

Chapter Thirteen

The Art Lesson

"Why, hello," said Bobby. "Fancy meeting you here!"

Laura looked up, as surprised as Bobby had been a moment before. Her hair was pulled into a sleek updo and her black evening coat was open over a blue striped cocktail dress with a plunging neckline. She even wore gloves.

"Why, it's Coach Bobby." The Art Mistress was equally taken aback, but after a moment she tucked her surprise away with the paperback she'd been reading. "Come sit over here." She patted the spot on the bench next to her. "I thought I was the only one who'd escaped from Metamora tonight. Mona gave me a ride to the station after dinner."

"I took a cab, before." Bobby sat next to Laura, thinking of Enid, who'd probably driven into the city with Rod. Perhaps Metamora's entire faculty was roaming the streets of Bay City tonight. "I had a dinner date with some old classmates," Bobby explained. "Then we—we went bowling." She was glad she had the bowling bag to excuse her almost masculine attire.

Laura didn't seem to have noticed Bobby's casual dress.

"I went to a—a gallery show in Riverside," she said as if she felt the need to explain her own finery. "I couldn't stand being cooped up with that mob of immature adolescents any longer. I needed the stimulation of the city. The cultural stimulation, I mean. The paintings I saw were terribly provocative, they gave me all sorts of new ideas—"

"Where's Ken?" Bobby asked, to divert the Art Mistress from her discussion of "provocative" art. Bobby knew nothing about modern art, except that she didn't like it.

"Ken's away for the weekend, inspecting a newly discovered mound on a farm near Mink Lake." Laura's disdain for her husband's hobby was hardly concealed by her attempt at an indulgent smile. "Haven't you heard him talking about it? He's been more excited than an Eagle Scout with a new patch."

Bobby rarely paid attention to what Ken said, having taught herself to tune his monologues into a relaxing drone. "Oh, how nice for him," she said politely.

The innocuous pleasantry was the spark for an unexpected explosion from the temperamental Art Mistress.

"Nice for him! Oh certainly! But what about me?" Laura struck her heaving cleavage with a clenched fist. "Is this any life for an artist, stuck in Nowheresville, away from the creative stimulation of the city, all because of some old Indian mounds?"

"Why, I don't know. Can't you paint your pictures anywhere?" Bobby asked cautiously. She'd often wondered what had drawn Ken and Laura together, but it had seemed impertinent to ask. Now, however, Laura was clearly feeling confidential.

"No, you can't," she told Bobby firmly. "You need a place with some artistic life—like Bay City, or Paris. We went there for our honeymoon, but only because Ken wanted to hear Albert de Mitraille, the famous French anthropologist, lecture! I spent most of my time being dragged along to some *académie* or other, listening to someone drone on while we looked at slides of pygmies. We spent one afternoon at the Louvre, one!" Laura looked bitter at the memory. "When we got back, Ken insisted on taking this job at Metamora. Why couldn't he write about mounds from a distance, the way Professor de Mitraille does about the pygmies?"

"So it was mounds that brought you to Metamora?" Bobby pieced it together.

"The Pottawatomi Mound near Beaver Junction," said Laura mournfully. "Mother always said marriage required sacrifices, but I never dreamed that would mean I'd be spending my Friday night alone, on the nine twenty back to Adena, while my so-called helpmate climbs around on some Indian burial mound!"

"Speaking of the nine twenty, they're calling the Muskrat River Local." Bobby rose and held out her hand to help Laura to her feet. They made their way to platform 9, and Bobby thought regretfully of her own plans for that evening.

"I didn't think I'd be on this train either," she confessed to Laura as they climbed aboard. In her mind's eye she saw again those girls, those faceless, welcoming girls who had awaited her at Francine's before Enid and Rod so cruelly deprived her of their companionship. "But at least we can be company for each oth—oh! I'm sorry—"

"Excuse me, I—"

"Ouch!"

As the train jerked into motion, Bobby lurched heavily against the other teacher, and the two mistresses fell into a tangled pile on the nearest seat. Laura's hands pushed at her ineffectually as Bobby tried to pull herself off the squirming artist.

"Gee, I'm sorry, that was awfully clumsy of me." Bobby

extricated herself at last, her face beet red, her whole body trembling—but not with exertion. The brief moment of physical intimacy with the brunette bombshell had caught her off guard and unleashed a wave of lust so powerful she worried that if she even looked at Laura she'd gobble up the Art Mistress the way Tiny had gobbled up the meatballs a few hours ago.

Bobby put her bowling bag on the rack over the seat and made a pretense of arranging it while she tried to regain her self-control. It looked like another night of restless tossing and turning while the sheets became hot and crumpled beneath her. How many midnight laps could she run? How many cold showers could she take?

"You're certainly strong, aren't you?" Laura said as Bobby sat back down. The Art Mistress was tucking a loose lock of hair into the knot at the crown of her head. "You remind me of my roommate in college—she was a real sports enthusiast." Pulling a compact out of her purse, Laura redid her lipstick carefully. Bobby watched Laura, mesmerized. Suddenly the Games Mistress's wish for a roomful of women was whittled down to just one—this one.

"What were we talking about, before that little *faux pas?*" asked Laura, putting away her purse. "Oh, yes, the compromises I've made for my marriage."

Look, don't touch, Bobby cautioned herself. Luscious Laura was like some delectable cream puff you spot in a bakery case when you're in strict training. "How long have you been married?" she asked.

"Five years," sighed Laura.

And yet, why not? After all, Bobby had decided to dispense with engaged women. Laura wasn't engaged, she was merely married—and to a man who neglected her shamefully, it seemed.

"We got married my senior year," continued Laura.

"After I had my miscarriage, I wondered why I'd bothered. I had to drop out just before graduation, and so I never got to put on a senior show, like the rest of the girls in the art department. I'd been working on a series of murals—in the Mexican style, you know—only instead of peasant labor, my theme was a debutante cotillion. My painting professor said that giving such a subject the monumental treatment was quite unique."

On the other hand, Laura isn't even my type, the gym teacher reflected. Bobby had always gone for petite, wholesome girls. She'd never had much patience for the tall, artsy girls who threw around foreign phrases like *faux pas,* as if American words weren't good enough.

But that was when I had my pick of girls, Bobby reminded herself. Before her college glory had faded like a hockey tunic left out in the sun. Besides, what was it Pat had said that evening, that distrust of others stemmed from a basic lack of confidence in oneself?

"... and we didn't even get a big wedding, because of the rush to the altar," Laura was saying. "Most of my sorority sisters got twice the presents I did! I registered for the most darling coffee service and all I got was the creamer. Then Ken was too cheap to ..."

It's not just physical attraction, anyway, Bobby argued with herself. There was something about the sultry beauty's obvious disappointment with married life that tugged at Bobby's heartstrings. She'd always suspected marriage wasn't all it was trumped up to be. Here was Laura, tied to a man who preferred mounds. Mounds! Bobby's lip curled into a sneer. What kind of man would leave Laura languishing alone for a mere mound?

Distracted by the jumble of contradictory thoughts in her head, half hypnotized by Laura's husky voice and the clickety-clack of the Muskrat River Local, Bobby hardly paid attention to what the Art Mistress said. As her fellow teacher poured out her tale of disappointed dreams, Bobby found her gaze drifting distractedly to the voluptuous thighs straining against the flimsy silk sheath as Laura uncrossed and recrossed her legs, or her red lips, as she pursed them in a picturesque pout.

The gym teacher was imagining how Laura might look with her hair down, her eyes closed, and her full lips parted, when the conductor blared, "Adena," shattering the picture in her head.

"We're here already?" Bobby helped the Art Mistress to her feet. Laura was still recounting the solo show she'd organized in Adena the year before. ". . . and everyone said it was as good as anything you see in Bay City," she told Bobby, following her off the train and into a waiting taxi. "It's all about who you know, really."

As the cab pulled away, Laura told the gym teacher, "But I believe my talent will force those Bay City bigwigs to pay attention one of these days!"

"Of course it will." Bobby slid close to the Art Mistress, inhaling her intoxicating scent.

"I get no encouragement from Ken," Laura continued bitterly. "He thinks my painting is just a hobby." Suddenly she turned and buried her face on Bobby's shoulder. "You don't know how frustrated I feel sometimes!"

"Sure I do," Bobby soothed the distraught faculty member, smoothing her hair with one hand. She trailed a finger down the nape of Laura's neck and the Art Mistress gave a delicate shudder.

"Oh, Bobby—you're so strong, and yet somehow gentle too. You understand how a woman feels."

It was a familiar moment to the ex-hockey player. Back at Elliott College, how many co-eds had she consoled when they returned to the dorm after a disappointing date? Every fiber of Bobby's being told her to take Laura Burnham in her arms and rain kisses on her disillusioned face.

Not in the cab, she reminded herself. She settled for patting the heaving shoulder soothingly. "Of course I understand. Aren't I a woman too?"

The campus was dark and quiet. The red taillights of the cab faded down the drive, leaving only the dim glow of the old-fashioned lanterns hanging over the dorm doorways. It was eleven, lights out. As they walked toward the quad, Bobby saw a lit window in Cornwall wink out.

"Would you like to join me in the art studio for a nightcap?" Laura proposed.

"I shouldn't," protested Bobby weakly. "I ought to go to bed." She couldn't make up her mind about making a play for the Art Mistress. Would it be breaking training, or much-needed practice? Would it be a foul or a clean shot into the goal?

"Oh please—I want to show you some of my paintings. I think they'd really speak to you." Laura took Bobby's hand. "Come with me."

Bobby allowed herself to be pulled along, knowing full well she shouldn't go anywhere alone with the alluring Laura. "Just for a minute."

They tiptoed through the silent quad, and as they passed the sundial the ex-hockey star instinctively tightened her grip on the Art Mistress's hand. "You know, I've always wanted to tell you, when I made that remark about the tower that first day we met, I didn't even know how Miss Froelich had died! Mona had told me—"

Laura halted and put her hand on Bobby's mouth to stop her words. "Please don't talk about it. I'm terribly sensitive about these things. I know this kind of morbid curiosity is common, I don't hold it against you."

"But I wasn't curious, I just didn't know—" Bobby

tried to explain again. Laura shushed her, and Bobby decided not to pursue it. She didn't want to upset the Art Mistress's sensibilities. They were passing under Mona's sitting room, and a rectangle of light fell on the path, which they instinctively circumnavigated.

"And those awful rumors the students are spreading," Laura continued in a whisper. "Half the student body should be in the care of a psychiatrist, in my opinion. I confiscated a note the other day in clay modeling. The girls were actually voting on the likeliest motive for Miss Froelich's suicide!"

"Really!" Bobby was half horrified, half fascinated. "What was winning?"

"That she was possessed by a demon ghost. Although," Laura tried and failed to repress a snicker, "there was a strong write-in vote for Miss Rasphigi as murderess! Poor Miss Rasphigi, without a thought beyond her titrations!"

They'd left the quad behind, and were passing the corner of Essex, which housed the chemistry lab and faced Kent Tower. It *was* ridiculous, Bobby told herself. But she couldn't suppress a sudden vivid image of Miss Rasphigi's cold eyes and hawk nose, her lips compressed as she shoved an indistinct, gray-haired woman over the crenelated battlement and watched without emotion as she tumbled end over end into a dark void.

Dizziness gripped Bobby and she stumbled along the dark path blindly, clinging to Laura's hand like a lifeline. There was something terribly familiar about this walk through the dark, as if she'd traveled this path before. When was it? Where was it? A dark night, a pretty girl . . . Why, it was her dream! But exactly! Bobby felt cold all over. Laura dropped her hand, and the vertigo-stricken coach bent her head and closed her eyes in an effort to maintain her equilibrium. Where was the cliff edge?

"Here we are." Light streamed out from the low building's glass walls. Bobby blinked. She was standing on flat land, just outside the old chicken coop that a forward-thinking young architect had transformed into Jersey, the Metamora art studio. Unsteadily, Bobby climbed up the concrete steps to the big room with its three walls of glass, its rows of drawing tables, and the smell of turpentine. Laura's hair, she noted with gratitude, had not changed its color. The Art Mistress was opening a door in the back wall.

"Welcome to my lair," she said coyly, standing in the doorway with one arm outflung, indicating that Bobby should squeeze past her into the cozy corner office. The first thing Bobby noticed was the glass wall at the rear, which during the day must look out on the wilderness that led to Mesquakie Point, but now was a looming black square. Bobby, still recovering from her attack of vertigo, was glad when Laura pulled dusty red velvet drapes over the emptiness and switched on a modern floor lamp. There were canvases leaning against a combination cabinet-bookshelf, and an old-fashioned chaise longue, upholstered in green velveteen. Bobby perched uncertainly on one end of it.

"*Voilà!*" Laura stood up from the low cupboard brandishing a bottle of red wine and a corkscrew. She handed them to Bobby while she rummaged for glasses.

Bobby, who was more accustomed to flipping caps off beer bottles, struggled for a few minutes before extricating the cork. "*Vin du table,*" she read. "What does that mean?"

Laura wasn't listening. "*À votre santé,*" she said, handing Bobby a glass. "Let me show you my paintings."

Bobby looked obligingly through the pile of canvases as she sipped the sour wine. She was still feeling dizzy, and she tried to distract herself by studying Laura's work.

She stared at a landscape, the trees painted in vivid violets and oranges, until it started to shimmer before her eyes.

"That's Mesquakie Point, at dusk," said Laura. She pulled out another canvas. "That's a creek in the woods." Another. "That's farmland, in the spring. You can see Adena in the background."

"Is that a train, there?"

"Yes, it's a reference to Monet's *Gare St. Lazare.* Those are all from last year, my fauve period. I've moved on to portraits and figure studies." She turned to the next stack. "Mona."

Mona's hair was crimson and she had a green stripe down her nose.

"Miss Rasphigi—that's mostly from memory. She refused to pose."

"I like it," Bobby said, glad to be able to express some honest appreciation. The black and white semi-abstract canvas had somehow captured Miss Rasphigi's stony expression.

"And this is Enid. I did her last week." Enid was a slash of ink black bangs and a yellow nose. Laura looked at it thoughtfully, and laid it aside, turning Enid's face to the wall. She took a long swallow of red wine, and then said, as if just struck by the idea, "I wonder, Bobby, would *you* pose for me?" She picked up a sketchpad and a charcoal pencil. "Just a quick sketch, to capture that—that Bobby essence." Her long eyelashes fluttered over her cheek as she spoke and a pulse pounded in the hollow of her neck.

Bobby surrendered to the inevitable. Ken was off digging in his mound, and here was his lonely wife, asking for Bobby's comfort, even if she didn't realize precisely what that comfort might entail. A shiver of familiar anticipation went through Bobby as she contemplated introducing the unhappy Art Mistress to a whole world of unimagined pleasures.

"How do you want me?" Bobby asked.

"On the chaise," Laura pushed her back onto it. "Half reclining. Your hand—"

"Here?" Bobby put her hand around Laura's neck and pulled the Art Mistress toward her. Laura yielded to the pressure of her arm, like an obedient schoolchild to a crossing guard's signals. "Like this?" She nibbled on Laura's ear, and the bohemian bombshell responded like an instrument tuned to its highest pitch. "Exactly," she moaned as she half fell, half threw herself into Bobby's arms.

The charcoal stick and sketchpad fell to the floor. The wineglasses stood untouched on the bookshelf, next to a monograph on Etruscan statuary. The bodies of the two mistresses met and melded in the white heat of passion long thwarted. "I've—never—felt anything—like this!" panted the insatiable Art Mistress as they nearly fell off the narrow velveteen chaise longue in their thirst for each other. Bobby scarcely heard her, so swamped was she in the pleasure of Laura's warm and willing flesh. The sex-starved gym teacher wanted this interlude to last forever, and the beauteous bohemian evidently shared her sentiments. "Don't stop," she cried in a strangled whisper.

And Bobby, too busy to reply, obeyed her command.

Yet too soon, their appetites were satiated enough that they paused in this gymnastic competition, whose only scorekeeper was desire.

"I should go." Bobby sat up, her conscience smiting her. "What time is it?"

Languorously, Laura lifted her arm to look at her wristwatch, the only thing she was still wearing. "It's only one A.M. Oh, Bobby, no one will miss us. Stay a while longer." Her voice was redolent with promises of further joys.

But Bobby's responsibilities came rushing back to her, and even the sight of Laura with her hair down, her eyes closed, and her full lips parted couldn't blot them out.

"It's Debby Geissler," she confessed. "She often sleep-walks . . . if something happened to her, I'd never forgive myself."

"Oh, all right." Laura sat up. "You better leave first." She brightened. "After all, Ken's gone all weekend. We can continue your . . . sitting tomorrow." Her salacious smile turned Bobby's stomach to jelly. "I'll see you at breakfast, Bobby."

Closing the studio door behind her, Bobby couldn't believe how well things had turned out. Instead of picking up some hard-bitten bar habitué like in the books, she'd brought out a sophisticated, older woman! Laura had taken to the games of pleasure Bobby had taught her with surprising speed. *I ought to thank Enid and Rod,* the Games Mistress thought with a smile as she climbed the path back to the quad. Besides, it was a relief to discover she hadn't lost her touch. Actually, she felt just like she was back in college again.

Bobby frowned. There was something wrong with that. She'd read something the other day in her psych book, something about police. Arrested development—that was it. Was it bad to repeat at Metamora the social-sexual relationship patterns she'd developed at college?

She was between Essex and Kent when she saw something that drove her worries about psychological development completely from her mind.

A glowing bicycle, ridden by a dark shapeless figure, floated across the quad and disappeared behind Kent.

After a split second of shock, Bobby ran after the apparition. But when she rounded Kent, all was dark. The bicycle was gone.

Chapter Fourteen

The Missing Locket

"I have a special request to make," the Headmistress announced at breakfast the next morning. "A valuable gold locket has been lost by one of our students. I'm asking everyone in the Metamora community to keep a vigilant lookout for a heart-shaped locket on a sixteen-inch pearl and platinum chain. If you should happen to find it, please turn it over to any staff member without further ado. Thank you."

Miss Craybill sat down and immediately a buzz of chatter started up around the dining hall.

"So, you haven't found your necklace yet?" Bobby asked Kayo absentmindedly.

She was thinking about her encounter with Laura just before breakfast. The Art Mistress had been hanging her corduroy car coat on a hook in the cloakroom when Bobby came up behind her and slipped her arms around the Art Mistress's sweater-clad waist. "Good morning, Laura," she murmured into her neck.

Laura whirled out of her grasp, stumbling backwards over Madame Melville's fur-lined boots. "Bobby! Not here," she said hastily. "Ken's back."

Bobby's whole body sagged in disappointed disbelief. "What about his mound?" she protested.

"It wasn't a real mound, just some farmer with a pile of dirt and some fake arrowheads he wanted to sell. I'm sorry, but—"

"Honeybun." Ken poked his head through the doorway, interrupting their low-toned conversation. "We're at the table by the window."

"I'm coming," Laura said brightly. "See you later, Bobby." She threw an apologetic glance over her shoulder at the forlorn Games Mistress as she hurried after her husband.

Now Bobby watched Ken and Laura eating their scrambled eggs and sausages with a familiar sense of frustration. This *was* just like college—eyeing her paramour from across a room, waiting for the next stolen moment. And even worse, Ken wasn't a date, he was Laura's husband!

"What?" asked the gym teacher with a start. Kayo was saying something. She pulled her gaze away from Laura and turned to her team captain, sitting, as usual, at her left.

"I said, no, I haven't found it," said Kayo. Her eyes slid to look at Angle at the far end of the table. Angle was shoveling eggs into her mouth with her usual wolfish appetite.

"You didn't happen to notice anything, did you, Lotta?" Bobby asked perfunctorily. As usual, the Savages' faithful water girl was sitting across from Angle, paying more attention to her idol than her own breakfast. She jerked around, dropping her fork. "I didn't see anything, Coach!" She gulped.

Before Bobby had time to wonder at Lotta's uneasiness, Beryl said, "I just hope that whoever 'found' it has the *decency* to turn it in—which I doubt!"

"Beryl, that's a terrible insinu—insinu—suggestion," Bobby reproved the boisterous right wing. "Metamora's honor code is sacred to all the girls."

Abruptly, Angle pushed her chair back and stalked out of the dining hall. Lotta scrambled after her.

"Angle, Lotta! You forgot to excuse yourselves," Bobby called after them. "Seems like everyone's gotten up on the wrong side of the bed this morning!"

It was a relief when the sound of scraping chairs across the dining hall signaled a general exodus. Bobby let the room empty around her as she sipped her second cup of coffee.

Saturday mornings, after room inspection, the students of Metamora spread over the campus like a flock of chattering magpies. The common rooms were always full of girls playing bridge, doing their nails, and gossiping. Even as the days grew more chilly, a group of determined sunbathers continued to stake out the sloping lawn behind Somerset, the library, while inside that building studious girls whispered to each other as they wandered the dim stacks. Artistic girls painted in Jersey, literary girls congregated in the *Tower Chimes* office in Cumberland. Before lunch Bryce would lead a nature walk for the Green Thumb club, and after the midday meal Mona would drive the blue bus, filled with girls who had town privileges, to Adena in time for the Bijou's matinee.

And at 3:30 the Savages would gather for field hockey practice. Bobby propped her chin on her hand, feeling glum. How would she fill the hours until then? The "art lesson" with Laura was clearly canceled. Next to last night's delights, the daily routine that usually satisfied her seemed unappealing. She didn't want to study her psych texts. She didn't want to sit in her office in the gym, refining her strategy for the team. She didn't even want to exercise!

Dragging herself out of Dorset, Bobby attacked room

inspection with less than her usual zest. "I thought you read this one," she said wearily as she pulled *A History of Sexual Customs,* disguised as a science text, from Sandy's shelf.

"Are you okay, Coach Bobby?" asked the bookworm with concern.

She was trudging back to her suite with her haul when a group of third formers stopped her. "Will you play gin rummy with us today, Coach Bobby?"

"Sorry, girls, I—I just can't," said Bobby. The juvenile company of the third formers was *not* what she wanted.

"At least tell us again about the five points of perfect posture?" one disappointed girl called after the departing gym teacher.

Bobby dumped the contraband in her footlocker and headed for the gym. A morning of quiet equipment maintenance in the deserted building, testing the knots on the rope ladder and pumping up deflated balls—that would soothe her spirits, she decided.

However, when she reached the gymnasium she found she had company.

"What size are the grid squares, Miss Butler?" Two students were standing beneath the basketball hoop holding the ends of a tape measure. On the other side of the gym, more Metamorians wandered slowly across the floor, bent over, with their eyes on the ground.

"Twenty by twenty, *please,* try to remember." The Math Mistress sounded impatient as she frowned at the clipboard in her hand.

"What's all this?" asked Bobby, trying to stay calm. This invasion of her athletic domain by the troublemaking Math Mistress was the last thing she needed this morning.

"Oh! Good morning, Coach Blanchard." The other teacher seemed somewhat flustered. "The Problem Solvers and I are applying the grid search method, used by archaeologists and scuba divers, to find Kayo's lost locket."

Bobby noticed now that the gymnasium floor was covered with a network of string, dividing it into a series of squares. She took a deep breath, fighting down her annoyance at the disorder in her otherwise orderly empire. As she groped for the words to tactfully tell the Math Mistress to get lost, Lotta emerged from the locker room. "All clear!" she reported. "Shall I do Coach Bobby's office?"

"That won't be necessary, Lotta," Enid said quickly.

"But you said the scientific method required no exceptions," persisted the precocious youngster.

"Miss Butler," interrupted Bobby, fuming inwardly, "a private word with you, in my office?"

When she'd closed the door after Enid she spun around and snapped, "What are you trying to pull now, Enid? You want those girls to think I'm a jewel thief?"

"No, no." Enid was on the defensive. "That's not it at all. I'm just trying to quell the rumors—"

"What rumors?"

"Surely you've heard—those DAP girls are spreading the story that Angela took Kayo's locket. The whole school is repeating it."

"Ah." Bobby sat down. So that's what was behind Beryl's comment and Angle's abrupt departure at breakfast. "But how are these squares of string going to help?"

"The best way to refute this vicious rumor is with calm, cool logic," Enid declared. "The Problem Solvers and I are going to divide the whole campus into a grid. We'll either find the locket or prove that it's not here. It's actually quite a nice problem in geometry. I have the girls reading blueprints and looking at topographical—"

Bobby had listened with mounting disbelief and now she interrupted. "Are you cuckoo? All you're going to do with this crazy 'scientific' search is stir up unwholesome suspicions! These kids aren't thinking about topographical maps, they're getting an unhealthy thrill, wondering which of their friends—or teachers—is a thief. You're not quelling these rumors, you're fanning the flames of gossip!"

"You always underestimate the adolescent's intellect and overestimate the impact of emotion," protested Enid hotly.

"Besides which, your whole scheme is full of holes! Where's Angle?"

Enid had convinced Angle to join the Problem Solvers—some whispered that she'd bribed her with excuses from Chapel—but Bobby hadn't seen her in the gym.

"Angle went for a bike ride." Enid lifted her chin.

"At least she had the common sense to stay out of this. Do you know what the girls are going to say if you don't find the locket? They'll say Angle had it hidden on her all the time. You weren't planning to strip-search the students, were you?"

"Certainly the method has its limitations, but we can at least categorically prove—"

"And what about the honor system?" Bobby grew more indignant. "This—this—vigilante investigation is against every idea of individual responsibility and character development that Metamora fosters!"

"You're certainly welcome to take your concerns to Miss Craybill," Enid retorted frostily.

At that Bobby blew up. "I'm not a backstabber! I'm not the kind to run to the Headmistress and tattle on another teacher, or try to trip her up! That's your play, not mine!"

Red spots stained Enid's cheeks. "I don't know what you're talking about."

"I think you do." Bobby got up. "I'm leaving. I can't

stand to even watch your 'scientific' witch hunt. Do me a favor and take every strand of string with you when you go!"

Bobby rushed out of the gymnasium, the startled faces of the Problem Solvers blurring as they jumped out of her way. She stormed away from the campus, across the field, and into the woods. The narrow path and heavy underbrush soon forced her to slow her furious pace and her pounding pulse sank back to its normal rhythm. Gradually, her temper calmed as she wandered in the woods, but her spirits sank lower than ever. For the first time, she dreaded hockey practice. She wished she could wander all the way to Mesquakie Point and forget about the factions and feuds of Metamora, the pettiness of spirit. For the first time in a long time she thought of Elaine and that picnic they'd shared before school began. How halcyon that day seemed in her memory!

"Would being a golf pro have been so bad?" she muttered.

"Hello! Is that Coach Bobby?"

The voice came through the trees. Bobby went around a sugar maple and found herself in Bryce's garden, behind the old Amundsen homestead. Bryce was wearing a torn straw hat and a brightly flowered shirt as he turned the withering pea vines and tomatoes under the rich brown loam.

"Gosh, I guess I've been walking in circles," said Bobby.

"Ole's just baked up some *eplekake* and brewed a pot of coffee. Go ahead in, you look like you need some," Bryce ordered her cheerily.

"Is it that obvious?" Obediently Bobby climbed the steps and went into the old-fashioned log cabin. It was almost a twin of the replica cabin at the Mesquakie Point tourist concession, which Ole's sister Freya managed.

Ole was untying an apron as she entered the kitchen. He smiled at her and poured a mug of coffee. "Here," he said, slicing a piece of warm, fragrant *eplekake* and putting it on a china plate.

Bryce came in, wiping his muddy feet on the braided rug. "Ah, *eplekake!*" he exclaimed. "Nothing beats fresh *eplekake* and a cup of coffee on a Saturday afternoon!"

Bobby realized she'd missed lunch and was ravenous. When the Biology Master heard that, he and Ole fussed around her, feeding her *rakfisk,* and *kjøttkaker* with a berry sauce. Bobby felt herself relax in the happy, domestic atmosphere of Bryce and Ole's little cabin. She found herself telling the pair about her recent quarrel with Enid and her fears that the misguided Math Mistress would only make the rumors about Kayo's necklace worse.

Bryce agreed with her. "What was Enid thinking? As if things weren't bad enough at Metamora with Miss Craybill in the state she is, and the rumors about Miss Froelich haunting the campus!"

Ole said, "Enid isn't having it easy."

Bobby protested, "What do you mean? Enid's the girl with all the answers."

Ole merely shook his head. Bryce said, "If only Miss Craybill was her old self . . . Did you notice how she didn't even touch her eggs this morning? Mona says she refuses to eat anything bird related. She's losing weight, in addition to her other difficulties."

"She still wants to clean our cabin," reported Ole.

"If this keeps up, I'm going to be seeing ghosts too!" Bryce's laugh wasn't quite natural.

"It was indigestion," said Ole. "I think last night's *svinekoteletter* were too rich."

Bobby wondered what they were talking about. Was it a private reference, just between the two of them? Looking around the room, she caught sight of the old-fashioned grandfather clock. "Is that clock right? Gosh, I'd better run to make practice!"

She refused another slice of the delicious *eplekake* and hurried down the path back to Louth Athletic Field. As she strode along, she thought of her strange nocturnal vision, the ghostly cyclist she'd seen as she crept back from Jersey to Cornwall. Of course it must have been an ordinary cyclist, and some trick of the light had given the illusion of glowing levitation. But who? And why was this cyclist prowling around the campus at one in the morning? Could this mystery somehow be connected to the loss of Kayo's locket?

A figure was approaching her, moving through the dappled shadows. It was Miss Craybill, walking in that peculiarly aimless way she had, head down, hands behind her back, eyes fixed on the ground.

"Good afternoon," she greeted Bobby, raising her eyes to the young gym teacher's face after encountering her sneaker. "How go the young Savages? Swimmingly? Swimmingly?"

"Yes, Miss Craybill," said Bobby. "Speaking of swimming, I've been thinking about what other sports we might introduce in the spring curriculum. Is there any interest in a swim team, do you think?"

"We don't have a swimming pool," Miss Craybill reminded her.

"Or what about, oh, bicycling? Any champion cyclists on campus?"

Miss Craybill's blue eyes filmed over with sudden tears. "Miss Froelich was an avid cyclist," she said. Bobby felt goose bumps form on her arms. "She almost never walked when she could ride. How often would I look out my window and catch sight of her sailing like a great black bat across the quad—" Miss Craybill broke off the flow of reminiscence abruptly. "Excuse me, I must visit the utility shed." She turned around and hurried back toward the campus.

Bobby decided she would put aside the question of the cyclist for the moment. Any mention of a midnight rider would only feed the insatiable appetite for the occult that had gripped so many students. And wasn't she as bad as Enid, making a mountain out of a molehill? Kayo had lost her locket somewhere and it would turn up or it wouldn't.

The best strategy, she decided, was to ignore the lost locket entirely. She would exhaust the Savages with exercise and leave them with no energy for speculation and suspicion.

With this resolve, Bobby hurried around the corner of the gymnasium, just in time to see Angle slap Kayo so hard that the field hockey captain staggered and almost fell.

Chapter Fifteen
Student-Teacher Conference

"What is going on here?" Bobby cried in shock, and the tableau broke apart. Angle ran like a wild creature toward the woods, while Kayo, white-faced, walked stiffly to the bleachers and sat down as a pandemonium of voices broke out. The girls flocked around their captain, asking her if she was all right and volunteering to run after Angle and drag her back. Lotta stood on the sidelines, her mouth open, a pile of clean towels in her arms.

Bobby pushed her way through the cluster of concerned Savages and knelt beside Kayo. "Look at me," she ordered. She took hold of Kayo's chin and waggled it gently. "Does that hurt?"

"No," whispered the captain. Her sapphire blue eyes were brimming with unshed tears, and she trembled at Bobby's touch. The coach saw that the usually self-assured teen was fighting to maintain her self-control.

"Lotta." Bobby beckoned the faithful water girl. "Take Kayo to my office and get her a glass of water." She watched as Lotta held the gymnasium door for the shaken girl. When it had closed behind them, she turned to the squad, hands on her hips. "Now, who can tell me what happened?" she demanded.

There was dead silence as the Savages glanced uneasily at each other. No one wanted to be a tattletale!

"Annette," Bobby picked out the French Mistress's daughter. "You tell me what led up to this unfortunate fracas." The levelheaded left wing was neither a DAP nor an ally of Angle's. She was as neutral as Switzerland.

"Well, Kayo, she have us start the drills, and Angle, she fall down twice during the block and pass play, and then she say, maybe it's on purpose, and lotsa girls say no, no, no, and Kayo say to keep drilling, and then Angle slap her." The French girl concluded her account with a Gallic shrug of incomprehension.

Bobby noticed that Annette's accent seemed thicker than usual and that this diplomatic account mentioned no names other than Angle and Kayo. "Does anyone have anything to add?" She looked narrowly at Beryl, but the right wing stood mute, eyes downcast. "Practice is over for the day," said Bobby tersely. "You girls can go."

Stymied, she watched the girls trickle back inside. If she forced one of the girls to break the code of silence, she'd only splinter the team further. But she was burning to know why Angle had hit Kayo.

Lotta emerged from the gymnasium. "Kayo's in your office drinking water," she reported.

"Lotta!" Bobby pounced. "You tell me what happened."

"I don't want to be a fink," worried the brainy fourth former.

"Here's what we'll do—you don't have to name names, just tell me what was said and done," Bobby proposed.

"Well, Ber—one girl hit Angle in the shin with her stick, accidentally-on-purpose, and then Hel—then she got tripped on the next play, and then Angle threw down her stick and said if they wanted to beat her up why didn't they use their bare hands and stop pretending to play field hockey, and Li—one of them said, 'Well, why don't you just give the locket back,' and Angle said if she wanted cheap jewelry she'd go to the five-and-dime in Adena and everyone started to yell at her and Kayo told them to be quiet and stop picking on Angle, who only acted so disagreeable because her mother ran away with another man and her parents are getting a divorce, and that's when Angle slapped her." Lotta furrowed her brow. "And I don't understand why Angle slapped Kayo when Kayo was the only one sticking up for her!"

Bobby didn't have time to explain the intricacies of adolescent psychology to the puzzled water girl. She dismissed the anxious youngster and headed to her office, glad that she'd reread Chapter 14, "The Structure of Student Values: Adult Impact on Effective Socialization," in *The Adolescent and His Society* only last week. It made a lot more sense this time around!

Kayo was sitting in the straight-backed chair facing Bobby's desk, holding the picture of the Spitfires in her hand, studying it intently. When Bobby entered she hastily put it back in its place next to Bobby's pencil cup.

"That was taken after we won the 1962 Midwest Regional Women's Field Hockey League championship," Bobby said as she pulled the chair from behind her desk and set it next to Kayo's. The last thing she wanted was the desk acting as a barrier of age and authority between them. She intended to follow the book's recommendations, to appeal to Kayo as an adult instead of treating her like a child. Kayo wielded tremendous influence over her teammates, over all Metamora, in fact. If Bobby could persuade Kayo to champion Angle, her job as coach would be a lot simpler.

"That's you, in the middle?" Kayo indicated a smiling, tousle-haired Bobby. "You look so young."

"Do I?" Bobby studied the photo with new eyes. "It's funny, I don't feel much older now! In fact, I'm at my wits' end with the situation on the team, and I'm here to ask for your help."

Kayo's eyes glowed. "I'll do anything I can to help you, Coach Bobby."

"Could you be friends with Angle?"

Kayo's face changed as swiftly as a prairie sky when a fast-moving storm approaches. "Angle," she repeated.

"Look, I know that was quite a blow you just took. I know you didn't deserve it. You probably didn't realize that exposing her private problems like that was the worst thing to do—"

A small smile twitched the corner of Kayo's mouth and Bobby stopped, aghast. Kayo had known exactly how provoking her words had been. What was the cause of this deep-seated enmity for Angle?

"Kayo." Bobby changed tactics abruptly. "You don't really think Angle stole your locket, do you?"

"I honestly don't know," Kayo declared. "But I do know she's had it in for us DAP girls since she got here. She's a troublemaker. You saw how she behaved during the game with the Holy Virgins! She's just not a team player. Honestly, Coach Bobby, don't you think the team would be better off without her?"

Is it Angle's defiance of her leadership that Kayo can't stand?

"What about your pass to Annette in the fourth quarter, when you bypassed Angle?" Bobby pointed out. "That wasn't very good teamwork either. Should I kick you off the team?"

"Oh, you're always defending her," Kayo broke out bitterly. "You're always giving her special coaching, having those long talks, just the two of you, treating her like your special pet!"

Why, Kayo's jealous! Bobby was dazed with the sudden realization.

"I work like a dog to get the girls to come to the extra practices and make them do their drills. I'm behind on organizing the regional DAP luncheon, I've fallen asleep at a Prefecture meeting, my grades are starting to slip, and you don't even notice!"

"Why, Kayo, of course I notice! I couldn't get along without you as my captain," Bobby hastened to reassure the resentful teen queen. "And if I've leaned on you so much that your other activities are suffering, we'll certainly have to make some—"

"Oh, I don't mind!" Kayo interrupted vehemently. "I'm willing to do anything for you—if only you could see me as more than just the captain of the squad!"

Kayo was leaning toward Bobby, her face flushed with passion. Her lips were parted and her breath came quickly. The hockey coach was suddenly struck by the teenager's uncanny resemblance to her aunt Dot. She put out a hand to restrain the panting girl, but Kayo snatched it eagerly and pressed it to her breast.

"You think of me as a schoolgirl, but I feel like a woman!"

Bobby's blood ran faster and she found herself breathing shallowly as her body responded against her will to this radiant young creature who had slid out of her chair and was kneeling before her.

"Kayo, I—" Bobby rose to her feet as she spoke, intending to beat a hasty retreat behind her desk, but Kayo rose with her, and instead Bobby found herself backed up against the big wooden desk.

Bobby gripped the edge of the desk with both hands to keep herself from reaching for the captain of the Savages.

The force of her sudden desire was like the heavy pressure of a raging river on a fragile earthen dam when the caretaker has forgotten to open the sluice gates.

"I can't be satisfied anymore with pashes, or exchanging mash notes, or even fooling around in the bicycle shed! Since you came to Metamora this fall, you're all I think about, all I dream about." Kayo bit her lower lip with her pearl-like teeth. "Maybe you think there's something wrong with me—"

"There's nothing wrong with you," Bobby hastened to reassure the ardent student. "At your age, it's perfectly normal to have crushes."

She smoothed Kayo's hair back from the girl's flushed face in a gesture meant to be motherly. But somehow her hand slid down Kayo's back to her rounded buttocks and Bobby gave the girl a tug that pulled the field hockey captain against her coach. "Perfectly normal," she murmured as she tasted the salty sweat on Kayo's neck.

She scarcely heard Kayo's low moan of delight. The scent of teenaged sweat had suddenly transported Bobby back in time, to her freshman year at Elliott College, when her craving for Madge Madison, the assistant field hockey coach, had driven her half mad. Then came that wonderful day when Madge took her to the nurse's room to tape up her twisted ankle. Bobby still couldn't say how it had happened, but one moment Madge was all business, and the next moment the roll of tape was on the floor and she and Bobby were kissing each other hungrily. . . .

Kayo's mouth was a voracious vortex of pleasure. Her hands were in Bobby's hair. Bobby yanked open the teen's white uniform blouse and Kayo gasped in startled excitement.

Bobby had been unable to believe her good fortune that afternoon, as she and Madge shed their hockey kilts and Madge taught her the rules and regulations of this new sport. And when Madge had pushed her down on the paper-covered exam table . . .

Blindly, the young coach swept the surface of her desk with one arm, pushing pencils and paper out of the way. She hoisted the quivering center onto the desk. Kayo's kilt was hiked up around her waist, and Bobby stood between her firm thighs, feverishly fondling the full young breasts as she probed her captain's mouth with an avid tongue. Kayo clung to Bobby with one hand, and braced herself with the other, her breathing uneven.

"I want—" she panted when they came up for air.

"I think I know," muttered Bobby hoarsely. Kayo fell back on the desk, pulling Bobby astride her. Dimly, Bobby heard the metal stapler clank on the floor as she concentrated on the supple, athletic body beneath her. . . .

It was like being hit by a hurricane, she'd thought that day. The Bobby she knew had been wiped out and rebuilt, like a small Kansas town after a tornado. Madge had taught her things about her body and physical capacities she'd never have figured out on her own. *Maybe that's when I was bitten by the teaching bug,* Bobby thought, *even if I didn't realize it. . . .*

"Oh!" cried Kayo. "Oh! Oh! Oh!"

While Bobby had been woolgathering, revisiting happy memories, habit had kept her hands busy, and now Kayo lay spent and satisfied beneath her.

"Feeling better?" inquired Bobby, just as Madge had asked her five years before. She helped Kayo sit up, remembering how her own muscles had felt like Jell-o as she'd staggered off that faraway exam table.

"Oh, yes!" said Kayo, and then added dazedly, "Is that someone at the door?"

For the first time Bobby was aware of a persistent knocking. "Who's there?" she called as she began scooping up scattered play lists, attendance rosters, and league schedules from the floor. "Button your shirt," she ordered Kayo, who still sat limply, as if in a dream.

"It's Angle," came the subdued reply.

"Just a sec." Bobby pulled down her sweatshirt and smoothed her hair. Kayo was doing likewise. "You're missing a button," Bobby tossed her a cardigan. "Put this over your blouse."

When Kayo had buttoned the borrowed garment over the evidence of their impetuous passion, Bobby opened the door. Angle recoiled at the sight of Kayo, who beamed at her blissfully.

"I know you'll think about what I said," Bobby told Kayo. The blond beauty looked bewildered. "About using your influence," Bobby reminded her.

"Oh! Yes, absolutely." She meandered off down the corridor as Angle stepped inside warily.

Oh, cripes, Bobby thought as she watched the retreating girl. *That was my Spitfire letter sweater I loaned her.* This was just the sort of thing that could cause jealousy among the squad.

"Sit down, Angle." Bobby turned her attention to the troubled teen.

Angle sat in the chair Kayo had occupied just moments before, while Bobby placed herself safely behind the desk. "I'm sorry I ran off," began the young hooligan, "but I'm not sorry I slapped Kayo! My parents are none of her business!"

"I know it's awful to have people gossiping about your private affairs," Bobby replied, "but in a small school like Metamora, gossip is hard to stop. You'll have to learn to ignore what people say instead of resorting to violence."

"I don't let anyone walk all over me," Angle snarled.

"Listen to me, Angle! Real toughness doesn't always mean hitting back. Real toughness means taking it on the chin without falling down!" Bobby could tell by Angle's stillness that she was really listening. "Besides, I'm sure Kayo meant well."

Angle snorted. "That's a good joke."

Bobby should have known Angle wouldn't be fooled either. "Well, your response was out of bounds. I can't have my hockey players socking each other, under any circumstances!"

Angle wilted. "Are you going to kick me off the team?" She reached down and picked the Spitfires photo from the floor and placed it carefully on the desk.

"Maybe I ought to, but no, I'm going to give you another chance." Bobby spotted her stapler and nudged it under the desk with her foot. "I'm suspending your town privileges for the rest of the semester. I'm benching you until you apologize—"

"Apologize!" Angle's head shot up.

"—and you and Kayo will have special one-on-one practices until you learn to get along."

"Kayo's going to blow a gasket when she hears that," Angle predicted, not without pleasure.

"I think Kayo will be quite cooperative," Bobby retorted. A picture of Kayo, splayed out on the desk, flashed across her mind in spite of herself.

After Angle left, Bobby stared at the picture of the Spitfires, recalling those olden days. She was glad she'd been able to restore Kayo's self-confidence, to reassure the girl that she was an asset to the team. However, now she recalled the aftermath of her affair with Madge. How upset Tiny had been! She'd tackled Bobby viciously during a practice scrimmage. And then there were the whispers of favoritism when Bobby was made a first-string sub. She hadn't thought of that in a long while.

Bobby hoped that particular part of history wouldn't repeat itself.

Chapter Sixteen
The Blown Fuse

Several weeks later, Bobby was sitting at her desk in her suite in Cornwall with a pile of clippings and a pot of paste. It was a cold night, and the wind rattled the panes of glass and echoed down the chimney. Bobby had decided to spend the evening updating her scrapbook.

Her hand hovered over the first clipping in the pile. "What esteemed Prefecture President was dealt a geometrical blow last Saturday? (and we don't mean metaphorically!)" read the item.

It was from *The Metamora Musings*'s popular "Guess Who?" column. Alice Bjorklund had apologized to Bobby—"Honestly, I don't know how I missed it"—but Bobby couldn't blame the newspaper's faculty moderator for the anti-Angle sentiment that had taken hold of the student body. The latest episode in the Angle-Kayo feud would have spread like wildfire, even without the help of the printed word. Only Miss Craybill, who grew vaguer and more distracted every day, was unaware of it. Kayo told everyone that it was "just a misunderstanding," but the student body was unconvinced. Angle had the distinction of being the least popular student on campus.

The truculent teen didn't help matters, refusing to apologize to Kayo. "I have no intention of apologizing," Bobby heard her tell a reporter from the *Musings,* quite coolly. The coach was at a loss, confronted with this contrary creature, who *would* not behave like any teen she'd read about in *Adolescent Development Patterns,* or even *The Adolescent and His Society.* It was almost as if she reveled in the suspicion and disdain with which most of her classmates viewed her. She even seemed to get a twisted satisfaction from the one-on-one practices with her nemesis, Kayo!

The Harvest Moon Mixer with the Patton Military Academy for Boys was approaching, the Games Mistress reminded herself hopefully. Weren't adolescent girls supposed to be interested in experimenting with the opposite sex? Would the big fall dance distract any of the Metamorians from this field hockey soap opera? Somehow, she doubted it.

She picked up the next clipping. "SCIENTIFIC METHOD FAILS TO FIND MISSING NECKLACE." When she'd cut this out, she'd felt a grim satisfaction in seeing her prediction come true. But she'd have endured Enid's triumph with equanimity if it had cleared away the cloud of suspicion that still shrouded Angle!

"SAVAGES STRIKE AGAIN!" "SAVAGES WIN OVER AMES TECH." "SAVAGES' WINNING STREAK CONTINUES."

Bobby laid the three articles side by side, savoring the progress they charted. Despite Angle being benched, despite the lack of cohesiveness, the Savages had done quite well so far this season. Surprisingly well, in fact. *Unbelievably well,* Bobby thought, a slight frown creasing her forehead.

The fact was, they'd been aided by a series of lucky coincidences. First it was their game with Rockford. The Raging Robins had been too exhausted to rage that day—because of some snafu in the school's schedule, the team had participated in a rock-climbing field trip right before the game. After three hours spent picking their way over the treacherous bluffs, they could barely walk, let alone defend their goal against the energetic Savages.

Or take the game with Ames Tech. The Industrious Ants were a tough team—the Holy Martyrs had beaten them in last year's championship by a single point. The only way the Savages had managed a win was that the Ants' three best players were benched. According to the story that circulated in the stands, the trio had been discovered dead drunk at the local sweet shop the night before. Peering at the three girls sitting on the bench with hangdog expressions and bleary red-rimmed eyes, Bobby could tell the story was true. It was shameful behavior—the more so because the star center refused to accept responsibility, claiming that someone had spiked the malteds they'd ordered on the night in question.

And then there was last week's game, with Peasley Prep. The Pea Pods were known for their brilliant coach, Gladys Tanklow, whose innovative strategies made the most of her small team's skills. But on the day of the game an inexperienced assistant principal stood in for Coach Tanklow, who'd been called to her sick mother's bedside. Everyone had been relieved to hear that Mama Tanklow's illness was nothing more than a bad cold, but it didn't change the score.

She should be grateful for the good luck, Bobby knew, but sometimes she couldn't help wondering about this series of helpful coincidences. The Kerwins' aunt Dot, a regular in the bleachers at her nieces' games, celebrated each victory with gusto. She pooh-poohed Bobby's concerns and had invited the coach more than once to have a drink with her and talk strategy. Bobby turned her down. It would have upset Laura.

Bobby frowned. Of course, she liked Laura lots, but

she couldn't get used to the teacher's temperamental mood swings. The evening after Kayo entered the dining hall wearing Bobby's Spitfire letter sweater, the Art Mistress had appeared at Bobby's door demanding, "Who are you going steady with—Kayo or me?" Yet in the faculty lounge or dining hall—whenever Ken was around—she avoided the Games Mistress.

Sometimes Bobby wondered if Laura's special friendship was worth the trouble. But she couldn't help feeling sorry for the neglected wife. "You don't know what it's like, living with Ken," the Art Mistress sobbed one night. "The excruciating boredom! I'm going to divorce him, just as soon as I find a way to tell Mother."

And what would she do without those stolen moments when the shock of Laura's heated flesh against her own, her searching lips, her hoarse cries, the collision of their two bodies, released Bobby's pent-up desire from its cage?

Without the sultry Art Mistress, it would certainly be harder to resist Kayo, who was waiting, always waiting, for another moment alone with her coach. Bobby tried to show the Savages' captain by her businesslike behavior that the scene in the coach's office would never be repeated, but she wasn't sure Kayo was getting the message. Should she speak to her? Remembering their last encounter, Bobby didn't think another student-teacher conference would be wise. Besides, Kayo was playing better than ever these days, and her coach certainly didn't want to jinx that!

After pasting in the last of the *Musings* clippings, Bobby turned to the first issue of *The Tower Chimes*, the school's literary magazine, which had just come out. Leafing through it, she saw that the field hockey drama had permeated even the remote world of literature lovers. Munty Blaine, of all people, had written an "Ode to Field Hockey," which featured a:

*"heroic figure, silhouetted by the sun,
who, to girls like god to time, makes us run."*

And Lotta's poem, written in the modern, non-rhyming style, was even more telling. "The Solitary Girl" began:

*"She stands alone
the solitary girl
against the faceless mob."*

Skimming the long poem, Bobby's attention was caught when she came to these lines:

*"venturing on two wheels
into woods dark and drear,
where none dare follow."*

The hairs rose on the back of her neck as the image of the eerie, glowing bicyclist rose unbidden in her mind's eye. Could it have been Angle she'd seen that night?

She closed the magazine and stared unseeingly at the trophy on her mantelpiece. A few days after she'd seen the glowing cyclist, she'd questioned Mona discreetly about the most frequent bike borrowers. Where did they go? What were they doing?

"Most of them go to the Mesquakie Massacre Gift Shoppe, to buy fudge or saltwater taffy," the housekeeper had explained with a smile. "Over the years they've worn quite a trail through the woods. It's against the rules, of course, but girls will be girls!"

So there was an explanation. And yet—

It had been past midnight. The Mesquakie Massacre Gift Shoppe would have long since closed; and—

Who among the student body was brave enough to venture into the haunted woods after dark?

Why had she dressed in a flowing black robe?

Why was she glowing?

A knock at the door made Bobby jump. Who could it be at this hour? Swinging open the door, she saw Enid, looking harried in a worn blue bathrobe she'd pulled on over some striped flannel men's pajamas. Rod's, perhaps? Bobby felt her usual rush of resentment at the sight of the anti-sport Math Mistress, and thinking about Enid's well-dressed boyfriend made her even more bad-tempered.

"Yes? What is it?" she asked shortly.

"I'm sorry to bother you." Enid was apologetic. "I think a fuse must have blown over in Manchester. Do you have a flashlight? I can't find mine."

"Just a sec." Bobby left Enid standing in her doorway while she retrieved her flashlight from the emergency supplies—tissues, candles, melba toast, sanitary napkins, sedatives—that she kept in her bedside drawer. She returned and held it out to Enid. "Here you go."

"Thanks." Enid took the flashlight but didn't leave. "The thing is," she bit her lip and Bobby realized the Math Mistress was ill at ease, "I've never changed a fuse."

"Where's Ole? Have him do it." The advice came out more dismissively than Bobby intended.

"I can't find him. I've looked all over."

Bobby couldn't help smiling at the picture of Enid tramping around the dark, chilly campus in her striped pajamas and bathrobe.

"Never mind, I'm sure I'll be able to figure it out." Enid turned to go. Bobby reached out to stop her, regretting her obvious amusement, and Enid flinched at the touch of Bobby's hand on her shoulder. Goodness, the Math Mistress was even more prickly than usual tonight!

"Wait, I'll show you, just let me slip on my sneakers," said the field hockey coach, suiting action to word. "It's not complicated, but we don't want you electrocuting yourself!" She almost added that two dead math mistresses in a year would be too much for Metamora, but stopped herself. "Let's go."

Enid led the way to Manchester. Inside the dorm all was dark, and Bobby flicked the hall switch on and off to no avail. Muffled giggles told her she and Enid were not alone. Taking the flashlight from Enid and switching it on, she caught a group of pajamaed fourth formers in its powerful beam.

"What are you girls doing up?" she queried. The girls responded in a startled chorus. "Gwen had to go to the loo—" "The lights were off—" "And she was scared—" "We were keeping her company!"

"Well, head back to bed now and stay there," said Bobby firmly. "Miss Butler and I are going to fix the lights, so you won't have any more excuses to be roaming around!"

"Yes, Coach Bobby," giggled the fourth formers as they dispersed. Gwen Norton hung back to ask, "Will you come and say good night to us before you go?"

Bobby had established a tradition of visiting Cornwall's bedrooms in turn, a different one each night, to say a special good night to the occupants. It was good for morale; the reward of a bedtime visit from Coach Bobby was more powerful than any number of reprimands for the high-strung third formers of Cornwall.

"All right," agreed Bobby. "But only if you girls stay in bed, all of you. I'm counting on you, Gwen, to maintain order while Miss Butler and I are in the basement."

Gwen's eyes in the glow of the flashlight were shining with devotion. "I won't let you down, Coach Bobby!"

As the two teachers descended the narrow, winding stairs to the basement, Bobby apologized to Enid. "I'm sorry I took over like that, in your dorm, it's just—"

"Forget it," said Enid tersely. "I'm sure it was more expedient than waiting for me to attempt discipline!"

Bobby knew Manchester had a reputation as a particularly rowdy dormitory, but she'd put it down to fourth-form high spirits. Was Enid having discipline difficulties?

The Math Mistress held the flashlight as Bobby efficiently changed the fuse. "There," she said as she pushed the main service switch back on and the storeroom was flooded with light. "You'll be able to do it yourself next time." She dusted her hands and closed the fuse box.

Enid seemed to have lost interest in learning the ins and outs of fuse replacement. She held out the flashlight to Bobby. "Take this, will you? I've got something in my eye."

Without the protection of her heavy spectacles, Enid looked lonely and lost as she stood in the dusty storeroom rubbing one eye.

"You'll just make it worse," said Bobby. Pulling out a handkerchief, she gently pushed Enid's hand aside and dabbed delicately at her reddened, watery eye. "How's the math club doing? Angle seems to be enjoying it."

Enid made no reply. Her breathing was erratic. *Goodness,* thought Bobby. *Have I set her off again?* "Angle—I mean Angela—told me all about that tree height problem," she tried again. "What was it, something about measuring the shadow?"

Enid grasped Bobby's upper arm in a vise-like grip. "Would you shut up about Angle?" she ground out between clenched teeth.

"Why—why—I thought you were interested—" Bobby faltered. Enid was looking at her with a strange intensity.

"My God, Bobby, what do you think I'm made of?" Enid groaned harshly. "I'm only flesh and blood!"

Her grip on Bobby tightened, and as if magnetized, Bobby drew closer to the Math Mistress, who was vibrating with a strange passion Bobby had never suspected she possessed. Bobby's mind was in a whirl. Did Enid—was Enid—?

Enid's mouth fused to Bobby's, and the gym teacher's thoughts were blown away by this gale-force passion. This was no palpitating schoolgirl, Bobby realized dimly as the whirlwind of desire engulfed her, no married woman sneaking illicit thrills. Enid's lips were fierce, seeking, hungry. They set Bobby on fire. The gym teacher's response was immediate. She put her arms around the other woman, and the flashlight fell to the floor with a crash.

The noise seemed to startle Enid back to her senses. Suddenly she pushed Bobby away from her. "I can't do this," she said unsteadily. "I don't want to do this."

Bobby couldn't believe her ears. All of the Math Mistress's actions added up to Want with a capital W—what obscure calculation could divide them now, leaving Bobby with a big fat zero?

"Wait a second," she said, moving toward Enid. A sound above made them both stop and cock their ears. Someone was coming down the staircase. A second later, Gwen Norton appeared in the doorway of the storage room, her eyes wide and so breathless with fright she could hardly gasp out her message: "Coach Bobby—Miss Butler—the third-floor corner suite is empty! Linda Kerwin, Penny Gordon, and Sue Howard have disappeared!"

Chapter Seventeen
Kent Tower

There students missing! Gone from their beds well after lights out! This was a serious infraction of the rules—or something worse.

The two teachers nearly collided with each other in their haste as they raced up the staircase, with Gwen at their heels. At the first floor Bobby easily took the lead as she sprinted to the second floor, leaving the less athletic Enid and the panicked fourth former behind. The third floor's hallway was shorter than the second floor's, and the corner suite at the end of the corridor consisted of two bedrooms connected by a tiny sitting room. The sitting room's bay window surveyed the quad, which was shrouded in darkness at this hour. Bobby switched on the light and cautiously opened the door to one of the bedrooms. Dead silence met her. A sweep of her flashlight revealed bodies huddled under the covers. But no—not bodies. Bobby turned on the lights and poked at the nearest mound. Pillows covered with blankets.

Enid and Gwen arrived, breathless, as Bobby emerged from the second bedroom, where she'd found the same clumsy deception.

"Gwen's right, they're gone," she reported grimly. "The old pillow trick. But where?"

Gwen began to cry. "They've been taken!"

"Don't be ridiculous," snapped Enid. "They clearly went of their own free will."

"They should have been back by now! Something must have gone wrong! I told them what they were doing was dangerous!"

The teachers exchanged a look. "You'd better tell us what you know, Gwen," said Bobby firmly.

Gwen blubbered it all out. Linda had received a replacement ouija board that day—she'd ordered it from a novelty company several weeks ago. It was common knowledge throughout Manchester that Linda and her occult-minded friends were planning to hold a séance as soon as the board arrived. Just where, Gwen wasn't sure, except that it was a place with powerful spiritual associations.

As Gwen wept quietly, sure that her classmates had been swallowed by the spirit world, Enid and Bobby stood in the sitting room at a loss, trying to figure out where the would-be mediums had gone for their séance. Bobby thought of Mesquakie Point, but at the mental image of the three girls stumbling through the forest in the pitch dark, she discarded the idea. Not even Linda would have the stomach for that trip. It must be somewhere on campus. . . .

"Look!" Enid grabbed her arm. "Did you see that?"

Even in the midst of this crisis, Bobby's thoughts flashed back to that moment in the Manchester basement when Enid had first grabbed her by the arm. She would never be able to look at Enid the same way again. The math teacher's hand burned into Bobby's arm like a branding iron. As if she'd read Bobby's mind, Enid released her grip immediately.

"What? Where? I don't see anything," Bobby stuttered.

Enid turned off the lights in the suite's sitting room where the little group was standing. "There." She pointed out the window. "Kent Tower!"

Now that the room was dark, the faint light in the tower was clearly visible. Of course. Morbid-minded Linda would choose that location for her otherworldly activities!

"That's them," said Bobby grimly. "Let's go."

The quad was dark and empty, yet somehow unquiet, alive with tiny noises: the scrunch of Bobby's tennis shoes on the dry grass, the ominous chirping of the crickets, the sudden rustle of some small mammal in the bushes. Bobby and Enid crossed it rapidly, driven by an unspoken sense of urgency that had no basis in the harmless hijinks of the irrepressible fourth formers. As they swung open the door to Kent and the squeak of Bobby's shoes on the tile echoed through the empty hall, Bobby asked in a low voice, "How do we get up into the tower? I've never been." Enid replied, "I have. The stairs are over here." She led the way to a small medieval door that Bobby had always assumed hid a closet, but which now revealed a narrow circular stone stairway. Wondering why Enid had been exploring the tower, Bobby hastened after the young mathematics instructor, whose blue bathrobe was already disappearing around the first curve. If she cupped a hand behind her ears, she could hear above them a faint mumble of voices. As they climbed higher, Bobby began to distinguish words. "E," said a voice that might be Linda's, "L. I. C. H." What strange alphabetical games were the fourth formers playing? "It's her," gasped the terrified voice of Sue Gordon. "It's Miss Froelich!"

Miss Froelich. In her mind's eye, Bobby saw again the body tumbling through space. Instinctively, she looked down—over the stair railing, down through the center of the twisting stairway, more than fifty feet down to the floor.

Her vision blurred, and she sagged against the rounded wall of the tower, away from the drop. Above her she heard Linda's quavering voice, "Are you at peace?"

The dizzy Games Mistress tried to force herself along but only managed another step and stopped there, frozen, clinging helplessly to the railing. Her face was covered in a cold sweat. "Look, it's moving!" She heard Penny's eager voice. And then a chorus of voices: "No!"

"Bobby? What's the matter?" Enid had returned and her grip on Bobby's arm was a lifeline.

"Just a—touch of—vertigo," Bobby gasped.

"Don't look down. Lean on me." Enid put her arm around Bobby and practically hauled the stricken Games Mistress up the remaining steps by brute force. Bobby clung to her fellow mistress as a drowning woman might cling to an inner tube. The two of them fell through the door to the narrow platform that encircled the turret.

"It's her!" shrieked Sue, and the three girls recoiled in terror, knocking the board askew and sending the planchette skittering across the uneven stone paving. Linda was the first to recover. "No, it's Miss Butler," she corrected, a tinge of disappointment in her voice.

Bobby pressed herself against the cylindrical wall of rough stone that enclosed the stairs, as far away as she could get from the crenelated battlement. The three friends, wrapped in blankets and supplied with cookies as well as candles and a flashlight, were huddled on the west side of the tower.

"The séance is over," Enid said peremptorily, picking up the planchette. "And you don't need a soothsayer to predict that you girls are in serious trouble!"

"We were just going to ask the spirit world where my

sister Kayo's necklace is," Linda explained glibly as the two other fourth formers gradually recovered from the shock of seeing two of their teachers, one bent over and clinging to the other, appear on the tower.

"We'll discuss that in the morning. Right now you must all get back to bed as quickly as possible. It would have been better for you if you'd stayed there in the first place."

The dismayed girls began to collect their occult paraphernalia. "Give me that," Bobby managed to croak, pulling herself upright, when she saw Linda attempt to hide the ouija board in the folds of a blanket. The amateur spiritualist handed it over reluctantly. "We were just getting somewhere," she muttered.

"And I'll take that." Enid held out her hand for the flashlight. "Out of bed after lights out—playing a forbidden game—climbing the tower, which is off-limits, as you well know! And on top of that filching school property!"

"We were going to return it," protested Penny weakly.

"Let's go, girls. Stop dragging your feet, Linda, you go first. Miss Blanchard and I will bring up the rear." As the cowed girls began to descend the stairs, Enid asked low in Bobby's ear, "Can you make it?"

Bobby nodded. "I'm all right." She wasn't, but the need to maintain her status with her students stiffened her spine. Closing her eyes and keeping a tight grip on Enid, she felt her way down the stairs, trying to picture the hockey field, flat, level, plainly marked with orderly chalk lines.

Even so, the descent seemed to last forever. Bobby could hear Penny Gordon snuffling—worn out by the late hour, the excitement, and the prospect of serious punishment. Suddenly Bobby felt Enid stop. "Miss Craybill!" Linda's voice exclaimed. Bobby's eyes flew open.

She was four steps from the bottom of the spiral stairs, and Miss Craybill was framed in the stairwell doorway, her face unearthly white in the glow of Enid's flashlight. Her gray hair was down her back in two braids, and she had on a surprisingly elegant quilted silk dressing gown in a deep shade of eggplant.

"What's all this?" she demanded. She, too, carried a flashlight, and Bobby blinked as the Headmistress played the light over their faces.

"I'm afraid these girls have broken quite a few rules," said Enid. "Miss Blanchard and I found them up in the tower having some sort of—"

"Midnight feast," interrupted Bobby. Her instinct told her that saying the word "séance" to Miss Craybill at this eerie hour as she confronted them with a wild look in her eye would be a bad idea.

Alas for her caution. "It was Linda's idea," sniveled Penny. "Her and her stupid ouija board!"

Miss Craybill recoiled as if struck, then she leapt upon poor Linda before either of the teachers could interfere. "What have you been doing now, you wretched girl? Why can't you leave her in peace? Why can't you leave her in peace, I say?"

"She's—she's not in peace," the white-faced girl quavered. Bobby had to admire Linda's courage as she contradicted the crazed Headmistress. *She really must believe in that ouija board stuff,* the gym teacher thought.

Miss Craybill flinched, and for a second seemed cowed by the young girl's assertion. She grasped the collar of Linda's terry-cloth bathrobe and pulled the shivering student toward her. "She's not? How do you know? What did she say?" She thrust her face close to Linda's and whispered hoarsely, "Did she mention me?"

The two teachers had been frozen in appalled silence, but now they sprang into action. "Perhaps tomorrow—" began Enid, edging herself between Miss Craybill and the terrified girl, while Bobby descended the steps and took

Miss Craybill by the arm. "The important thing right now is to get these girls back to bed, I know you'll agree." Miss Craybill went along automatically, all the while stealing half-angry, half-supplicating glances at Linda as the little group moved down the wide hallway of Kent, the portraits of the founders and benefactors glaring down in the flickering flashlight.

"No, but it's ridiculous, irrational," muttered Miss Craybill to herself, shooting another queer look at Linda. Suddenly she stopped. "What have you got there?"

Bobby looked at Linda, but Linda was looking at her, and so was Miss Craybill. She looked down. It was the ouija board, tucked under her arm, that had attracted Miss Craybill's attention, and before Bobby could react the Headmistress snatched it from her. "We'll put an end to this nonsense once and for all," she said, pushing open the door to the quadrangle. She hurled the flimsy game board to the ground and took the candle and matches from Sue's limp hands. They all watched helplessly as their Headmistress managed to get the cardboard burning. "Let this be a lesson to you!" cried Miss Craybill triumphantly as the flames rose. "Do not seek to cross the divide that God has erected between our world and the next! Do not meddle," her voice rose over the crackling of the fire, and Bobby detected the sharp note of hysteria in it, "with things beyond your ken! Do not—"

"Look," said Linda, pointing. The dancing flames of the burning ouija board revealed a glittering necklace draped over the sundial, the heart-shaped locket swinging gently.

Chapter Eighteen
In the Locker Room

Tuesday afternoon the blue bus with the words "Metamora Academy for Young Ladies" lettered on each side wheezed out the Academy's front gate and roared up Route 32 toward Miss Mellyn's Seminary in nearby Beaverton.

Bobby sat up front, glancing over her shoulder at the subdued Savages. Angie slumped next to her, in her customary attitude of sulky defiance, and Lotta was across the aisle, stealing glances at the object of her affections. Except for a low-toned conversation here or there, the team was unusually quiet. Bobby glimpsed Kayo staring out the window, absently fingering the locket that hung around her neck.

Despite her and Enid's best efforts to hush up the circumstances, the story of the dramatic reappearance of the locket had rocketed around the student body. Linda was something of a celebrity. The credulous students told each other that the semi-successful summoning of Miss Froelich's spirit was somehow connected with the return of the locket.

"Don't these kids think anything through?" Bobby

asked Mona despairingly. "How could a spirit pick up a necklace and carry it around?"

"Well, they have thought it through pretty thoroughly," Mona reported. "The theory now is that Miss Froelich possessed someone who put the locket on the sundial, and since they were possessed they have no memory of it at all."

Bobby had to admit that it was a foolproof explanation—if you believed in the spirit world. She didn't, she'd told herself firmly.

And yet after talking to Mona, Bobby found herself climbing the stairs to the second floor of Kent where the class photos hung, and studying the class of 1963. There was Miss Froelich, in the bottom row, seated on Miss Craybill's left. A round-faced woman wearing what looked like an old-fashioned pince nez, her gray curls and fixed smile revealed nothing.

All the mistresses wore academic gowns. Bobby compared them in her mind's eye to the ghostly bicyclist. Certainly, the mysterious cyclist and Miss Froelich shared the same wardrobe.

I'm being ridiculous, Bobby told herself. *Trying to ID a ghost from a photograph!*

She wandered down the hall, pausing in front of each picture long enough to find Miss Froelich. 1962, 1961, 1960 . . . 1949, 1948, 1947 . . . Miss Froelich's hair grew darker and longer, her wrinkles melted away and her glasses disappeared. Next to her, Miss Craybill seemed to grow taller, and plumper, smiling at the camera with vivacity.

Bobby kept going. At the far end of the hall, Miss Craybill and Miss Froelich were students, the two friends now in separate rows. Miss Froelich stood with the sixth formers, Miss Craybill in the row in front. Bobby looked carefully at the young Nerissa Froelich. The dead Math Mistress was a tall, lanky girl, and the camera had caught her in motion, her head half turned, a mischievous smile on her face. She looked energetic, athletic—alive. For the first time, Bobby felt genuine sorrow at the thought of this girl's unpleasant death. How had it happened? What rash act had tipped her off the tower?

Suddenly the weight of these long-ago Metamorians, many of them probably as dead as Miss Froelich, was too much for the young field hockey coach. She fled the dim hallway and hurried down the stairs to the faculty lounge, seeking solace in sherry hour.

There, too, the only topic of conversation was the superstitious sentiment sweeping the campus.

"I confiscated another ouija board replica in Art II," Laura declared, sitting up straight and holding out her glass for more sherry. "Cynthia Fellowes, one of my best students. She was supposed to be working on the design for the Harvest Moon Mixer poster, and instead this! She tried passing it off as a color study."

"On the positive side, the fourth formers hung on my every word when my American history class covered the Salem witch trials," remarked Ken Burnham from his seat next to Laura. He seemed bemused by the novel experience.

"Oh, there's nothing positive about this ridiculous state of affairs," moaned Miss Otis. "Don't you realize what this will do to Metamora's reputation? We must quash this craze before the Old Girls' Tea. If the Old Girls get hold of this ghost story, they'll spread it to the ends of the earth! Before you know it, people will start to think there *was* something funny about Miss Froelich's death. And then—"

An uneasy pause ensued, broken only by Madame Melville, who waved her cigarette airily and said, "I do not think you will flatten this gossip, Bunny. It must run its course, like a fever. *Et alors*." She shrugged her Gallic shoulders. "Maybe there is a ghost. Did not your poet write, 'There are more things in heaven and earth . . .'"

That quote again, thought Bobby. *Everyone knows it but me.* She felt suddenly overwhelmed by her own inadequacy in the face of this latest crisis. She stole a glance at Enid, sitting below a gargoyle, correcting papers. Enid was hardly ever at sherry hour these days. She'd had a date with Rod almost every night this week.

She'll probably be announcing her engagement any day now, Bobby thought bitterly as Serena and Hoppy joined in the debate over the spirit world. Looking at Enid, Bobby felt shaken by a mixture of rage and desire. Why was she, Bobby, attracted to this woman who despised her? Why was she so bored by Laura? Why did Kayo's adoration only worry her? Why had Enid kissed her that night?

"There's a scientific explanation for everything," a voice observed dispassionately.

For a moment Bobby thought it was a spirit voice, answering the questions churning around in her head. But it was only Miss Rasphigi, interrupting the debate Madame Melville had started.

The teachers turned simultaneously. Miss Rasphigi stood at the edge of the circle, wearing a white lab coat over her usual shapeless black dress, a face mask around her neck. She surveyed the teachers with her cold dark eyes as if they were strangers, as indeed they were. Miss Rasphigi rarely attended faculty gatherings.

Now her eyes settled on Mona. "My expresso," she said with a hint of reproach.

Mona got to her feet. "Oh, Connie, I'm so sorry, it completely slipped my mind."

"What is the explanation for our ghost?" Enid challenged Miss Rasphigi.

Miss Rasphigi was following Mona out the door. "I have to get back to my spores."

The teachers laughed uneasily after she was gone. "Her spores," repeated Miss Otis. "When the school's reputation is at stake! If I thought she knew something she wasn't saying, I'd wipe her petri dishes clean with bleach!"

Bobby was rehashing that discussion in her head as the bus pulled into the parking lot of Miss Mellyn's Seminary. She wondered what Enid thought. Did the Math Mistress believe in the Metamora ghost?

"Everybody out!" called Mona cheerfully as she set the parking brake. The versatile housekeeper shared bus driving duties with Ole Amundsen, who was occupied that afternoon resodding the scorched patch of the quad. Bobby put her uneasiness aside and led her team off the bus.

The next half hour was the usual flurry—greeting the coach of the Mellyn Nuthatches, the scorekeepers and umpires, getting her team warmed up and making sure Lotta was set with towels and water. She saw Mona sitting in the stands, laughing and chatting with a group of suburban matrons including the Kerwins' aunt Dot. Bobby glanced at the svelte blonde disinterestedly before turning back to the business at hand. *Even Aunt Dot doesn't excite me anymore*, she thought glumly.

The game should be a shoo-in, Bobby knew. The Nuthatches, nicknamed the Birdbrains, were at the bottom of the league. Miss Mellyn's school had a reputation as a haven for girls endowed with more money than mental ability. These daughters of the well-to-do whacked the ball about in a leisurely manner, as if whiling away the time until the next debutante dance. There were one or two players with talent—an energetic halfback and a wing with nice ball-handling skills, but they were no reason to worry. So why couldn't Bobby get rid of this uneasy feeling?

The squad's silly superstitions were getting to her, Bobby thought. Going to Miss Mellyn's locker room to hurry the stragglers, she came upon a scattering of Savages debating whether or not Kayo should wear the necklace during the game. "Miss Froelich wanted it returned," Linda spoke with authority. "So it will bring us luck." She was pulling her crimson knee socks on over her shin guards.

"But what if it's become possessed?" asked Penny. "We never got the chance to figure out if Miss Froelich's spirit is malevolent!" She looked nervously at Kayo, who was putting her school uniform in a locker.

Kayo turned on the two girls angrily. "You're being too silly for words," she said. "I'm going to wear it. I don't want to lose it again."

Bobby, who'd been on the point of saying something, simply clapped her hands. "Hustle, Savages, hustle. Let's get warmed up."

Where was their focus? Bobby worried as she took her seat next to Angle and the game began. Where was that healthy competitive spirit? That desire to stomp the opposition? That bloodlust that made a winning team?

She clapped routinely as Annette scored a goal. The Savages were playing sloppy. Linda should have been in position for the rebound.

As she watched, the Nuthatch with the ball-handling skills slipped around Helen and drove the ball into Savage territory. Angle tensed beside Bobby, and the next moment the coach and the squad on the sidelines had leapt to their feet as the stands gasped, "Ohhhh!"

The Nuthatches had shot on goal, and in one of those freak occurrences, the ball Edie blocked had rebounded off the goalpost and thwacked the Savages' stalwart goalkeeper just above her left shin guard. She clutched her leg and fell to her side.

"Is that a goal? Does that count?" Angle was shouting

as Bobby signaled for a time-out and raced to the stricken goalie's side. Edie was gasping in pain, hugging her leg to her chest as she sprawled on the ground.

"Just a bad bruise," reported the umpire, who had reached the fallen girl first. Indeed, the red swelling of a hematoma had already made a visible lump on the side of Edie's leg. As her anxious teammates helped the wounded goalie limp off the field, Bobby tried to decide which player she should sub in. Penny Gordon was more adept than stolid Dodie Jessup, but Penny was as high-strung as a half-broke thoroughbred filly, and with superstitions swamping her good sense, she'd be seeing ghosts at the penalty mark. Still, reasoned Bobby, maybe goalkeeping would snap her out of her distraction. "Penny!" she called, deciding in favor of skill. "You're in for Edie."

When the halftime whistle blew with the score 3–1, the Savages clustered around Edie, who sat next to Angle, an ice bag on her knee.

"It's just like when Hector slew Achilles," commented Lotta. "It always seemed kind of far-fetched to me, that he got stabbed in the one spot he was vulnerable. But look at Edie! Getting whomped in the one spot her pads don't cover."

"That ball was *helped*," declared Linda suddenly. "Do you realize who we're playing?"

"The Birdbrains, so what?" Shirley Sarvis was skeptical.

"The *Nuthatches*. The very bird species Miss Froelich was observing in the tower when she fell!"

Bobby, who'd been listening with half an ear, turned to intervene, but Angle beat her to it. "You kids make me sick," she scoffed. "Blaming ghosts for your own lousy playing. Miss Froelich wasn't even looking at nuthatches!"

"Well, what was she doing up there?" Helen Wechsler challenged the team outcast.

"I dunno." Angle shrugged. "Maybe she jumped on purpose."

"That's enough!" Bobby was next to Edie in two strides, wishing she'd spoken up before Angle's unfortunate remark. "Angle, you're running laps before dinner for a week." It was getting harder and harder to find a free period to punish the troubled teen. "And the next person who mentions Miss Froelich, or ghosts, or Kayo's necklace is benched!"

"But—" began Linda.

"You're benched!" shot back Bobby, as the whistle blew. "Joyce, you're up!"

It was a demoralized tribe of Savages who straggled onto the field. Two second-string players in key positions, a captain wearing a cursed necklace and the burning question unsettled in their mind: demon possession, or suicide? Neither possibility rallied their sinking school spirit.

The Nuthatches, on the other hand, had been infused with a new vigor by their unexpected goal and the freak accident that had taken out the enemy's goalie. The second half saw their transformation from aesthetes to athletes. The goalie dived for the ball enthusiastically. The center with the pink nail polish gripped her stick like she meant it. Kayo won the bully, but lost the ball when she glanced toward her coach for approval. Bobby could only gnash her teeth as the team captain fouled repeatedly in her effort to repair her error. Beryl charged in to help her friend, leaving a hole the Nuthatches flew through, and Penny misjudged every shot on goal.

Angle put her head in her hands, unable to watch. 5–4, a Nuthatch victory. Only Annette, Shirley, and Joyce kept the game from being a complete rout.

"It's too bad, Bobby," Mona said sympathetically as

the spectators dispersed around them. "Maybe some cocoa in the common room when we get back to Metamora will help perk up the Savages' spirits."

"Cocoa!" Aunt Dot appeared at Bobby's elbow. "What they need is a good talking-to."

Bobby prayed for patience. The last thing she needed was an alumna complaining about this embarrassing defeat.

"The girls had an off day, I guess," she said tersely. She headed toward the locker room, but Dot followed her.

"Off day! I expected a five-point win—I never dreamed you'd manage to lose!"

Bobby wondered how she had ever found this woman attractive.

"We alumnae have certain expectations," Dot told her. "I've studied the stats and I know what kind of performance the team is capable of, with the right coaching. Why didn't you play Angle?"

Bobby was speechless. The right coaching? Was the Kerwins' aunt blaming her for this debacle? Did Dot Driscoll think she could tell Bobby who to play?

Fuming inwardly, Bobby managed to get away from the interfering alumna, and entered the locker room in time to hear a different post-game analysis. "Don't feel bad," Linda comforted her friend Penny. "The spirits were against us."

That was the final straw. Bobby threw her clipboard to the floor where it landed with a resounding crash.

"You can't blame the spirits, you can't blame me, you can't blame anyone but yourselves!" she cried in a fury. "Do you know why you lost? Because you played like a bunch of *dopes!*"

The startled girls jumped and flinched, but Bobby was on a rampage.

"You played like you'd never seen a hockey ball before—and because why? Because instead of studying the game, you've stuffed your heads with this superstitious *bunk!* You spend all your time wringing your hands about unimportant things like missing necklaces, and dead math mistresses, and who likes who, while your opponents steal the ball from under your silly *noses!*"

"Miss Froelich's death isn't exactly unimportant," Linda ventured.

"A real hockey player would care more about smashing her opponent!" Bobby lashed out. "How do you girls expect to succeed in life, let alone on the hockey field, with this losing attitude?" She tried to think of the worst thing she could say. "I don't think *any* of you will ever make the National Women's Hockey Team. Not *one.*"

Even as she drew in her breath at the conclusion of her harangue, Bobby began to realize she'd made a serious mistake. She'd lost her temper with the Savages. She'd been unsettled by the occult rumors, let down by her love life, sore about the score, goaded by Dot Driscoll—and she'd taken it out on the team.

The Savages weren't used to such harshness. The stricken girls looked down at their hockey cleats. Kayo's blue eyes had overflowed, and Linda and Penny were clutching each other for support. Beryl muttered with forced bravado, "I can smash the opponent whenever I feel like it." Otherwise there was dead silence.

Sickened by herself, her anger spent, Bobby sought in vain for the words that might repair the damage she'd done. She looked at wounded Edie, who had never been anything but dependable, staring at the floor. Shirley, Annette, and Joyce, who'd done their darnedest, all looked like they'd been punched.

But it was Angle who twisted the dagger of self-reproach in Bobby's gut. Looking straight at her coach with disappointed eyes, she broke the silence. "I don't think I want to be on the National Women's Field Hockey Team."

Bobby sucked in her breath. Had she just destroyed all her hard work at integrating Angle into the team and life at Metamora?

"Let's hustle and get dressed, girls," she said in a voice not quite her own. "The bus leaves in five."

Turning, she hurried from the locker room. She leaned against the wall outside the door, trembling with panic and regret. How could she have said those things? It was as if she'd forgotten everything she'd read the past few weeks. They were just kids, schoolgirls—*adolescents!* In one crazy lapse of judgment she'd destroyed the respect and admiration she'd been so proud of.

Coach Mabel was right, Bobby thought, heartsick. She remembered the Coach's visit to her in the hospital, after the accident. "I don't know that I could ever trust you with responsibility again, Bobby," she'd said then. If Miss Watkins had known what had happened that night at the swimming pool, would she have ever placed Bobby at Metamora?

And the worst of it was, Dot was on the money. It *wasn't* the squad's fault they'd failed. It was Bobby's, pure and simple. Despite all her protestations to Enid, she *had* built the squad around the experienced DAP clique. When those players failed, the whole team failed.

I failed, Bobby reminded herself bitterly. She'd failed both as a coach and as a teacher. She'd failed Miss Watkins, Miss Craybill, and she'd failed herself. After this year was up, she'd resign, if the Headmistress and angry alumnae didn't send her packing first. The vision of the hot plate, the cheap hotel, the job handing out towels at the Y rose up before Bobby like a destiny she'd only postponed. Would it be like that book she'd confiscated from Sandy, when the girl sinks into drugs, degradation, and despair?

I can't face dinner in Dorset tonight, Bobby decided. *I can't even face the bus ride back to Metamora. I'll grab the train to Bay City from Beaverton and drown my sorrows at the Knock Knock Lounge. Get a glimpse of what my future looks like.*

"Yes—no—more—!" gasped the girl in the pink angora sweater. She arched herself against Bobby, who blindly tugged at the girl's skirt but was unable to get it up out of the way, so tightly entangled were the two of them in the tiny, not too clean bathroom. "Sorry, honey," she panted in the girl's ear, then in a flash of inspiration she hoisted the girl onto the sink and knelt down before her.

"Oh, Buddy, you're the best! The best!"

"It's Bobby," corrected Metamora's Games Mistress when she came up for air. Someone was pounding on the bathroom door. "Enough already! I'm going to get Jojo to break this door down if you two don't come out."

As Bobby retucked her shirt and straightened the collar, she reflected that this was the first unfriendly remark anyone had made since her arrival at the Knock Knock Lounge a few hours ago. Was it because she'd dressed the way Pat had prescribed—fly-front pants, man's shirt, slicked-back hair? Was it running into her old teammate, Lon, who'd introduced her around? Bobby didn't think so. She had a feeling the gals at the bar of the Knock

Knock would have been just as welcoming if she'd arrived in a gym tunic.

"Let me buy you a drink, lover," said the girl in the pink angora sweater, snapping her lipstick case closed and leading the way back to the bar. Lon had called her Doreen—or was it Norine?

Drinking a beer with a pretty girl at her side, Bobby had to admit the life of a failed gym teacher wasn't as bad as it was painted. But as the euphoria from her tryst with Doreen faded, she couldn't help replaying in her head that terrible scene in the locker room. She shuddered. How could she have berated the Savages that way, like an unsocialized adolescent with deficient impulse control?

"What's the matter, honey?" said Doreen, sipping her beer. "Is it me, or do you have another girl on your mind?"

"A whole roster of girls," Bobby told her glumly. The faces of the Savages as they'd looked at her, white, shaken, dismayed, came back to her so vividly she winced. None of this—not the beer, Doreen, her new fly-front flannels—could drown out her realization. She was a failure as a teacher. *Damn Miss Watkins,* she thought angrily. *If she hadn't egged me on to try this teaching business, I'd never have known how much I liked it.*

Doreen was eyeing Bobby with new respect. "How many girls is a roster?"

"Eleven," said Bobby. "A goalie, a center, two forwards, two wings, two halfbacks, three fullbacks. Then there are the substitutes."

"Why, you must be all worn out!" Doreen seemed awestruck. "I'll get you another beer." She waved for the bartender. But beer couldn't stop Bobby from brooding over her teaching mistakes.

"Say, you took P.E. classes in high school, didn't you?"

"It was required."

"Did your instructors use the module or project method

to introduce you to, say, volleyball?" Bobby asked earnestly. "And do you think the particular pedagogic method they chose made it harder or easier for you to absorb the principles of a given game?"

"Huh?" Doreen's jaw dropped.

"Excuse me." Bobby turned at a tap on her shoulder, and found herself looking into hazel eyes behind a pair of horn-rimmed glasses. "I couldn't help overhearing your question, and I wondered if you'd read the recent article in September's *Secondary Pedagogy* which questions the project-based methodology." She turned to her companion. "Doris, maybe you have a copy?"

Standing just behind the girl with the horn-rimmed glasses, waiting for her turn to get the bartender's attention, was a familiar figure, trim as usual, in a greenish brown suit of cloqué wool.

"Miss Watkins!" gasped Bobby.

"Why, Bobby Blanchard!" Miss Watkins smiled in pleased surprise. "I've been wondering how you were getting on!"

Bobby concealed her inward astonishment at Miss Watkins's unlikely presence in this waterfront dive. Bobby had never even pictured Miss Watkins away from her desk and punch cards. What was she doing here?

Miss Watkins introduced her friend, the girl with the glasses who had mentioned project-based methodologies.

"This is Netta Bean, she teaches at the Eleanor D. Roosevelt School for Troubled Girls, where I do some volunteer counseling."

"This is Doreen, Doreen . . ." Bobby was embarrassed she didn't know the girl's last name, but she felt even sillier when Netta smiled and said, "Why, it's Norine Nemickas. Let's see, you graduated, what is it, two years ago?"

"That's right, Miss Bean!" Norine, formerly Doreen, sounded delighted. "After you barely passed me!"

"You must call me Netta now," said the inner-city school-teacher. "Won't you join us?" When they'd all sat down, Bobby couldn't help asking, "Do you come here often, Miss Watkins?"

"I like to check on Jojo." Miss Watkins nodded at the mannish bartender. "You see, I placed her in this job. She was working as a delivery girl before, but she had no penchant for early hours."

"What do you teach?" Netta Bean asked Bobby.

"Physical education," Bobby replied, wondering glumly how much longer that would be the case.

"Bobby is Games Mistress at the Metamora Academy," Miss Watkins put in. "Her first teaching job. And it sounds as though you've taken to it like a duck to water." The vocational counselor beamed.

"Metamora Academy—why, I think I know one of your colleagues," said Netta.

"You must mean Hoppy Fiske," Bobby realized. "She talks all the time about her summer stint at Eleanor D. Roosevelt."

"How is Hoppy? She talked about Metamora a lot too. We often discussed some way to bring together the students from the two schools, as a sort of cultural exchange. We think the girls would have lots to teach and learn from each other. Perhaps you might have some ideas?"

"I'm not the go-to teacher for good ideas," Bobby confessed. "The truth is, I've made a hash of my teaching responsibilities!"

"Have your reading scores fallen?" Netta asked, concerned. "I find peer tutoring a useful tool in those circumstances. Or have you lost a pupil? I took a group to the Bay City Art Institute and one of the girls got arrested for pickpocketing. My principal read me the riot act!"

"No, no, it's nothing like that," Bobby hastened to correct her colleague. She told the two women about restarting the field hockey team, the enmity between her two best players, the disappearing, reappearing locket, and losing her temper with her team.

"It sounds to me like you're making a mistake common to women who move from performing an activity professionally to teaching it at an amateur level." Miss Watkins soothing voice made Bobby's problems seem manageable. "I see this quite frequently in my profession. You're subconsciously trying to satisfy your frustrated ambitions through your hockey team. You're seeing your players as younger versions of *you*. They're not, and never will be."

"Why, that's true." Bobby felt as though she'd discovered something important. "They're just kids! It's way too soon for them to think about playing field hockey at the professional level!"

"And personality conflicts between students are tough for every teacher," Netta chimed in. "Especially when violence erupts! I've found it sometimes works to focus on the quieter, less demanding students, and often the troublemakers will come around on their own. It's also handy to know ju-jitsu."

"I've studied it," Bobby said. "And the truth is, I have been neglecting my classes in favor of field hockey. Why, I rushed through the third form's unit on tetherball, and I simply can't find a way to get the fourth form interested in peasant dance." She slumped back in her chair. "I'm just so far behind the other teachers in my pedagogical technique! No one else would lose their temper and make such stupid mistakes!"

"Bobby, Bobby!" Miss Watkins scolded. "Didn't I tell you you're your own worst enemy?"

Netta leaned forward. "I've made scads of mistakes, believe me! There was the time I failed to take a student's threat to assassinate the principal seriously—and the time I borrowed some records from the library and they got broken in a fracas—the time I let the kids use a real noose when they dramatized 'An Occurrence at Owl Creek Bridge' . . . oh, I could tell you loads of stories!"

"I wish wasn't stuck with Miss Fayne's curriculum." Bobby sighed.

"Rewrite it!" suggested Netta. "Starting with peasant dance. Maybe the reason you can't make it interesting to your students is that you're not interested in it yourself."

Bobby looked at Netta with respect. She'd hit the nail on the head. Bobby *hated* peasant dance!

Norine had left the table, bored with the shop talk, and had joined the women on the dance floor, gyrating to a popular song.

"Do you know the name of this tune?" Bobby asked Netta and Miss Watkins as an idea germinated in her head. But before either could respond, the bartender stopped by their table to issue a terse warning. "Cops outside. Probably just looking for a payoff, but I know youse got better things to do than spend a night in the slammer. The cellar's open."

"Thanks, Jojo," said Miss Watkins, getting to her feet. Netta followed suit.

"What's going on? What's she talking about?" Bobby asked, bewildered.

"A raid, maybe." Netta replied matter-of-factly. "Follow us."

A bevy of girls was already descending the narrow steps to the Knock Knock Lounge's musty cellar. "For crying out loud, not everybody," Jojo expostulated. "We don't want the fuzz to cop to the hidey-hole."

"I'm not hiding," said a woman with a crew cut, whom Bobby had noticed earlier. She rapped the bar. "Another beer!"

"I'm with you, honey!" cried a girl in a snug red sheath

who'd been standing uncertainly in the middle of the floor. Bobby didn't get to see their romantic reunion because it was her turn to carefully climb the worn wooden steps down into the dimness. She was the last one.

Abruptly the door behind her shut and the cellar was plunged into blackness. Bobby felt her way down the last few steps, listening to the titters and whispers below: "Is that you, Janet?" "Hey, keep your hands to yourself!" There was a crash and a dozen fierce "Shhh's!" Meekly a voice whispered, "Sorry—anyone want a broken bottle of beer?"

Bobby groped her way blindly to where she thought the wall might be, and her exploratory hand collided with a soft sweater. "Whoops! Is that you Doreen, er, Norine?" she whispered.

"Do you want me to be?" The answering whisper was slightly slurred, and Bobby smelled whiskey on the warm breath that fanned her face.

"Quiet already!" someone said sharply.

A hand felt for Bobby's bicep and tugged her closer until the warm whisper was right next to her ear. "Killjoy," the mysterious girl breathed. Her hand let go of Bobby's arm and encircled her waist. "Mind?" came the whisper. Bobby could feel the girl's lips brushing her ear as she added, "I'm a little unsteady."

Bobby couldn't stop her eyes from straining, fruitlessly, to see the mysterious new friend who stood inches away from her. But if she couldn't see, her other four senses were tingling. Cautiously, she put an arm around her cellar acquaintance, feeling the soft sweater that had made her mistake the girl for Norine. The girl was standing so close, leaning slightly on Bobby, that Bobby could feel the rise and fall of her breasts as she breathed. Underneath the whiskey there was a clean soapy smell. Bobby put her lips to where she thought the girl's ear might be, and bumped her nose on something hard. It took her aback for a moment until she figured it out. Glasses.

The girl next to her was shaking with suppressed giggles; Bobby could read the vibrations like a kind of Braille of the body. The young P.E. teacher felt for the girl's ear with her hand, pushing aside a silky curtain of hair before putting her lips close and whispering, "Oops." The body pressed against hers shook again. Then the girl turned her head suddenly, so that Bobby's lips trailed over a satiny cheek before encountering a soft, searching mouth.

Pleasure exploded in Bobby like fireworks in the night sky. Any concerns about the possible raid, her vocation as a teacher, or even lingering thoughts about how to make peasant dance relevant to teens faded from her mind. She tasted lipstick, whiskey (or was it rye?), and an ineffable sweetness that was the girl's own. All she wanted at that moment was this soft, warm, passionate creature who had swum up out of the blackness to meet her in mutual need. This was what she'd been heading for when she got on the train in Beaverton, when she changed into her new flannels in the chili parlor, when she walked into the Knock Knock Lounge; this girl and this sweet, melting feeling, this silent shuddering of desire, the beating of her own pulse in her ears, like a telegraphic signal pounding out a message of lust and longing, and the scratch of wool against Sanforized polycotton as the girl twisted in her arms—

The door above opened, sending a shaft of light into the cellar as Jojo called hoarsely, "All clear, folks." Instinctively Bobby and her new friend pulled back from their embrace to take a look at each other.

"Enid!" Bobby gasped.

Chapter Twenty

An Unexpected Encounter

Enid seemed even more astounded than Bobby. She stumbled backwards and would have fallen if Bobby had not caught hold of her arm.

"Bobby Blanchard!" Enid sounded almost indignant. "What are you doing here?"

"What am I doing here?" Bobby was affronted. "What are *you* doing here? After all, you're practically engaged to Rod!"

"Rod's as queer as a three-dollar bill," Enid retorted. When Bobby eyed her dubiously, she added, "If you don't believe me, go ask him—he's at the Café de Paris, the piano bar down the street."

"But—but I thought you were normal!" Bobby blurted.

"Normal! Where on earth did you get that idea?"

Enid sounded like her usual acerbic self, despite the fact that her hair was mussed, her glasses were crooked, and her lipstick was smeared. *Why—I did that!* Bobby realized. She felt confused, pulled in opposite directions by dislike and desire.

"What about the shove you gave me the other night, after I changed the fuse? You acted like I had leprosy and was trying to infect you!"

"I'm sorry, I—I—" Enid was at a loss. "Honestly, it had nothing to do with you," she told Bobby apologetically. "It's a developmental pattern problem. You see, I have this weakness—this attraction to empty-headed athletes, the gym teacher type. It stems from a role-confusion crisis my sophomore year of high school, which I've been working hard to overcome . . . Look, let's get out of the basement, shall we?"

Bobby followed Enid up the stairs wondering whether to feel complimented or insulted. The dance floor was full again, and women crowded three deep at the bar. The good-humored gaiety that made the Knock Knock Lounge so appealing had been restored. But Bobby no longer had any interest in lingering in the convivial atmosphere.

"Let's get out of here," she suggested. "We can catch the local back to Adena and you can tell me about your juvenile development and this problem of yours. Wait for me while I say good-bye to a friend."

She found Norine and thanked her for the pleasant time they'd spent together. Lon had long since disappeared. When she returned to Enid, she discovered the Math Mistress chatting with Miss Watkins and Netta as if they were old friends. Netta seemed delighted that Bobby and Enid knew each other. "How ideal!" She beamed. "Bobby, I hope to see you again soon, either here or at Metamora. Hoppy and I are going to have a real pow-wow about our socioeconomic exchange idea."

"Good-bye, Bobby, good-bye, Enid," Miss Watkins chimed in. "Enid, you can't deny Spindle-Janska. I'm calling my contact at Business Machine Corporation tomorrow!"

"How do you know them?" Bobby demanded as they walked along the dark, deserted street. Bobby zipped her jacket up to her chin against the icy dampness.

"In the gay life, everyone knows everyone, haven't you

learned that?" Enid said haughtily, wrapping a scarf around her throat.

"This was my first time at a place like the Knock Knock," Bobby admitted.

Enid relented. "Miss Watkins was my guidance counselor in high school, and coincidentally, Netta is going with Lois Lenz, a high school classmate. She was telling me that Lois is doing very well, working as a private secretary to a top advertising executive. Apparently she foiled some scheme—"*

Bobby was interested in Enid, not this friend of Netta's. "What did Miss Watkins mean, 'You can't deny Spindle-Janska'?" she interrupted.

"Oh—that." Enid grew thoughtful. "Miss Watkins was telling me this teaching job is a big mistake. She said my Spindle-Janska Personality Penchant Assessment showed that I should be in a job where I work solely with data, not people."

"But you know so much about teaching. The Spindle-Janska must be wrong!"

"Bobby." Enid stopped in the middle of the sidewalk and put her hands on her hips. "I'm a *terrible* teacher! You must be the only person in the faculty lounge at Metamora who hasn't figured this out. I can't keep discipline. Half of my third formers still can't solve a basic quadratic equation. I simply haven't your knack with adolescent girls! I don't even like them, most of the time."

She began to walk briskly, and Bobby hurried to catch up, trying to absorb this additional reversal of the Enid she thought she knew.

"The only reason I took this job was to save on living expenses. I need every dime I can get for graduate school— I want to study advanced probability theory, not drone on

* See *Lois Lenz, Lesbian Secretary*

about basic math. That's why I go out with Rod so much. We've been entering dance contests, for prize money."

Bobby spotted a little bean wagon through the mist of the waterfront, the lit window like a warm beacon in the chill. "I sure could go for a hot dog," she murmured. She needed sustenance to help her take in all this new information, and the bowl of chili she'd had earlier that evening seemed very far away. "How about you?"

They each ordered a hot dog, piled high with sauerkraut, pickle relish, mustard, and catsup. After they'd munched a few minutes in silence, Bobby said, "So what happened to you with gym teachers in adolescence? Was it that teacher who made you run laps?" *Enid sure can hold a big grudge over a little mandatory physical exertion,* Bobby thought.

"No, it was her student teacher. When I was fifteen I developed a huge crush on Miss Schack, who came to Walnut Grove that year." Enid's expression grew dreamy. "She had short brown hair and blue eyes, and I loved the way her biceps bulged when she demonstrated rope climbing. I quit the math club that semester to join the Hi-Y Safety Squad she moderated."

"Well, what was the matter with that?"

A note of bitterness crept into Enid's voice. "As it turned out, she was carrying on with the captain of the swim team! A whole semester doing duck-and-cover drills, and for what? She was never going to notice a greasy grind like me. And even if she had, what was the probability of such a mismatch lasting? When I want to pair up—and I'm too busy for that right now—I'll do it based on logical criteria of shared characteristics. Meanwhile, I just have to get over this unfortunate fixation I have. I'm looking into psychoanalysis."

"What's on this logical criteria list?" Bobby asked with interest. "What kind of girl rates with you?"

"Well, first of all, she must share my basic values, background, and goals," Enid declared.

Bobby nodded. That's what *Adolescent Development Patterns* said too.

"Shared intellectual interests are important." Enid continued to tick off items. "She must like to read, prefer foreign films to musicals, and have a good sense of humor. In addition, she should be a good cook, have a car—"

"What should she look like?" Bobby interrupted.

"Oh, tall and strong, kind of outdoorsy, with greenish gray eyes, high cheekbones, and—" Enid caught herself. "Actually, looks don't matter to me. Or they won't after I get over this—this odd attraction I have."

Bobby tried to picture Enid's ideal girl but the best she came up with was a cross between that actor from *Rawhide* and Miss Watkins. "Can you really be so calculated about love?" she asked.

"*I* think so," Enid replied, wiping mustard from the corner of her mouth. "But I'm betting you disagree, right?" She wadded up the napkin and threw it away.

"I generally go after girls without thinking at all," Bobby admitted.

As they walked to the train station, Bobby wondered if Enid had the right idea. If not for her ban on gym teachers as mates, they probably would have ended up in bed together and Bobby would have had nothing more than another notch on her belt. Instead, Bobby felt they might be friends. She'd never had a friend who wasn't a teammate. It made her feel hopeful, as if her development wasn't arrested after all.

"It's funny," Bobby thought aloud. "I always thought you had the teaching part of the job solid, and it turns out you don't even like it! And Rod—I was so sure the two of you were for real." She remembered that night she'd seen the two of them going down the stairs to Francine's and the bitter twist of jealousy in her stomach. "It's like the fellow said," Bobby observed wisely. "You can't judge a book by its cover."

"Well, if you're going to make the gay scene, you'll have to learn what to look for, how to identify other women like yourself."

"There's a method?" Bobby asked eagerly.

"Of course!" Enid was the knowledgeable instructor again. "Sometimes women wear a green handkerchief on the second Wednesday of the month; or they might mention liking Alexis Smith—"

"Who?"

"Or the movie *Young Man with a Horn*—"

"What?"

"Or if they're thick as thieves for no good reason, like Dot Driscoll and Mona."

"Really?" *I told Elaine they were playing for our team,* she thought triumphantly.

They were approaching the train station now, and as they reached the top of the stairs leading down to the waiting room, Enid added, "And of course that's why Miss Craybill is crazy with grief over Miss Froelich's falling to her death."

Without warning the flight of steps swung around and upside down, like a crazy kaleidoscope, and Bobby grabbed the brass banister to keep from falling. Through the pounding in her ears, she heard Enid's alarmed voice. "Bobby, are you all right? Can I do anything? Do you want to sit down?"

"Help me down the stairs," Bobby croaked. She closed her eyes and tried to slow her panicked breathing as Enid slipped her arm around the stricken teacher's waist and helped her down the marble steps. At the bottom, Bobby opened her eyes. Enid's dark eyes were wide behind her glasses.

"Can you walk, Bobby? They're calling the Muskrat River Local."

"I'm fine," she answered as the dizziness subsided. She felt embarrassed as they hurried toward platform 8. The big train station was empty at this time of night; the jumble of track announcements echoed hollowly and incoherently around her. Enid followed her onto the car without speaking, but once the tickets were collected, she leaned forward. "Have you always had such severe vertigo, Bobby?" There was scientific curiosity in her voice, but sympathy in her eyes.

"No, it only started this past spring, after I had a fall." Bobby leaned back, grateful for the support of her seat. "But I don't want to bore you with my problems. Tell me more about 'making the gay scene.'"

Enid was not distracted. "You won't bore me. I'd like to help." She leaned forward and there was that look in her eyes that had been there the night Bobby changed the fuse in Manchester. Bobby sat up, but Enid drew back immediately. And Bobby leaned back, reminding herself again that she didn't need any more flings.

"It sounds like you're suffering from a psychological block of some sort that would benefit from what analysts call the 'talking cure,'" Enid continued analytically. "Have you ever told anyone about this?"

"Not really," Bobby admitted. Of course Chick knew, and Pat, and the twins. But she'd never told anyone the whole story of that night. "I thought if I did some exercises . . ."

"Bobby, you can't solve mental problems with calisthenics," Enid told her firmly.

Why not tell Enid? Bobby reflected. She did seem to have some experience with deep-seated neuroses.

"Well, it was last May, just before finals," the young phys ed instructor began. "We'd wrapped up the softball season with a victory over the Weslington Wolves, and we were celebrating at The Old Crow—a pub where we used to go after games to drink a few beers.

"It was a hot night. You know how hot it can get in Bay City? Pat—she's our goalie on the Spitfires, I mean she was—Pat said how great it would feel to go for a swim. Then Frieda—she wasn't a team member, but she came to all the games, to cheer us on—she said couldn't I do something, seeing as I was the captain."

"She had a yen for you," Enid guessed.

Bobby didn't want to brag. "Oh, I don't know. She was pinned to a Sigma Tau boy." Briefly, Bobby wondered why it was that fraternity pins had never gotten in the way of fun in college the way engagements did in the real world. "She was an art history major," Bobby added irrelevantly.

"Go on," urged Enid.

"Of course, the gym's pool was closed at that time of night, but I happened to have the keys. I was Coach Mabel's right-hand man, and besides, I'd been doing a special project, a history of the development of gym equipment. So . . . I guess I wanted to show off a little, and I said I'd give us a pool party."

"Normal college hijinks," Enid observed a little enviously. "Of course, I had to study all the time to keep up my scholarship."

"We all trooped over to the gym, me, Pat, Chick, this girl Frieda, and the rest of the team. Chick brought along a dozen bottles of beer. I was a little worried about what Coach Mabel might say, but I'd earned my Red Cross Lifesaving Certificate the summer before, so I told myself it was the same as if a lifeguard was on duty. Besides, we were all athletes. We knew how to take care of ourselves."

Bobby paused, remembering how still the water of the pool had been, like a sheet of glass, until Pat shattered it with a cannonball; and how they'd left the light off, so as not to attract attention, and the way the moonlight streamed in through the big windows overlooking the empty tennis courts, making their bodies glow a luminous white.

"We didn't have our suits, so we went skinny-dipping. It's a great sensation. We had our beers lined up along the edge of the pool, and you had to take a swallow every time someone did a perfect swan dive. Frieda was swimming in her underwear—she said she wasn't used to swimming in the raw, but after a couple beers and everybody teasing her . . ."

This was the part that was blurry in Bobby's brain. She tried to remember every detail. "I was up on the dive, and I heard her say, 'Oh, all right, I'll take off my bra.' And then somehow I slipped and fell off the dive. I hit the edge of the pool and I broke my collarbone, my right humerus, and—"

"Just a moment," Enid interrupted. "You left something out—you were trying to get an eyeful of this art student!"

"No, no!" protested Bobby. "It was just the beers I'd drunk, and her voice distracting me, right when I was about to dive!"

"Oh, Bobby." Enid was laughing. "Your psychological block is quite simple. You associate your desire to look at a girl undressing with the physical pain and injury resulting from your fall. If only you'd been in the library looking at pictures of classical statues like me instead of on the high dive, none of this would have happened."

Bobby blinked. Was it really so simple? Suddenly she could see Frieda, reaching behind her back to undo the clasp of her bra. Had that picture been in her subconscious all this time?

"I hope you got a good look, at least," Enid was following her own train of thought. "The little exhibition-ist! I know the type."

"No, she was just a sweet kid," protested Bobby weakly. "Although I did think she could have come to see me in the hospital. That's when the dreams started."

"Tell me about these dreams," Enid ordered her.

Bobby told her about the mysterious girls who led her off the cliff. She didn't mention that sometimes her dreams featured Enid in that sinister role.

"Well, that clinches it, doesn't it? You have a guilt complex. You desire a woman, yet secretly fear pain, per-haps rejection. That's why they always lead you off a cliff."

"Really?" *Have I been desiring Enid all semester?* Bobby wondered.

The train swayed past the outer suburbs of Bay City, big houses nestled among tall trees. The stars were visible in the sky. "It would be nice not to have those dreams any-more," Bobby remarked. "They've been getting stranger. Sometimes the girl's on a bicycle, and I'm following her through the Metamora woods."

Enid eyed her narrowly. "Is it a glowing bicycle?"

Chapter Twenty-one

Breakdown

"You've seen it too!" exclaimed Bobby. "The ghostly rider on the glowing bicycle!"

"I've seen something," Enid corrected her. "But it's not a ghost. It must be a student who's somehow managed to get hold of some phosphorescent paint."

Phosphorescent paint? Was the explanation as simple as that? Bobby felt foolish for not thinking of the possibility sooner. "Of course," she said. "A phosphorescent adolescent. It certainly fooled me, all the same. When did you see it?"

"The first time was the night of your game with that Catholic school. I'd slipped out to the quad for a cigarette, and I saw it for just a second, entering the woods. Then a week or so later, I saw it again, this time from one of Manchester's third-floor turrets. It was quite late—I couldn't sleep, and I wanted to escape that cooped-up feeling dorm life gives me. The night was clear and the moon was bright. I saw the bicycle coming from the woods, heading toward the quadrangle. I ran down the stairs, but when I rushed out into the quadrangle, the bicycle was gone."

Bobby was thinking hard. Was it a coincidence that the

glowing cyclist appeared the same day the Savages competed in a field hockey match?

"I saw the cyclist the night of the Metamora–St. Margaret Mary's game too," she told Enid. "Only it was coming from the woods, after midnight, and it disappeared before it reached the quadrangle. Do you think this bicyclist is making round trips—maybe to Mesquakie Point and back?"

"But why?" wondered Enid. "At night the gift shoppe, the information booth, the replica cabin—they're all shut down. It would be deserted. What would be the point?" A thought struck her. "Unless Linda—"

"Linda wouldn't go alone," Bobby objected. The amoeba of an idea—a crazy, way-out idea—was wiggling around in her head. "And honestly, I can't see any student sneaking out repeatedly, for so many hours, after lights-out, without getting caught!"

"You think it's a teacher?" Enid laughed, and then stopped, when Bobby just looked at her. "You could be right," she said slowly.

"The night I saw it coming out of the woods," Bobby said, "it disappeared behind Kent!"

"You don't think it's Miss Craybill!" Enid looked horrified. "I know she's been acting strangely, but—"

"She's the most logical person," Bobby pointed out. "She lives alone in Kent, so no one would see her come and go. I imagine there's scads of space to hide a glowing bicycle in that building. And as everyone knows, she can't forget Miss Froelich!"

"But why? Why bicycle to Mesquakie Point and back in an academic robe, on a glowing bicycle?"

"Why dig up the pansies around the sundial? Why chase after every nuthatch that flies by? Why spend the school's first hockey game poking under the bleachers?"

They sat for a while in silence, a silence broken only by

the lonely sound of the Local's whistle as it racketed past the empty fields. Although she'd chalked up the midnight rides to Miss Craybill's eccentricities, Bobby couldn't help wondering if there was some darker explanation for the Headmistress's visits to Mesquakie Point. Was Miss Craybill hiding some sinister relic of Miss Froelich in the replica cabin? Bobby discarded the idea, only to be seized by another, more frightening one. What if Miss Craybill was possessed? It would certainly explain her strange behavior. Yet again, why would the spirit of Miss Froelich drive her to Mesquakie Point and back? What meaning did Mesquakie Point hold? What dark passions had driven the pair of them?

"I guess we ought to tell someone, Miss Otis, probably." Enid broke the silence. Bobby warmed at the "we" Enid used, as if they were a team. If only she could help Enid over her queer neurosis about gym teachers the way Enid had helped her!

Her thoughts had wandered back to Enid's ideal girl when the cab let them off at Metamora's closed gate and they headed up the road to the quadrangle. The blackness had a palpable quality, as if the pair of them were walking undersea, like in that Jules Verne movie that had played at the Bijou last week. It was like the blackness in the cellar earlier, so total that the other four senses were sharpened.

Enid reached for Bobby, and Bobby clasped her hand. The Math Mistress's ungloved hand was warm and dry. For an instant Bobby was suffused with happiness. She and Enid were truly friends, their petty rivalry and distrust now in the past. Then she wondered: Was Enid just holding her hand because of her fixation on that other gym teacher? Was Bobby a faceless substitute for that long-gone woman? For a second she wanted to fling the hand away. Then Enid gave her hand a little squeeze. Was she, too, remembering that moment in the cellar? Or had she simply tripped, and leaned on Bobby for balance? The darkness was alive with possibilities and pitfalls.

What's the matter with me? Bobby asked herself, astounded at the way a simple stroll in the woods with Enid had turned into a roller-coaster ride, with Bobby's heart in the front seat.

"What's that?" Enid said sharply.

"What?" A branch snapped in the woods to the right of the road. Enid's hand was tight on Bobby's as they both strained their eyes, peering fruitlessly into the dark.

"Probably just a skunk," Bobby whispered. "No, wait—"

Her eyes had caught a faint glow, an orange dot that brightened and dimmed. "Someone's there, in the underbrush." She raised her voice. "Whoever you are, come out of there right now." She waited. "You'll only make it harder on yourself if I have to come in and get you."

There was a long pause, and then, crackling and crunching through the dead leaves, the lurker walked toward them, and they could dimly discern her gangly outline. "It's only Angle," Bobby told Enid. She struck a match so that the Math Mistress could see the pale, dirt-streaked face of the troubled teen, a cigarette dangling defiantly from the corner of her mouth. Enid released her death grip on Bobby's hand.

"Angela, do you realize how many rules you're breaking?" Enid's voice was high-pitched with anger and fear.

"Plus, you scared the bejeezus out of us," Bobby broke in.

"Out of bed after lights out, out of bounds, smoking—"

"It's not so late," Angle protested sullenly.

"Listen," Bobby intervened. "We're all tired, and the woods aren't the best place to discuss discipline. Put out the cigarette, come along to bed, and stop by my office at lunchtime tomorrow to take your medicine." She turned away, without waiting to see if Angle would follow, pulling Enid with her.

"God, you're good," murmured Enid admiringly. "That was textbook reverse psychology." Bobby glowed inwardly, making a mental note to look up the term.

Sure enough, after a few paces, Angle came scuffing up behind them. She took a last drag on her cigarette and then squashed it underfoot. "I wasn't just smoking, you know," she said argumentatively. "I thought I heard something, and I came to investigate. I thought maybe whoever took old Kayo's necklace and then returned it was going to play another trick."

"You're not afraid of the ghost?" Enid asked.

"Nah. Something's screwy, but it's not a ghost, I don't think."

They walked a few paces, and now they could see the faint glow of the dorm lights. Angle spoke again. "You know what Linda and the rest of her crew are saying now, don't you? That Miss Froelich jumped because of her guilty conscience. They say she was racked with shame over her unnatural friendship with Miss Craybill." Angle slid a sideways look at the teachers. "Linda's been all hepped on this unnatural friendship biz ever since Sandy loaned her this book—"

"*We Too Are Lonely,* utter trash. I confiscated it this morning, but clearly it wasn't soon enough." Enid spoke vehemently.

"You don't think it's true?" Angle asked diffidently.

Both teachers spoke at once.

"What happened to Miss Froelich," Bobby began, but Enid interrupted.

"Angle, that book is arrant nonsense. The author is no authority—just a hack writer trying to sell copies to readers who get a cheap thrill from the idea of two women—"

"The point is," Bobby took over, feeling Enid was veering off topic, "that what happened to Miss Froelich was an accident, pure and simple. She was bird-watching, observing the white-breasted nuthatch, and she fell. It's regrettable, tragic even, but it was an accident."

"Well, I don't know about the unnatural friendship bit," said Angle dispassionately. "But Miss Rasphigi says it's impossible that Miss Froelich was looking at white-breasted nuthatches when she fell."

They'd reached the top of the rise, where the road leveled out as it met the Quadrangle. "Why would Miss Rasphigi—" Bobby began, but at the same moment, they all became aware of a distant sound, a faint screech, screech.

"That's it! That's what I heard!" Angle cried.

"Hush," warned Bobby, "I think—" She ran toward the quadrangle, Enid and Angle at her heels. At the far end, next to the sundial, stood Miss Craybill, wearing her eggplant-colored quilted satin dressing gown, a candle clasped in her hands. She was looking at the space between Manchester and Dorset. Down the path that led to the wild wooded forest between Metamora and Mesquakie Point rode the glowing bicyclist. Even knowing that the bicycle was merely smeared with phosphorescent paint, Bobby felt the back of her neck prickle. The bicycle seemed to float above the earth, and the homely screech, screech of the unoiled chain only made the black figure riding more uncanny.

"Nerissa!" quavered Miss Craybill. "Is that you?"

The bicycle abruptly turned off the path and disappeared behind the corner of Kent. Miss Craybill crumpled into a heap beside the sundial.

Chapter Twenty-two

The Confrontation

Bobby and Enid ran to the fallen Headmistress with Angle close behind. Miss Craybill's eyes were closed. Picking up her wrist, Bobby felt her pulse—a fluttering, erratic sign of life. Enid was repeating, "Miss Craybill! Miss Craybill!" as she gently patted the fallen woman's cheeks.

"She needs a doctor," said Bobby, dropping the inert hand. "Angle, go get help."

"Where? Who?" The young teen was jumping from one foot to the other in agitation. Without waiting for a reply, she shouted loudly, "Help! Help!" Bobby bit her lip in vexation.

"Stop that! Go get Miss Rasphigi." The Chemistry Mistress might have some medical training. At least the errand would calm the excitable teenager. Angle shot off in the direction of the science lab.

Lights were going on in dorm windows, and Miss Otis was hurrying across the quad. "What on earth," she began with her usual asperity, but stopped short at the sight of Miss Craybill lying prone in her eggplant dressing gown.

"Aggie!" Miss Otis fell to her knees beside the Headmistress. "Aggie, speak to me! It is I, Bunny!" She shook the unconscious Miss Craybill until Enid pulled her away. "Stop it, Miss Otis, you're not helping!"

A faint groan from the stricken Headmistress contradicted her. "She's coming to!" said a voice behind Bobby. Looking around, she saw Serena and Alice, in matching plaid bathrobes, clutching one another.

"Bunny, you must take prep for me. I have a splitting headache," said Miss Craybill weakly. "Tell Nerissa to bring me some aspirin."

"She's gone bonkers," said Laura in an awed voice. She stood next to Ken, who had his pipe in his hand. *He must sleep with it,* Bobby thought.

"Aggie! Aggie, do you know where you are?" shouted Miss Otis.

Miss Craybill looked at her, bewildered. "At Metamora, Bunny."

"That's no test of mental awareness," muttered Enid to Bobby. "Not when she's been here the past forty years."

"Has anyone called the doctor?" demanded Bobby in exasperation.

"I 'ave." Madame Melville was smoking a cigarette, as impeccably dressed as if it were sherry hour. "We should move her inside, out of the damp and chill, *n'est-ce pas?*"

Angle panted up, with Miss Rasphigi behind her. The Chemistry Mistress looked at Miss Craybill and remarked, "Medicine is not my field."

"Where is Mona?" wailed Miss Otis. "She's certified in first aid!"

"I'm certified—" *in first aid,* Bobby was going to retort, but then she paused. Where *was* the helpful housekeeper? How was it that she, right in Devon, hadn't heard this whole hullabaloo? Devon was right next to Kent—

Not only right next to Kent—it connected to Kent.

And if the mysterious cyclist wasn't Miss Craybill, who lived in Kent—

"Enid," Bobby whispered urgently, "The bicyclist must be—"

She could read the same realization in Enid's widening eyes.

"Mona!" she breathed.

The two teachers had instinctively moved a few steps away from the rest of the faculty, who were now squabbling over how best to move their Headmistress. Bobby noticed with a sinking heart that the dorm windows were filling with the heads of sleepy students. This latest quadrangle crisis had a growing audience.

"You stay here," she ordered Enid. "Get Miss Craybill inside, somehow! I'm going to pay a visit to our phosphorescent friend."

She ran to the rear of Kent, skirting the school bus and paneled station wagon, which were little more than hulking shapes in the darkness. She tugged at the metal utility door and to her surprise it opened. Had the cyclist grown careless in her haste? Stepping inside, she felt for a light switch. She was in a back corridor, near the records room. Bobby glanced around, and her eyes were caught by a curved smudge on the wall, just above the baseboard. A bicycle had rested there, if only for an instant. Bobby tried the door to the records room. Locked. Mona would have the key.

Bobby explored further. Where was the connecting door to Devon? It must be the heavy wooden door at the end of the corridor, arched like an entranceway. She tried the knob. Locked. At the end of her patience, Bobby pounded on the door with all her strength. "Open up! Open up in there!"

The crack at the bottom of the door showed a thin line of light. "Just a minute, for goodness sake," said Mona's muffled voice. Bobby heard her slide the bolt and the door opened, revealing Mona in an aqua-colored chenille bathrobe. Her big eyes were blinking, her hair was tousled, and her face was flushed with sleep. "Why, Bobby!" She began. Bobby pushed past her, into the room, and Mona shut the door behind them.

They were standing in a walk-in closet. On either side hung gay summer frocks, wool skirts, spare uniforms. There were piles of hatboxes, sweaters, shoes neatly arrayed on a rack, each toe stuffed with tissue.

"What on earth are you doing at this door?" Mona asked in bewilderment. "It's never used. It's just a fire exit."

Bobby began to wonder if she and Enid were off track again. "Didn't you hear the big brouhaha in the quadrangle?" Bobby asked. "Miss Craybill has collapsed."

"Oh no!" Mona clutched her bathrobe more tightly around her throat. "I didn't hear anything—I took a sedative this evening to help me sleep. What happened?"

"She saw a ghostly cyclist and it was too much for her." Bobby didn't mention the brand-new ouija board she had noticed at the base of the sundial. The fewer people who learned that Miss Craybill had been attempting to contact Miss Froelich's spirit, the better.

"Ghostly cyclist!" Mona exclaimed. "Bryce mentioned seeing a ghost, but he put it down to the pork fat from Ole's *svinekoteletter!*"

"Never mind the *svinekoteletter,*" snapped Bobby. "I want the key to the records room!"

"The key to the records room," Mona repeated blankly. "Now?"

"I think we'll find a clue to the ghostly cyclist there." Bobby was watching her closely, but the housekeeper didn't turn a hair.

"My housekeeping keys are in the sitting room. If the records room key isn't on that ring, we'll find Miss Otis. She'll have it."

Bobby waited for Mona in her bedroom, a gay bower in ruffled chintz. Miss Otis—was *she* the ghostly cyclist? She *had* appeared surprisingly quickly, fully dressed in her Metamora uniform.

It was exhausting, suspecting her colleagues! Bobby looked around the room, so feminine and cozy, with the pink-shaded lamp by the bed, the prints on the wall of people in old-fashioned clothes picnicking and swinging on swings, the braided rug on the floor, the bed, with its chintz-covered comforter turned neatly down. Nothing odd here.

Wait a second—what was with the turndown service? Bobby's suspicions came rushing back. If Mona had been deep in slumber, why was the bed so tidy? Bobby went to the bed and put her hand on the mattress. Cold. The pillow was askew and automatically Bobby straightened it. A piece of black cloth peeked out from underneath. Bobby threw the pillow aside and picked up the black academic robe that had been hastily stuffed beneath it.

"Here we are," Mona said, reentering the room, jingling a key ring in her hand. She stopped when she saw Bobby holding the black gown. "No—no," said Mona. Bobby strode toward her and, seizing the lapels of the aqua chenille bathrobe, she yanked it open. Underneath, Mona wore a full-skirted pine green wool jumper with a snugly fitted bodice, ideal for cycling.

A fierce look flashed through Mona's eyes as she pulled herself free. She shrugged off the aqua chenille bathrobe and threw it on the bed. "All right! I disguised myself as a glowing bicyclist! What's the harm? Is there a law against it?"

Bobby was aghast. "What's the harm? How can you ask that with Miss Craybill collapsed in the quadrangle?"

Mona paced the cozy bedroom like a panther in a cage. "That was an accident. She'll probably be fine tomorrow." She turned to Bobby and spread her hands be-seechingly. "It's not that I like playing dress-up! I had to. Maybe you can understand . . ."

"Understand what?"

Mona sat on the edge of the neatly made bed. "I'm in love," she said simply. "And she's married. The only times we can see each other are these late nights, at Mesquakie Point. It's a cold and lonely ride through the woods, but at the end of it, there she is, waiting for me in the replica cabin."

"I thought the replica cabin was closed at night," Bobby said.

"I have the key," said Mona. "Ole's sister Freya runs the concession there, and I borrowed the key one day and made a copy." Her eyes took on a dreamy quality. "It's just a bare little cabin, with a fake antique trundle bed, but to us, it's a little bit of heaven."

"But why the crazy dress-up?" Bobby demanded. "You have the keys to the Metamora station wagon. Why not just drive to Mesquakie Point in your regular clothes?"

Mona threw up her hands. "I would have been noticed immediately! You know how Metamora is—what excuse could I make for mysterious midnight drives, except my own mad passion? With a little phosphorescence from the Drama Club, I threw the gossipers off track. I never imagined so many people would spot me." Mona's merry laugh pealed out. "Is it my fault there's so much prowling around campus after lights-out?"

Bobby tried to get used to the idea that Metamora's housekeeper, who planned the meals, restocked the medicine cabinet, and poured out mug after mug of steaming cocoa, was in the grip of a grand passion. Yet was it so surprising? Hadn't she wondered about the housekeeper's predilections from the day they met? And after what Enid had told her tonight . . .

"Are you meeting Dot Driscoll?" Bobby asked.

The housekeeper sobered at once. "Why do you think that?" Bobby held her tongue. "Don't make me tell you," said Mona. "And please, please don't expose us. You'd put us in terrible danger. Give me a chance to explain to Miss Craybill myself. I promise you, I will."

Bobby hesitated only briefly. After all, was Mona sneaking off to Mesquakie Point so different from Enid and Bobby in the cellar of the Knock Knock Lounge?

"All right," said the Games Mistress. "But no more bike rides! You and your friend will have to figure out something else. And you tell Miss Craybill the whole story the minute she's coherent! You just can't let her go on thinking Miss Froelich is haunting the campus."

"The very second," Mona promised. She got to her feet. "I'd better go and do what I can to make her comfortable."

Bobby followed Mona out of Devon, the front way this time. On the steps Mona turned to her. Her face was veiled in shadow. "Thank you, Bobby. I won't forget this." She hurried away.

The quadrangle was empty now. The teachers had evidently gotten Miss Craybill inside. The dorm windows were empty too, the spectators gone back to bed. Despite solving the mystery of the ghostly cyclist, Bobby felt an uneasiness she couldn't shake. She looked at the sundial, glowing faintly white in the moonlight. She looked up at the tower, and in her mind's eye saw a figure in black plummeting to the earth. Someone had said something, earlier this evening—oh yes, Angle, quoting Miss Rasphigi—

The dizziness caught her unawares, and she almost fell over. Using the shrubbery to pull herself upright, Bobby lurched toward Cornwall, keeping her head down. Would she ever be cured?

Chapter Twenty-three

Peasant Dance, Again

Bobby put the record on the turntable and stood poised to drop the needle. "Class, we're going to try something new today," she said nervously.

The students looked at her blankly. Bobby could hardly blame them for their lack of interest when there was so much else happening at Metamora. The girls had seized on last night's drama and speculated and gossiped until Bobby barely recognized the facts behind the students' fevered imaginings.

Earlier that morning, in Cornwall, she had overheard Sandy Milston's version. "She was riding a flaming bicycle," Sandy was telling an avid group of third formers. "Her hair was glowing, and her face was like a skull, except she had glowing eyes. When she touched her, Miss Craybill fell down, like she was frozen, and she hasn't spoken since."

"Hurry up, girls, or you'll be late for breakfast," Bobby interrupted this horror comic account of the previous night. As the girls scattered obediently, Debby muttered, "Darn it, I miss everything." The unfortunate third former had sleepwalked through the excitement, ending up in Bobby's own bed. The Games Mistress had gotten quite a start when she'd stumbled into her suite well after midnight.

The prayer at breakfast, led by Miss Otis, competed with the buzz of whispering. And when the Latin Mistress concluded with a petition "for our Headmistress, that she may speedily recover from her head cold," the misguided attempt to hide the nature of Miss Craybill's illness was met with snorts of laughter. As she speared a sausage, Karen Woynarowski asked Bobby point-blank if Miss Craybill had "gone mental."

"Of course not!" Bobby said loudly. "She's overtired and is resting."

It was basically true, Bobby reflected. The only news from the sickroom was that Miss Craybill was still heavily sedated. Miss Otis left immediately after the prayer, and Mona was absent. With the senior faculty table heavily decimated, Gussie Gunderson was left to keep what order she could, but no one understood the admonitions she issued in Greek. Fragments of conversation swirled around Bobby as Dorset emptied out after breakfast. "Miss Otis fainted when she saw her." "*I* heard her shriek!" ". . . then Coach Bobby held up a cross." "Madame Melville tried to give her absinthe, but . . ." "It's fifty-fifty whether she'll ever regain consciousness, the doctor said." "*I* heard forty-sixty." "If Miss Otis takes over, I'm asking my folks to transfer me to Peasley!"

Bobby froze at the last comment. Without Miss Craybill at the helm, would the little world of Metamora shatter and disintegrate? What would Bobby do then?

"When Stalin died, they played classical music on the radio," Miss Rasphigi remarked to no one in particular as the teachers followed the students out the door. Bobby couldn't tell if the Chemistry Mistress meant the comment as a suggestion. *I don't think classical music would calm the situation,* thought the Games Mistress as she watched Miss Rasphigi retreat in the direction of Essex and the chemistry lab. She remembered what Angle had told her and Enid last night. Miss Froelich's fall had nothing to do with nuthatches, according to Miss Rasphigi. She took a step after the retreating Chemistry Mistress, then stopped. Best not to rake that business up right now. The last thing she wanted to do was to fuel more of these wild speculations that were so damaging to Metamora's reputation.

Bobby glanced at the newest edition of *The Metamora Musings,* which she'd picked up outside Dorset. META-MORA TO WELCOME OLD GIRLS, one headline read.

> On Friday, November 1, the Old Girls will descend on Metamora's campus like a plague of benevolent locusts. Festivities will include an Old Girl Tea, classroom visits, and the annual Old Girl Revue, which promises some delectable evening entertainment for Old and New Girls alike. Old Girls are expected from as far away as Valdez, Alaska, and Petropolis, Brazil . . .

What had Miss Otis said about the Old Girls? That they'd spread any unsavory rumors to the ends of the earth. What would they make of Miss Craybill, invalid after an encounter with a ghost?

Bobby sighed, and crushed the paper in frustration. She wished she could talk to Enid. She wanted to tell the attractive Math Mistress they'd been right about Mona, and about the Housekeeper's clandestine affair with Dot Driscoll. She wanted to ask her if she'd done the right thing, promising Mona secrecy. If only Enid would suddenly appear, maybe in that snug-fitting red sweater she'd worn last night. *I guess I've been lonelier for a real friend than I realized,* Bobby thought.

But the Math Mistress had been absent all morning. Hoppy Fiske had told Bobby and the Burnhams that just before breakfast Enid had discovered a large cache of lurid literature, wrapped in plastic and hidden in the toilet tanks of the third-floor washroom. Apparently bookworm Sandy, frustrated with Bobby's vigilance, had entered into a partnership with Linda, transferring her collection to Manchester. Linda had taken advantage of the hapless Enid's inexperience to establish a rental library, doing a brisk business. Only a stopped-up toilet had foiled their scheme. Enid had spent the breakfast hour combing Manchester for every last copy of Kinsey's *Sexual Behavior in the Human Female.*

All in all, it was an odd time to make innovations in the classroom, Bobby thought wryly, as she stood by the record player, the record arm in her hand. But if she was ever going to make anything of herself as a teacher, she had to stop hiding behind Miss Fayne's curriculum and try out some of her own ideas.

She set the needle gently on the grooved record.

> *"Come on baby, let's do the twist*
> *Come on baby, let's do the twist*
> *Take me by my little hand, and go like this."*

Now she had the girls' attention. "Let's begin. Right foot forward, left foot back. Now we're going to swivel our hips"—Bobby demonstrated for her fascinated audience—"while shifting our weight from front to back, back to front . . . Okay, let's try that much."

As the students began to swivel their hips, Karen Woynarowski waved her hand frantically.

"Coach Bobby," she said breathlessly. "Is this going to be on the final? Isn't this supposed to be *peasant* dance class?"

"What is a peasant?" parried Bobby. The question seemed made for one of the "enrichment opportunities" she'd read about. She stopped the record player and the twisting came to a halt. "Let's take a moment and try to say what 'peasant' means."

"It's like a serf, in Russia," volunteered Joyce Vandemar. The fourth formers were reading *Anna Karenina*.

"A lower-class person," Penny Gordon offered. It cheered Bobby that the fourth form Savages wasn't holding a grudge over yesterday's tongue lashing.

"But the serfs have an innate nobility," argued Joyce.

"Anyway, America doesn't have aristocracy and servant classes," put in Gwen Norton. "We're a *meritocracy*."

"Good points, all of you," interposed Bobby. "Actually, another way to look at it is that America is one big peasant class, because most Americans are descended from immigrants who were peasants in their own countries. So all Americans are peasants—"

"Even DAPs?" asked Penny, open-mouthed.

"—and American songs are all, when you get right down to it, peasant songs." Bobby put the music back on. "Now, let's try again."

The girls were all twisting energetically now, and Bobby felt a little wave of excitement. Why, peasant dance *could* be fun! She saw that Sally Stafford was frowning as she rocked stiffly forward and back. "The movement comes from the hips," said the Games Mistress, going to her. "Try to relax your upper body. Let it rotate naturally."

"I can't do it! I don't have any natural rotation!" cried Sally in frustration.

This was the real teaching challenge, Bobby realized. To convince a hopeless girl that her body was capable of more than she realized. Yet how to relate the dance to this girl's own experience? "Sally, you're a member of the Young Integrationists, aren't you?" Bobby asked. The discouraged girl nodded. "Pretend the top half of you is on the picket line," she told the teen, "and the police are coming to arrest you. What do you do?"

"Go limp," said Sally, doing so. Bobby caught her before she fell. "But just the top half," she reminded the teenaged agitator. Sally tried twisting again. "I think I've got it!" she exclaimed.

"You do!" Bobby felt just as pleased as the dancing girl. "Just don't forget the second point of perfect posture, tucked tummy."

I just love this job, the Games Mistress thought in a rush of emotion. What did it matter if she never knew who had dreamed of heaven and earth and philosophy? She had taught the Twist to the most uncoordinated student in her class!

And why stop there? Bobby was boiling over with ideas. Why not collaborate with Hoppy on a seminar, "Body Mechanics for Non-Violent Resisters"? And that hip-swiveling motion, with that little kick—how well it would translate to a feint followed by a push-pass. Bobby quickly sketched out a play on a piece of scrap paper. "Ready for the next move?" she asked as she put the paper in her back pocket.

"Yes!" cried the class enthusiastically.

Bobby was still riding the wave of her unexpected success after class when she ran into Kayo, coming from Jersey.

"Coach Bobby!" Kayo hurried toward her. "I've been looking for you—where did you go last night? I feel just awful about the game with the Birdbrains the other day. It was all my fault!"

"No, Kayo, you mustn't blame yourself—"

Kayo dropped her art class portfolio on the path and grasped Bobby's arm. "I read the riot act to Linda and her friends after dinner last night. You won't hear a peep about ghostly possession from them ever again! Linda's on to some new craze anyway."

"That's good." Bobby tried again to interrupt the tempestuous teen. "You know, I made mistakes too—"

Kayo overrode her. "And I promise you, I won't let myself get distracted again." She dropped her voice and moved closer to the Games Mistress. "It's just—I keep thinking about you and that day in your office . . ."

"Yes, I've been wanting to talk to you about that," Bobby temporized, wondering what on earth to say to the passionate center. She didn't want to hurt Kayo's feelings.

"Do you think about it too?" Kayo's eyes were limpid pools of blue, inviting Bobby to jump in and sound the depths. "Do you remember the way you tore my shirt open so the buttons popped off? Do you remember the feel of your flesh against mine, the way you pummeled every part of me with your punishing kisses?"

Bobby took a step back, her breath coming faster in spite of herself. Kayo must have been borrowing from her sister's lending library!

"I could meet you for a special practice—or a student-teacher conference," Kayo persisted.

Bobby looked wildly around for some rescue and spotted Enid walking briskly toward them. The Math Mistress was like a life preserver, floating amid the waves of passion that threatened to drown the field hockey coach.

"Enid! How are you today?" An edge of desperation made her cheery greeting shrill.

"Hello, Bobby, Kayo." Enid's measuring glance took in Kayo's flushed cheeks, the portfolio on its side on the ground, Bobby's wild eyes. Bobby wondered if Enid was remembering another gym teacher and team captain. She hoped not.

"Were you looking for me?" she asked eagerly.

"No." Enid glanced toward Jersey. "I need to see Mrs. Burnham."

Bobby felt disappointed, all out of proportion with the cause. "Oh. Well, I thought we could—consult, maybe—about that matter from last night?"

"Of course." Enid seemed distracted. "I'm free before dinner." She continued down the path with a hasty farewell.

"It'll be a relief when *she's* gone," Kayo remarked, looking after the Math Mistress with disdain.

"What are you talking about?" Bobby asked sharply.

"Scuttlebutt is that she's interviewing for a job with some big company in Bay City. If she gets it, she'll be gone next semester."

Bobby marveled anew at the way the Metamorians knew everything that was going on, practically before the events occurred.

"And a good thing too." Kayo's dislike for the Math Mistress was plain. "Everyone knows she's been down on the Savages from the beginning!"

With a sinking heart, Bobby realized she'd failed to conceal her feud with Enid from the students. Another teaching mistake! It seemed like for every step forward she took a step back.

"Miss Butler has always had Metamora's best interests at heart," she told the Savages' captain sternly. Kayo gave her a smile of complicity.

"Oh, sure," she said. "By the way, the old killjoy made me forget the rest of my news—Mrs. Gilvang told me the Ants lost to the Virgins the other day, so that means if we beat the Pioneers, we'll be up against the Virgins in the playoffs!"

"The Holy Martyrs beat the Ames Ants?" Bobby was

distracted from her emotional turmoil by this piece of intelligence. "Gee, I thought the Ants were supposed to be the stronger team."

"That's what everyone thought. Mrs. Gilvang said it was a terribly close game. She said that the Ames coach thinks there was something funny going on. Her forward line all got stomach cramps at halftime after sucking ice cubes from the same ice tray." Kayo looked at her watch. "I've got to tear," she said reluctantly. "I have a DAP confab before lunch. We're collecting money to send flowers to poor Miss Craybill."

"Wait a second, Kayo." Bobby put a restraining hand on the departing girl's shoulder. "Why was Mona— Mrs. Gilvang—at the game between the Ants and the Holy Martyrs?"

"She goes to all the games," Kayo explained. "She's the biggest fan field hockey has! She's always asking me about the other teams and players—who's injured, what the team mood is, who plays better in the rain." Kayo bent and picked up her portfolio, stuffing back into it the crude sketches of hockey players that had fallen out. "Just let me know about that student-teacher conference," she told Bobby. "I'm ready anytime."

Bobby watched the blond ponytail bounce up the path, but her mind wasn't on Kayo and her unfortunate fixation on her coach. Why was Mona keeping such close track of the Midwest Regional Secondary School Girls' Field Hockey League? What was the attractive housekeeper up to?

Chapter Twenty-four

The Sick Room

Bobby was still thinking about Mona's keen interest in field hockey that evening as she worked in her office in the gym, sketching out the new play she'd thought of in peasant dance. A tap at the door pulled her out of her reverie. "Come in!" she called, hoping it was Enid. The conversation they'd had before dinner had been unsatisfactory. Enid had chided Bobby for promising Mona secrecy—she'd been all for revealing the ghostly cyclist's identity to Miss Craybill that instant. Then they were interrupted by a penitent fourth former turning in a book called *Boarding School Hussies*, which she'd gotten from Linda. "It isn't like Metamora *at all,*" she'd said wistfully as she relinquished the book.

But instead of Enid it was Mona who entered, with her light, energetic step. "There you are! I've been looking all over for you."

"Oh?" Was Mona going to tell her she had confessed to Miss Craybill and all was well?

But Mona was there on other business. "You know the Harvest Moon Mixer is this Saturday," she began, seating herself on the edge of Bobby's desk and taking out a cigarette.

Bobby struck a match and lit it. "Yes?"

"Bryce and Ole were going to chaperone with the Burnhams, but Bryce has a terrible cold and Ole is staying home to nurse him." Mona drew on her cigarette and exhaled a cloud of smoke. "Truthfully, Ole's the big loss. He's a wonderful dancer, and *so* good with the wallflowers."

Bobby looked at Mona blankly. Where was all this going?

"So you and Enid will have to fill in," the housekeeper concluded.

"Me and Enid!" cried Bobby. Her pulse began to pound. *What am I getting so excited about?* she wondered.

"I know you don't get along terribly well, but really, there's no one else. Serena and Alice are going to Bay City—there's a performance of *Götterdämmerung* Serena's been wild to see and their tickets are purchased. Hoppy has a teacher friend visiting. Gussie, Yvette, Connie—well, they just won't add to the party spirit the way you and Enid will."

"I can't dance with the wallflowers," Bobby pointed out.

"Enid agreed to ask her beau Rod to come. Seems he's a terrific dancer." Mona got up and strolled behind the desk. "Honestly, I don't understand why the two of you are making such a fuss. It's a party." She peered at Bobby's playbook as she lightly kneaded the coach's tensed-up shoulders. "New strategy?" she asked. "Are you going to use it against Adena?"

"No, the girls need more practice with it first." Bobby shut the playbook. "Say," she added, trying to be casual. "I hear you went to the Ants–Holy Martyr game."

"That's right," said Mona. "The school nurse at Ames invited me over for afternoon bridge and then I kept her company at the game. She had her hands full with those sickened forwards!"

"I hear the coach suspects foul play," ventured Bobby.

"It did seem odd, all those players getting upset stom-achs at the same time," Mona agreed as she exhaled a cloud of smoke. "So I can count on you for the dance? Enid's already dusting off her mist-gray organza."

"I don't have anything suitable to wear," Bobby fret-ted, distracted from the idea of field hockey sabotage by the thought of Enid in organza. How could she let Enid see her in that old blue party dress she'd worn through college?

"Serena will have something that fits you." Mona stubbed out her cigarette and went to the door. "I ought to get back to the Headmistress."

"Have you had a chance to tell her the identity of the ghostly cyclist?" Bobby queried sternly.

"Oh, Bobby." Mona laughed gaily, pushing open the heavy door to the playing fields, and letting a cold wind sweep into the gym. "She's barely sitting up, and it was all I could do to coax her to eat some prune whip. I'm going to make her a nice blancmange tonight."

As Mona chattered away about invalid menus, Bobby couldn't help thinking that the truth about the ghostly cyclist would be a better tonic than all the blancmanges in the world. Yet the next morning, when Bobby repeated her question to Mona, the housekeeper put her off with egg custards; and another day it was beef tea. Mona kept telling her there was plenty of time, but Bobby's impa-tience grew.

"Have you heard?" Enid called to her on Saturday as Bobby was exiting Suffolk, a dry cleaner's bag over her arm. "Misako's father called to find out if the Headmistress was truly possessed by a ghost—seems his daughter wrote him about Miss Craybill's collapse. Miss Otis managed to convince him that it was a language misunderstanding. When is Mona going to tell Miss Craybill the truth?"

"I don't know," admitted Bobby helplessly. "You really think I should take matters into my own hands?"

"I would," Enid assured her crisply. "What have you got there?"

Bobby looked down. "It's my duds for the dance tonight." Diffidently, she added, "Should I pick you up at Manchester, and we can go over together?"

"Gee, Bobby, that would have been nice, but I promised Rod . . ."

"Oh sure," said Bobby quickly. "I'll see you there, then."

"See you."

Bobby stood a moment after Enid's departure, struggling with unfamiliar feelings. She was used to overwhelming waves of desire, fires of lust, the sensation of being passion's pawn. But why was she so disappointed that Enid couldn't walk across the quadrangle with her?

Glancing across the lawn to Dorset, where the mixer was to be held, she saw the building was already bustling with activity. She could make out the silhouettes of girls, the decorating committee no doubt, hanging garlands around the windows. In front of the building, Mona was deep in conversation with a stranger. Had Aunt Dot come for a visit? Bobby squinted. Why, it was Netta Bean, from the Knock Knock Lounge. She must be Hoppy's teacher friend. Did she know Mona too? The two women disappeared into Devon.

Bobby's glance moved right, to the two lit windows on the third floor of Kent. She could discern a silhouette there as well—the lonely shape of the Headmistress, propped up in bed.

Enid's right, she decided suddenly. *And Mona's being far too cavalier about her promise to come clean.* I'll *tell Miss Craybill the truth about the ghostly cyclist!*

Leaving her garment bag in Cornwall, she hurried to Kent and up the stairs to the unfamiliar territory of

Miss Craybill's private quarters. Pushing open a heavy paneled door, she found herself in what seemed to be a little anteroom. Birds were everywhere. Framed prints of birds hung on the wall, which was papered with a pattern of twining green vines. Stuffed birds seemed to perch amidst this two-dimensional foliage. Canaries twittered in a cage hung from the ceiling. Beneath a painting of a red-headed woodpecker, a uniformed nurse dozed in an over-stuffed armchair, upholstered in brown horsehair.

Bobby crept past her and slipped through the half-opened door next to the nurse. She was in Miss Craybill's bedroom. Quickly she took in the dark wood walls, the red Turkish rug, the fire burning in the big fireplace with the portrait of a falconer over the mantelpiece. Opposite the fireplace was Miss Craybill, looking smaller than ever in a large four-poster.

"Miss Craybill," Bobby said softly. "May I speak to you?"

"Hello, Bobby." Miss Craybill looked at her without interest and then turned back to the picture she was studying. As Bobby approached the bed, she could see that Miss Craybill's counterpane was covered with photographs of Nerissa Froelich. In some she was garbed as Bobby had seen her in the school portraits. Others were evidently snapshots from summer vacations. Often Miss Froelich was holding a pair of binoculars and pointing at something outside the frame.

"How are you, Miss Craybill?" Bobby asked, easing into a straight-backed chair by the bed. Miss Craybill picked up another picture.

"This was taken right after she'd spotted her first snowy owl, in Thunder Bay, Christmas, fifty-six." She handed it to Bobby, who studied the photograph, not knowing what else to do. Miss Froelich was seated in the booth of what looked like a woodsy restaurant, grinning ear to ear.

Bobby put the picture back on the bed.

"Miss Craybill, I found out who was riding that bicycle, pretending to be a ghost." She waited, but Miss Craybill showed no interest, continuing to pick up and put down photos as if she were playing some queer game of solitaire. "It was Mona, Miss Craybill! She was biking to Mesquakie Point to see a—a friend. She'll tell you herself, if you ask her. She put phosphorescence on the bicycle to make it glow." Bobby raised her voice. "Phosphorescence, do you hear me?"

Miss Craybill turned her head slowly to look at Bobby. The Games Mistress had never seen an expression of such melancholy sadness. Sadness had soaked into every pore, leaving the Headmistress sodden, like a dead leaf in the rain. Her eyes were windows onto a terrible void.

"It doesn't matter," she said. "Nothing matters."

"But Miss Craybill, what about Metamora?" Bobby felt shaken and helpless. "Don't you care what's happening? The staff is in a disarray! The students are running amok! The rumors they're spreading are getting worse! By next week they'll have everyone saying that Metamora is haunted and that the ghosts of savage Indians pushed Miss Froelich to her death! Think of the damage—"

She got no further. "Savage Indians, pah!" cried the Headmistress, suddenly agitated. "I killed Miss Froelich!"

Chapter Twenty-five
Miss Craybill's Confession

"You!" Bobby was aghast. "But that's impossible!" For a moment she pictured Miss Craybill pushing the hapless Math Mistress over the tower's parapet and then running fast enough down the twisting stairs to reach the body before anyone else. The image made her dizzy. "How? Why?"

"I killed her with my thoughtlessness. I murdered Nerissa with my blind self-regard," sobbed Miss Craybill. "I might as well have pushed her—I drove her to jump!"

Bobby tried her best to calm the hysterical Headmistress. "You're overwrought." She poured a mug of hot milk from the thermos on the bedside table. "You don't know what you're saying."

Miss Craybill pushed away the hot milk with renewed vitality. "I know perfectly well what I'm saying and I'm not going to keep quiet anymore!" she cried. The milk spilled over the rim of the mug, spattering a photo of Miss Froelich and Miss Craybill astride a tandem bicycle.

"Nerissa wanted to retire last year, but I wasn't ready to give up Metamora just yet. I told Nessa it wasn't the right time—there was no one to succeed me. The truth was, I'd never groomed a successor, because I couldn't bear the idea that one day I'd have to give it all up, this little world I've made mine, the power to hire and fire, the best suite on campus, the travels to educational conferences, the adulation of the Old Girls, the endless succession of new girls, blanks ready to be stamped with the Metamora imprint."

Bobby had never heard Miss Craybill speak so volubly about her profession. The Headmistress favored the Socratic method in her Senior Seminar, preferring to pose a question rather than answer one. Now however, stories poured out, like an unquenchable public fountain, endlessly burbling. The torrent washed over Bobby so swiftly she could only catch an occasional fragment like a piece of flotsam in a storm—Miss Craybill's lonely childhood, a pet cat who had died, her delighted discovery of Metamora, her first meeting with Nerissa, then a homesick transfer student. Bobby gave up trying to interrupt and just listened, hoping that this confession would at least ease Miss Craybill's tormented mind. Miss Craybill spoke reverently of Miss Froelich's love of birds, and how the dead Math Mistress used to bicycle to Mesquakie Point, rich in kingfishers, dippers, herons, and even an occasional bittern.

"Ah, those halcyon days! Those blissful years! We only differed on one thing—birds. For me, birding was a hobby. But increasingly for Nessa it was an avocation, the career she wished she'd pursued. She subscribed to dozens of birding periodicals, and even contributed an article to *Midwest Marsh Birds*."

"But you were happy," Bobby reminded her.

"Until last spring. Nessa had an invitation to join a party of bird-watchers going to the Amazon this fall. They must be at Manaus by now," the Headmistress added irrelevantly. "She reminded me of my promise to retire. I told her not yet. I said, 'One more year.' Nessa grew morose. She was older than I, and worried she wouldn't be fit for such strenuous birding expeditions for much longer. The week before her death, I drew up the schedule for the following year, putting both of us down for our usual classes. She wouldn't speak to me beyond what was necessary. She even slept on a cot in her office. She took long bicycle rides and would be gone for hours. I didn't take it seriously—I believed it was just a peevishness that would pass. We had planned to go to Florida to seek a glimpse of the purple gallinule after school was out in June. I was sure she'd recover her good nature before then.

"And then came that awful Thursday. I was sitting in my office, writing a letter to a parent about some contraband peanut brittle. I heard a shriek—for an instant I thought it was the cry of some rare bird, and I hoped Nessa would see it, and that it would cheer her. All that passed through my mind in the split second before I heard a heavy thud." Miss Craybill shuddered and put her hand over her eyes.

"I still think you're jumping to conclusions." Despite her protest, Bobby felt badly shaken by Miss Craybill's revelation.

"Jumping," repeated Miss Craybill dully. "Jumped." Tears leaked out the corner of her eyes and trickled down her lined cheek unnoticed. "I drove her to it," she repeated. "I know. I ran through the grass to her body. Her eyes were open. She reproached me. She said—" Miss Craybill couldn't finish her sentence.

"She was dead when you found her!" Was it possible Miss Craybill, her mind overpowered with guilt, had imagined her dead friend's reproaches?

"She wasn't," contradicted Miss Craybill. "But Mona said we should keep it quiet—for the good of the school. She said it wasn't my fault. You all say that. But you're wrong."

Mona again. Bobby made a mental note to ask the happy housekeeper what she knew about Miss Froelich's last words.

Miss Craybill went on unheedingly. "I thought she might have left me a note—some final farewell. I searched everywhere, on the sly. There was nothing. Now I don't care who knows. It *was* my fault. I did it. I don't deserve to be Headmistress anymore. Everyone should know what an evil woman I am. I did it. I might as well have pushed her—"

"What was it she said, exactly, Miss Craybill?" Bobby interrupted the mantra of self-reproach. But the Headmistress was too absorbed in her own misery to reply, and the next instant it was too late.

"Bobby, what are you doing here?" Miss Otis hurried across the room, the nurse at her heels. "Agnes—Agnes, Mona's made you a delicious rice pudding. Do you feel hungry, Agnes?"

Miss Craybill continued to repeat her confession like a religious creed. "I did it. I don't care who knows. I might as well have pushed her. I did it . . ."

"I'd better give her another injection." The nurse took out a hypodermic needle and a little glass vial. Miss Otis herded Bobby to the door.

"You shouldn't be here Bobby. Miss Craybill's not herself. She doesn't know what she's saying. She needs rest." The Latin Mistress was practically pushing the young gym teacher. "Aren't you chaperoning the Harvest Moon Mixer? Hadn't you better get ready?"

The last thing Bobby saw, before the door closed, was the nurse sliding the needle into Miss Craybill's unresisting arm.

Chapter Twenty-six
The Dance in Dorset

"May I present Henry Long?"

"How do you do?" Bobby shook the moist palm offered to her. The line of girls and their dates seemed to stretch on interminably. The Games Mistress was at the end of the receiving line and was conscious of Enid and Rod, on the other side of the Burnhams. Enid, a vision of geometric loveliness in a floating gown of black and gray rhomboids on a pearl gray ground, had been the first to shake this hand.

With the image of Miss Craybill's lax body still vivid in her mind, the gaiety and color of the Harvest Moon Mixer seemed slightly bizarre to Bobby. She felt self-conscious in her borrowed evening attire, even though Serena and Alice had assured her that the black brocade jacket over the ruffled white blouse was just like a tuxedo. Bobby kept worrying she'd trip over the matching skirt, which fell to the floor.

"May I present Curt Hudgins?" Kayo slid into place in front of the bemused gym teacher. "Curt is my cousin," she added, with a wink. "Miss Blanchard, my . . . coach." Bobby shook hands with the bespectacled youth, helpless before Kayo's proprietary air. The Savages' center was radiant tonight, in a full-skirted, ballet-length formal of ivory lace over smoky blue taffeta. Surely, thought Bobby with a shiver of fear, she wouldn't force a one-on-one with her coach at the *mixer!*

As the combo struck up a tune, Bobby watched Rod and Enid gliding among the students like the dance-contest winners they were. Rod looked darkly handsome in a tux with tails as he twirled Enid with a showy flourish. How Bobby envied him that tux!

The gay crowd turned blurred as her thoughts reverted to the Headmistress. Miss Otis couldn't keep her sedated forever. How long would Metamora survive once the parents learned that Miss Craybill blamed herself for the Math Mistress's supposed suicide? True or not, the girls would be yanked out of Metamora faster than Bobby could strike out batters in softball season. She felt a little like someone in that creepy Edgar Allen Poe story Sandy Milston had told her about, watching the students dance, unaware of their approaching doom.

Darn Miss Froelich, darn Miss Craybill, darn Mona even, Bobby thought sadly, helping herself to some of the pink punch. *Just when I was getting somewhere with this teaching stuff!*

Laura came and stood next to her. Her deceptively simple strapless satin seemed more suited for a glamorous movie premiere than the Metamora mixer. "I knocked on your door the other night," the Art Mistress murmured, a hint of reproach in her low, husky voice. "Where were you?"

"I must have been busy." Bobby avoided the Art Mistress's soulful look. "You know what an uproar the students have been in this week."

The truth was, she'd completely lost interest in Laura. Was she fickle, or was this a sign of maturity? She couldn't decide.

"I've been looking over those books Enid confiscated," Laura pursued. "They're quite thought provoking."

Bobby was searching for Enid on the crowded dance floor. Some of the couples were dancing awfully close, but Bobby couldn't be bothered to shove a phone book between them, whatever Miss Otis said. Rod was dancing with Beryl Houck, but where was Enid?

"Oh? That's nice," the Games Mistress said belatedly, realizing Laura was waiting for a response. The dance ended and as the dancers applauded, Rod and Beryl joined the two teachers at the punch bowl.

"A glass of punch, Miss Houck?" Rod proposed.

"I'd rather have a beer," Beryl grunted.

"Beryl!" reproved Bobby.

"Ah, Coach Bobby! May I have the next dance?" Rod took Bobby's hand and skillfully twirled her away from the ill-mannered right wing and the frustrated Art Mistress.

"I like your tux," Bobby told him as they triple-stepped over to the other side of the floor.

"I *adore* your brocade with the gold thread. Simple, yet stunning. And you carry it off marvelously!"

"Enid looks lovely tonight," Bobby ventured, hoping to draw Rod out about the enigmatic Math Mistress.

"Thank you! I'm going to be an egotist and take all the credit, since I picked her dress out. In fact, I created Enid's look. She was a thorough frump in high school, not to mince words. You know, baggy skirt, wrinkled blouse. But to win dance contests, you need some style!"

Bobby thought that Enid looked good whether she ironed her clothes or not. But all she said was, "Well, she has her mind on things of the mind. I mean, ideas and stuff."

"So she says. But then why the sudden fascination with field hockey?"

Bobby was so startled she stumbled. Recovering her balance, she automatically took the lead. Rod fell easily into the follower's footwork.

"Fascination?" asked Bobby, swinging Rod into a reverse turn. "What do you mean?"

"Well, she's been reading up on the topic." Rod looked at Bobby sideways as they danced a few steps in cuddle position. "I thought *you'd* know something about this new passion. C'mon Coach, give!"

"Honestly, I haven't a clue," Bobby babbled as the song ended in a blast of brass. "I always thought Enid was dead set against anything athletic!"

"So she's always said," replied Rod as they came to a halt. "But the heart has its reasons, that reason knows not, right?" And he dived into the crowd, on the prowl for gossip and wallflowers.

Bobby scarcely saw him go. It was like a flashbulb had gone off in her head. All semester she'd been puzzled by the attraction she felt for the sharp-tongued Math Mistress. It was different than the desire that had driven her fling with Madge, those clandestine trysts in college, the disastrous affair with Elaine.

I don't want another notch on my belt, she realized. *I want a steady!*

She wanted to go roller-skating with the Math Mistress, she wanted to hold hands at the double feature, and ride the Ferris wheel with her at county fairs. She wanted to park with her on Glen Mountain Road!

Why hadn't she seen it before? Bobby was amazed at her own blindness. *We share the same socioeconomic background, the same basic values. Sure, there are surface differences, and maybe I can't cook and don't own a car, but we enjoy the same activities, like going to the Knock Knock Lounge and solving school mysteries. And we're*

both trying to change the unfortunate psychosexual pat-
terns we developed in adolescence!

She had to share her discovery with the Math Mistress.
"Ken, have you seen Enid?" she asked the History Master, after searching the room to no avail.

"She's on the trail of the kids who stepped out to the
terrace for 'fresh air.'" Ken laughed paternally. He waved
his pipe at Bobby. "Do you know that in Samoa the
youths frequently—"

Bobby didn't wait to find out what the teens did in
Samoa. "I'd better give her a hand," she said hurrying
away, skirt swishing.

Outside on the terrace there were a few couples sitting
on the flagstone wall, talking quietly. Bobby spied the editor of *The Metamora Musings.* "Peggy, did you happen
to see Miss Butler?"

"She went thataway." Peggy gestured vaguely down
the steps.

A few paces from the bottom of the terrace was the
path that led to the Mesquakie Point Woods. Bobby wandered along it, enjoying the cool night air on her flushed
face. She turned and looked back at Dorset. The big windows framing the whirl of movement and color were like
living paintings.

"Bobby? Is that you?"

"Enid?"

Enid was a faint glimmer of silvery gray at the base of
a big pine tree. "Will you look at this," exclaimed the
Math Mistress. "One of those kids stashed a cache of beer
here!" She nudged something with her foot, and Bobby
heard the clank of bottles. *That Beryl!* she thought. But
reprimanding boozy Beryl was the last thing on her agenda.

"Enid, I've been thinking," she said in a rush. "We like
each other a lot, there's no denying it—"

Enid straightened up. Her face, in the faint moonlight, was serious. "I've been thinking too—" She took a step toward the brocade-clad gym teacher.

"I know I'm not your ideal girl," Bobby continued.

"I'm not anyone's ideal girl," Enid admitted with a twisted smile.

"Don't say that," contradicted Bobby hotly. "What I'm saying is, I've been trying to change my interpersonal interaction patterns, and it sounds like you want to do the same—"

"It's true, fighting my predilection has brought me no satisfaction," muttered the Math Mistress.

"So why not try getting together?"

"You're right." Enid slid into Bobby's arms, and the Games Mistress felt like a banked fire suddenly stirred into flame. "What I need is to forget logic and embrace the purely physical side of an affair, like you have!"

"No, no!" Bobby tried to pull away, but Enid's kiss was like a match to a fuse, burning a path of molten desire to Bobby's core and causing an explosion of hot delight that took the young gym teacher by surprise. "Enid!" she gasped incoherently, "I don't want another tawdry affair! I want a mature relationship that can survive the light of day!"

She struggled to pull away, but the Math Mistress had a foot on the hem of the brocade skirt. "Hush," whispered Enid, sounding suddenly like the girl in the cellar of the Knock Knock Lounge. Her hands were like red-hot branding irons, burning through Bobby's borrowed clothes and marking her as Enid's own. "Whenever we try to talk, we quarrel."

The explanations, the arguments all flew from Bobby's head like a flock of alarmed quail fleeing an out-of-control campfire as Enid's heated kisses burned away her last coherent thought. The Games Mistress's awareness of time and place was suddenly limited to the urgent softness of Enid's breasts, pressed against her own, the tight grip of Enid's fingers on her arm, the cold dampness around her ankles from the dew sodden skirt, the heat at the core of her being. Bobby felt strangely exposed under the voluminous skirt. She responded against her will to Enid's touch, helpless as a nerve when the doctor taps your knee with his little hammer. At the same time she felt giddy, like she'd gotten on a carnival ride and couldn't get off. Giving up her halfhearted resistance, she gave herself over to the Tilt-A-Whirl sensation, the wild spinning, the lurches up and down.

Without knowing how she got there, Bobby was kneeling on the ground, lips fused to Enid's, who knelt facing her. Suddenly Enid pulled away and yanked Bobby's skirt up. "So many petticoats," she panted as Bobby skidded sideways. "Are they really necessary?" Bobby's head spun. *Am I having a vertigo attack?* she wondered. But the dizziness, instead of sickening her, intensified her pleasure. "I wouldn't know," she whispered breathlessly. "It's a loan from Serena." Then, as rational thought briefly rose from the flames of desire, she cried out, "Enid this is wrong, wrong—"

"You're not one of those touch-me-not girls, are you?" Enid was on top of her, and Bobby felt a delicious topsy-turvy helplessness seize her as Enid's seeking hand found her most sensitive spot. "No—I don't think so—oh yes, yes!" Bobby moaned in astonished ecstasy.

Then, just as abruptly as it began, it was over, leaving the two teachers still radiating heat, like coals in a barbecue, after the flames from the lighter fluid have died down. "We should get back to the dance," Bobby said, helping Enid to her feet and brushing ineffectually at her skirt. *I'd better send the brocade to the dry cleaners before I give it back to Serena,* she thought.

"What's your rush?" Enid sighed, nuzzling her face into the taller girl's neck. It was all Bobby could do to say, "Enid, I've got to be square with you, this isn't what I had in mind—" Then she stopped.

Footsteps were approaching, crunch-crunching up the path. "Yoo-hoo, Coach Bobby," called a voice softly.

The two teachers sprang apart as Kayo's ivory lace formal materialized on the path, but not quickly enough. In any case, their mussed hair and crumpled skirts were enough evidence of their activities, and Kayo was a quick study. She stopped short, with a little gasp. "Not Miss Butler!" she protested. "Not Miss Butler!"

Turning, she fled, not to Dorset, but into the Mesquakie woods.

Chapter Twenty-seven
A Visit to the Chem Lab

Bobby walked back to Cornwall after the dance, brooding over the misunderstanding with Enid. How could the Math Mistress think Bobby would accept yet another affair based solely on physical pleasure? Did she think Bobby had learned nothing from *Adolescent Development Patterns*?

It was too bad she'd been unable to clear things up back there under the big pine. But Kayo had twisted her ankle—tripping over a tree root on her headlong flight to the forest—and they'd had to carry her to the infirmary. *I ought to reconsider my strategy for Thursday's game against Adena,* the coach thought distractedly as she recrossed the quadrangle. It wasn't just Kayo's ankle—there was also her hysterical declaration that she never wanted to see Coach Bobby again. But surely the Savages center would think better of her hasty words? Kayo had been overwrought, that's all. Thank heavens Miss Craybill's nurse had been handy with her hypodermic when they'd arrived at the infirmary!

Her thoughts returned to Enid. How could she make the Math Mistress take her seriously as a prospective steady? Should she ask her out on a real date? Or should she wait for Enid to make the first move? Should she play hard to get?

She wondered if Enid had returned to Manchester by now. She really ought to drop by and tell her what Miss Craybill had said earlier that evening.

The Games Mistress paused irresolutely, near the entrance to Essex. Light fell from the window above. Looking up, she saw Miss Rasphigi in the window, examining a beaker.

Bobby picked up a pebble from the path and tossed it against the window. She watched Miss Rasphigi put down the beaker and open it.

"What do you want?" asked the Chemistry Mistress. "I've already told you, I have no medical training, and I'm in the middle of an experiment."

"Don't worry, Miss Rasphigi, no one's collapsed," Bobby reassured her. "And I won't take up any time. I just want to know what it was you said to Angle to make her believe that Miss Froelich wasn't up in the tower looking for nuthatches."

"You or Angle are inaccurate," said Miss Rasphigi. "I said Miss Froelich wasn't observing nuthatches when she fell."

"How can you be sure?" persisted Bobby.

"The white-breasted nuthatch is an inhabitant of large deciduous forests. It feeds on insects in trees, which it descends head first. If Miss Froelich had been observing nuthatches, she would have been on the western side of the tower, which overlooks a large maple tree; not on the eastern side, which overlooks the quadrangle, where there's nothing taller than a shrub."

"So, Miss Froelich *wasn't* bird-watching." Bobby was dismayed. She hated to think that Miss Craybill was correct—that the former Math Mistress had jumped to her death. "But what about the binoculars?"

Miss Rasphigi was already closing the window. "The data are insufficient for definite conclusions," Bobby heard her say before it shut.

"Maybe no conclusions, but plenty of—of inferences," Bobby muttered to herself, groping for the word, and wishing Enid had been there to hear her use it.

This was no time to play hard to get, she decided. She'd go to Cornwall, check on her charges, shed her borrowed finery, and visit Enid for some help probing the Metamora mystery. She owed it to the school!

All was quiet when Bobby reentered Cornwall. She stripped off the borrowed brocade, now quite bedraggled, and paused before her closet, frowning. The gray sweatshirt, or the navy blue? Before she could decide, there was a soft tap at her door.

"Who is it?" she asked throwing on her bathrobe and opening the door. "Why, Enid! Come in, come in!"

Enid entered Bobby's sitting room diffidently. She had changed too, into her red sweater and a pair of black ski pants. "I just wanted to ask after Kayo."

"Of course! Do you want some peanut brittle?" Bobby proffered the candy she'd confiscated that morning.

"No, thanks." Enid sat down, casting a sidelong glance at Bobby's collection of trophies, medals, and banners. "How was she when you left her?"

"That ankle may prevent her from playing against Adena next week. It's too bad, because they're a tough team."

"I meant was she still so—distressed? I think she must have had a crush on you."

"Oh that. Yes, she was still pretty upset." Bobby didn't want to think about Kayo's unhappiness. She had a bad feeling she should have prevented it somehow. Should she talk to the confused girl, or would that make things worse? *I'll think about it tomorrow,* she decided. "Listen, we have more important things to talk about," she told Enid.

"Oh?" Enid looked expectant.

"I finally told Miss Craybill about Mona being the ghost, but she didn't even care."

"Oh, that," said Enid.

"She believes she drove Miss Froelich to suicide! She says Miss Froelich had planned a big bird-watching trip this fall, and when Miss Craybill put the kibosh on it, Miss Froelich jumped!"

"Really!" Enid looked interested now.

"And that's not all! Miss Rasphigi says that if Miss Craybill had fallen from the tower because of birds, she would have tumbled on the other side. Something about nuthatches nesting in the big maple."

"Interesting. But I'm not sure I buy it." Enid tucked her feet underneath her. "First, what kind of mathematician kills herself over birds? Second, we don't know for sure what species of bird she was looking at that day, or which side of the tower she'd be on. We just don't have enough data."

"That's what Miss Rasphigi said." Bobby felt proud of Enid's acumen. "But we can infer, can't we?" She brought out the word with a flourish. "Anyway, I forgot to tell you Miss Craybill said Miss Froelich said something kind of reproachful before she died."

"What?"

"I don't know." Bobby wished she'd wrung it out of Miss Craybill. "Miss Otis threw me out before Miss Craybill could tell me. All she said was that Mona said they should hush it up."

Enid thought for a moment. "Can we infer that Mona witnessed Miss Froelich's last words too?"

Bobby looked at Enid agog. "So we can find out from Mona! Do you think Miss Froelich looked over the battlement and saw Mona doing her ghost bit, and that made her fall? No, wait, it was daytime." The coach was crestfallen.

"Maybe we're making too much of this," said Enid.

"I don't think so." When Bobby thought over Miss Craybill's description of hearing Miss Froelich fall, there was something that didn't jibe. Something that didn't make sense. What was it?

"She screamed!" Bobby exclaimed. "Why would she have screamed if she jumped on purpose?"

A knock on the door made them both start.

"Probably just Sandy, to say Debbie's sleepwalking again," murmured Bobby. But it was Laura, still wearing her strapless satin. She pushed her way past the startled hockey coach.

"Bobby, I had to come. You've been so distant lately. I told Ken I'd forgotten a glove in Dorset." She stopped when she saw the Math Mistress in Bobby's armchair. "Oh! Hello, Enid."

"Hello, Laura," the Math Mistress replied.

There was an awkward silence while Laura looked back and forth between Enid and Bobby, and Enid watched Laura. Bobby rearranged the trophies on her mantel, desperately trying to think of a way to get rid of the interfering Art Mistress. "Enid is—is helping me with some field hockey strategy, Laura. We're kind of busy."

Laura's eyes gleamed. "Couldn't I help as well?" she suggested huskily. "After all, three heads are better than two! And I've been reading this book, *Strange Triangle*—"

"You'll have to count me out of any triangular doings." Enid got up from the chair. "I should get back to my charges. Who knows what those hellions in Manchester have gotten up to?"

Bobby was helpless to prevent the Math Mistress's departure. Darn that Laura! "Well, thanks for all your help." She followed Enid to the door and lowered her voice. "I'm awfully sorry we got interrupted."

Enid looked over Bobby's shoulder at Laura, who was redoing her lipstick. "You know, don't you, that she'll never leave Ken, no matter how much she complains about him?" she murmured softly. "That wedding ring is as permanent as the mole on her right thigh."

Bobby stared after the departing teacher, open-mouthed. How did Enid know about Laura's plans to leave Ken? How did she know about that mole?

Chapter Twenty-eight
More Discoveries

The hot water pounded on Bobby's tired muscles and the sound of the shower echoed through the empty locker room as Bobby scrubbed under the spray.

It was very early Sunday morning. After a fitful night's sleep, Bobby had risen at dawn to run off her uneasiness.

After she'd suggested to Laura last night that they just be good friends, the Art Mistress had departed in one of her temperamental huffs and Bobby had gone to bed still puzzling over Enid's remark. Immediately she was deep in a dream of chasing Miss Rasphigi up the steps of the tower, going around and around, yet never reaching the top, until finally she woke up, covered in sweat. When she fell back asleep, she dreamed she was at the top of the tower, and Mona was there, serving cocoa to Enid and Laura. Leaning against the wall behind them was a skeleton in an academic robe. Bobby had jerked awake with a gasp. She'd punched her pillow and tried to think of sheep. But when she closed her eyes, she was falling, falling from the tower toward the sundial. Then somehow her momentum slowed. Enid, standing where the sundial had been, pushed her back up in the air, like a volleyball player setting a ball. "Ups-a-daisy," said the Math Mistress with a smile.

Am I getting better, Bobby wondered as she turned off the shower, *or worse?*

In the stillness Bobby heard the locker room door creak open. A prickle of fear ran down her spine. Who would visit the gymnasium at seven a.m. on a Sunday morning? She stood tensely as footsteps approached the shower stall. Wrapping herself in a towel, she yanked aside the shower curtain. Lotta, opening a locker, jumped around with a little scream.

"Coach Bobby," she gasped. "You scared me."

Bobby felt ashamed of her nervousness. The Metamora atmosphere was beginning to affect her. "Sorry, Lotta," she replied. "What are you doing in the locker room so bright and early?" She asked the question casually, but Lotta stuttered her answer.

"Nothing! I mean, I just wanted to leave Angle a present. It's her birthday today."

"Really?" Bobby saw that Lotta held a small gold box. "What did you get her?"

Shyly, Lotta took off the lid. Inside was an expensive calfskin wallet, the initials "A.C.O." embossed in gold.

"Nice," commented Bobby. "Throw me my shirt, will you?" Lotta handed the teacher her shirt and then turned back to the locker and carefully tucked her gift next to Angle's shin guards. She closed the locker and locked the padlock, giving the combination dial a little spin.

"Handy, you having Angle's combination," Bobby remarked, her voice muffled as she toweled her hair dry.

"I have everybody's combination," Lotta explained. "So I can gather up the equipment for the away games and let the players save their strength."

Bobby had a flash of insight. "You're the one who took Kayo's locket!" she exclaimed. "But why?"

"I—I—" The precocious student was tongue-tied.

"Was it because of Angle? Did she ask you to do it?" pursued Bobby artfully.

"No!" Lotta leapt to her idol's defense as Bobby knew she would. "It was my idea—I don't know why I did it. Kayo sent me to get her spare pinny, and I saw her locket hanging from the hook, and I—I took it. I don't even like lockets! Will I be expelled?" Lotta looked ready to cry.

"Why did you have to return it in such a dramatic fashion?" Bobby asked. She thought she understood Lotta's motives better than the brainy but emotionally mixed-up teen. The ever-helpful water girl had been pining after Angle and stewing with resentment on her behalf all season while the rest of the squad treated her like an errand girl. It was a wonder she hadn't done worse!

"First I threw it in the Mesquakie woods," Lotta gulped. "Then, when everyone was saying Angle must have taken it, I was worried that if someone found it there it would clinch the suspicions against her, because everyone knows she goes there all the time. So I looked—I used Miss Butler's grid method—and I finally found it again the day Linda and her friends were having their séance. While you and Miss Butler were chasing after them, I snuck out and put it on the sundial, where someone would be sure to see it."

Bobby shook her head, thinking of the superstitious frenzy unleashed by this misguided crush.

"Well, Lotta," Bobby sounded as stern as she could with her damp hair still dripping, "I'm afraid this unfortunate impulse will have serious consequences—"

"Please, please don't expel me!" Lotta burst into tears. "Kayo got her stupid locket back, and what Beryl did, sneaking beer into the mixer, is much worse!"

Mentally, Bobby kicked herself for forgetting to grab the illicit beer when she and Enid carried Kayo to the infirmary. "Lotta, you're not going to be expelled, there's no need to rat out your fellow students. I want you to apologize to the whole squad for putting them in an uproar, and especially to Kayo. And of course you'll resign as water girl." She had to look away from the misery on Lotta's face as the anemic teen repeated in disbelief, "Re—resign as water girl?"

"Run along to breakfast now," Bobby ordered gruffly, pretending to be busy zipping up her Windbreaker.

The power of love! Bobby thought as she headed back to Cornwall. It had led Lotta to theft and Miss Craybill to a nervous breakdown. On the other hand, it had motivated Kayo to drive the Savages all season, putting them in the running for the regional championship! It had given Mona the energy to bike to Mesquakie Point in the dead of night, on a bicycle coated with phosphorescence.

Mona, she remembered. *I have to ask her what Miss Froelich said before she died.* If she could convince Miss Craybill that Miss Froelich had not jumped on purpose, maybe the Headmistress would recover and Metamora would be saved!

It seemed like an ordinary Sunday at Metamora, Bobby thought, watching the girls at breakfast. Only someone accustomed to the small nuances of teen behavior would pick up on the edge of unhealthy excitement in the mealtime chatter, the growing disregard for Miss Otis's authority. Bobby saw Beryl doctor her orange juice with a small flask, while around her the distracted teachers conversed among themselves.

"The situation's getting worse," she told Enid grimly after the meal was over. "I'm going to talk to Mona."

"I'll try Miss Craybill again," Enid said.

Bobby found Mona in the kitchen, inspecting a grocery delivery from the A&P in Adena. "Look, graham crackers!" She brandished a box at Bobby. "I thought we'd

have s'mores over the rec room fire after the game with
Adena."

"Sounds good." Bobby bore straight to the business at
hand. "Mona, when—"

Mona interrupted her with a laugh. "Bobby, you've got
to be patient, it's still much too dangerous to tell Miss Craybill anything that might upset her. She *is* doing a little
better—I must say I think my idea of getting her a pair of
budgies was inspired—but she's hardly—"

"It's not about that." It was Bobby's turn to interrupt
the prattling housekeeper. "I only wanted to ask: When
you and Miss Craybill found Miss Froelich lying by the
sundial, what did she say? What were her last words?"

For an instant, Mona's face took on that hooded, wary
look Bobby had seen when she'd guessed the identity of
the housekeeper's illicit lover. Then Mona was all wide-
eyed surprise. "Last words? Miss Froelich was dead
when Miss Craybill found the body. Anyway, I—"

"You were there too," Bobby told her. "I saw Miss Craybill and talked to her. I told her about your cycling es-
capades, and honestly, she didn't seem to care much. She's
blaming herself for Miss Froelich's death—because of something Miss Froelich said, something you both decided to
hush up."

"Forgive me, Bobby, I didn't know you knew," Mona
said instantly. "I didn't want to lie to you, but Miss Craybill and I thought the fewer people who knew that Miss
Froelich had—you know—the better. And honestly, if
Miss Craybill didn't tell you what Miss Froelich said, I
don't know that I should. It was—personal. You do understand, don't you?" She glanced at her watch. "Goodness,
I'd better get these groceries put away. Isn't it nearly time
for first period?"

Bobby left, frustrated by the housekeeper's sudden attack of high-mindedness.

Wait a second. She stopped in her tracks outside Dorset. *There aren't any classes on Sunday!* Was there more to the housekeeper's moral stance than met the eye?

She hurried to Kent. Perhaps Enid had had better luck.

Enid was coming down the steps outside Kent, and Bobby's heart contracted at the sight of her all over again. *I love that girl,* she thought, heartsick. *From her black-framed glasses to the tips of her scuffed penny loafers!*

"No go," Enid reported. "The Headmistress is better guarded than Fort Knox."

Bobby groaned. Miss Otis and her clumsy attempts to protect Metamora's reputation! "Mona was a wash too. There's something up with the housekeeper—something's bothering me about her, but I can't quite put my finger on it."

"Really?" Enid was intrigued. "Maybe we could go for a walk in the woods and put our heads together over the problem."

"Sure!" Bobby's pulse pitter-pattered. Then she remembered, "Oh, I can't—field hockey practice starts in ten minutes. But—later?"

"I have a meeting with the Problem Solvers," Enid told her.

The two teachers looked at each other for a moment. Was the disappointment Bobby felt mirrored in Enid's eyes?

Metamora, thought Bobby, trudging disconsolately to the gymnasium. It had brought them together, but it also pushed them apart.

Her thoughts were so busy with Enid that it took her a second to remember why Lotta's eyes were red-rimmed, and why she wasn't bustling around with towels and water. Then the morning's discovery came rushing back.

"Are you ready to apologize to the team?" Bobby asked her, putting an encouraging hand on her shoulder. Lotta nodded, struggling to maintain her composure. Bobby blew her whistle, interrupting the players' calisthenics. "Savages, gather round, Lotta has something to say."

As Lotta confessed in a broken voice, the players gasped and muttered amongst themselves. Some of them stole covert glances at Angle, who stood a little apart as usual, her face as impassive as one of Mr. Burnham's Iroquois braves.

As the chattering Savages returned to their calisthenics, Bobby reminded Lotta, "And don't forget to find Kayo and make amends with her as well. She's probably still in the infirmary." She felt again that worm of anxiety at the thought of Kayo.

"Can I—can I go to the Adena game to cheer at least?" Lotta begged. Bobby had to harden her heart. "No, Lotta," she told the girl. "Not this time."

The coach was glad to return to drilling the Savages in the Twist Push-Pass Feint. The new play was going to be a humdinger when they got it right. "No, no," she explained again to Shirley Sarvis. "You pass in the *opposite* direction of your twist. Otherwise there's no surprise, do you see?" She demonstrated again.

"It's like trying to rub my stomach and pat my head at the same time," said Shirley, good-naturedly trying the move again.

Misako, Bobby observed with some surprise, had the new play down perfectly, and could switch directions as needed, without a second thought. Joyce Vandemar wasn't half bad either. Perhaps it was because they were both in her peasant dance class and had studied the Twist so thoroughly.

At the end of practice, Angle came up to Bobby. "Coach, I've decided to apologize to Kayo."

Bobby blinked in surprise. "Angle, that's terrific news! What made you change your mind?"

"Now that everyone knows Lotta took the locket and not me, it won't be like I'm saying I was guilty. And I want to beat those Holy Virgins again." She paused and shuffled her feet. "Besides, I—I was walking by the infirmary last night, and I heard Kayo crying!"

The worm of anxiety in Bobby's stomach gave a wriggle.

"I bet that Curt Hudgins she dated for the dance tried something she didn't like." Angle's eyes flashed angrily. "And him her first cousin!"

"You see now that Kayo has problems and confusion about her identity just like any girl on the verge of womanhood," Bobby told the teen, wondering how Angle knew so much about Kayo's escort. "Your empathy is a real sign of maturity."

Angle looked at her keenly. "Kayo's confused about her identity?"

"I just meant it as an example," Bobby hastened to say. "What I mean is, I'm happy you're finding things in common with your classmate."

"Well, I believe in showing the enemy a united front," Angle concluded, "even when there are ideological differences."

At least now she didn't have to worry about benching Beryl for that beer, Bobby thought, feeling relieved. She began to rewrite her starting roster for the Adena game. Even if Kayo was out . . .

"Coach Bobby?"

Bobby looked up from her desk. "What is it, Edie?"

The goalie hovered uncertainly in the doorway. "I just wondered . . . did Kayo tell you about Thursday?"

A feeling of foreboding filled the hockey coach. "What about Thursday?"

"It's the annual DAP luncheon in Bay City, for all the DAP girls in the region. We elect new officers, and get awards for the money we've raised, and have the *glögg* ceremony for new members . . ."

Bobby leaned back. "Kayo said nothing about it."

"That's what I was worried about." Edie knit her brows. "She said she was going to arrange for us to leave early and be in Adena in time for the game, but when I visited her in the infirmary this morning, she said we had to stay for the whole thing. She said we couldn't neglect our DAP duties any longer."

"Thanks for letting me know, Edie," Bobby managed to say.

When the goalie had gone, she looked down at the roster. Who was she left with? Angle, Annette, Shirley Sarvis, and a bunch of second-string fourth formers. Even with Angle it wouldn't be enough.

Unless . . . She picked up her pen and began adding names to her starting list. "The fourth formers know the Twist Push-Pass Feint," she said aloud. "We'll have to use the Twist Push-Pass Feint!"

Chapter Twenty-nine

The Old Ivy

"The Savages are coming,
Better run, better hide,
They have a firm grip on their sticks
And won't be satisfied
By anything less than victory,
So their enemies woe betide!"

The Savages sang their fight song triumphantly as Ole drove the blue bus up the bluffs back to Metamora.

"Three cheers for Coach Bobby!" piped up Joyce Vandemar. "Hip hip hooray . . ."

The cheers shook the bus. The team had been cheering ever since they'd left Adena and showed no signs of slowing down.

"Some victory, huh?" Ole said to Bobby.

"Yeah." Bobby was still too dazed to do more than repeat, "Some victory."

One part of her rejoiced at the Savages' stunning victory, the other part fretted over the latest bit of bad luck affecting the Midwest Regional Secondary School Girls' Field Hockey League. When they'd arrived at Adena High, the Savages had been greeted with the news that several of the first-string Pioneers were out of the game due to a bizarre outbreak of poison ivy. "It was all over their legs," Adena's coach told Bobby. "It was like someone had rubbed their shin guards in the stuff!"

Bobby was more convinced than ever that someone was sabotaging the field hockey games. But who? And why?

At least this lets Mona out, Bobby thought. The housekeeper had stayed at Metamora today, to prepare the s'mores party.

The bus was bumping through the big stone gate posts and now the team burst into the Metamora school song:

> *"Hail to thee, Metamora,*
> *O mother of our minds,*
> *From here to Bora Bora*
> *Her faithful daughters finds,*
> *Brave-hearted, always willing . . ."*

They swung into the parking lot behind Kent, and the Savages tumbled off the bus. "We won, we won!" they shouted to several DAP girls, who were descending from a taxi, still dressed in their Bay City best.

"You did?" Edie, Penny, and Linda were surprised and a little jealous. "Without us?"

"Darn Kayo and her DAP loyalty," flung out Linda. "I wish we'd been there!"

"Well, thanks to us, you'll probably play in the championship game," Joyce reminded Linda generously. Misako took Edie's arm.

"Come, Edie," she said. "S'mores for all the Savages! DAPs too!"

Bobby followed her team, looking anxiously around for Kayo. But instead she bumped into Hoppy outside the entrance to Dorset. The Current Events Mistress was with Netta Bean from the Knock Knock Lounge.

"Why hello, Netta!" The coach paused to greet the bespectacled inner-city school teacher. "How nice to see you again!"

Netta was certainly becoming a frequent visitor at Metamora. Anxiety seized Bobby. Did she teach math as well as English? Did she have her eye on Enid's job?

"Bobby! Just the person we were looking for." Hoppy pulled the Games Mistress to one side as the Savages streamed past them.

"Say, Hoppy, did you hear how well Misako played in the game today? Her performance of the Twist Push-Pass Feint was perfection!"

"Never mind that now." Bobby felt a twinge of resentment as Hoppy brushed aside Misako's achievement. "Netta and I have had a real brainstorm. We want your help in putting together a friendly field hockey competition between the Savages and some of the students from Eleanor D. Roosevelt."

"With a goodwill fellowship party afterward," Netta chimed in. "I think incorporating sports into the cultural exchange will be an invaluable way to emphasize the student's commonalities, even as they explore their differences."

"Well sure, okay." Bobby wondered at Hoppy, planning her cultural exchange as if nothing was wrong at Metamora. "But what about Miss Craybill?"

"Look." Hoppy turned serious. "We all know Miss Craybill is *non compos mentis,* who knows for how long. If this cloud has a silver lining, it's the opportunity to try out some really progressive educational ideas while Metamora lasts!"

Bobby was shocked at Hoppy's cold-blooded practicality.

"Netta, let's go to the s'mores party, I'd like you to observe Metamora's social status systems in action," Hoppy proposed to her friend. "And our housekeeper makes a mean cup of cocoa."

"I'd love a cup of cocoa." Netta followed Hoppy into Dorset.

Bobby stayed outside, deep in thought. Was Hoppy an exception or the norm? Had the rest of Metamora's faculty given up on the school too?

"Bobby! There you are!" It was Enid, breathless, her cheeks red with excitement. "I think I may have the means of putting Miss Craybill back on her feet!"

Relief filled Bobby. At least Enid was still in there pitching. The Math Mistress was unfolding several sheets of flimsy stationery.

"I found this letter today, tucked into the *Dictionary of Named Effects and Laws in Chemistry, Physics, and Mathematics.*" She thrust it at Bobby. "Read it!"

It was dated May 30 of that year. "Dear Myra," it began.

"Who's Myra?" asked Bobby.

"That part doesn't matter, just read!"

> Dear Myra,
> Term's over at last, and once I finish entering grades, I'll be able to devote all my time to the pursuit of the elusive short-billed marsh wren. My envious congratulations to you on your pair of Hooded Mergansers! That is a coup indeed. They say their territory stretches south to our fair state, but I've never been fortunate enough to see one, much less a pair.

"It's all about birds," Bobby objected.

"Skip ahead, here." Enid put her finger on the paragraph.

> As you know, I'm planning to join Seeley Sedgewick on her expedition to the Amazon this fall. I thrill when I think of the Macaws, Nightjars, and Blue Crowned Trogons that await me.

*Aggie will be terribly disappointed, I fear. I've
been rather avoiding her, since I dread breaking
the news of my defection, but I ought to tell her
soon, as she'll have to hire a replacement Math
Mistress for next term. Perhaps your kind invitation for August will help soften the blow. And of
course*

The letter ended there.

"So she *was* going to the Amazon!" Bobby gasped. "Which means—"

"Miss Craybill's belief that she drove her friend to suicide is false!" Enid finished.

"We have to show this to the Headmistress immediately," Bobby declared. "This will be the shot in the arm she needs—and it will do her a lot more good than the shots she's been getting."

Enid was shaking her head. "I tried, remember? Miss Otis has two nurses relaying each other on round-the-clock duty, and a specially appointed sub-prefect patrolling the third-floor corridor. And now she's gone to a meeting with the Old Girls' Weekend Organizing Committee and won't be back until who knows when."

Bobby looked up at Kent, her mind rapidly running over the possibilities. A rope from Kent's roof down to Miss Craybill's room? Too long to rig. Should she rally the Savages to overpower the nurse and sub-prefect? No, they deserved to enjoy their victory celebration without being dragged into the deranged Headmistress's problems. If only Enid had some acrobatic circus training . . .

"I know—the ivy!"

"The ivy?" repeated Enid blankly.

"Sure—see how thick it is there?" Bobby pointed at the green leaves that covered the building. "It should hold our weight. Didn't you ever scale the ivy at your school to sneak into the dorm after curfew?"

"I was never out after curfew," said Enid stiffly.

"Well, curfew is ringing now at Metamora." Bobby grabbed Enid's hand and pulled the dubious Math Mistress from Dorset's entrance to Kent.

"Miss Craybill's room is above the infirmary," Bobby said, tugging Enid up the steps and into the building. "If we go out through its window, we won't have to climb all the way from the ground."

"I don't know," began Enid as the Games Mistress flung open the infirmary door. The two teachers stopped on the threshold. Kayo was inside the sterile white room, pilfering painkillers from the medicine cabinet.

"What do you two want?" demanded the Savages' captain rudely.

Bobby felt her stomach drop at the expression of suffering on Kayo's face. She'd been acting like a coward, avoiding the teen ever since the Harvest Moon Mixer. How could she have been so callous? Her own memories of Madge should have taught her that a broken heart didn't heal like a bruised ankle!

She pushed Enid toward the window. "You go first, I have to talk with Kayo," she whispered.

"Me?" Enid was horrified. "But I've never climbed ivy in my life!"

"It's just like climbing a ladder. You'll be fine." Bobby waited until the Math Mistress's dangling feet had cleared the top of the window frame before she turned to Kayo, who'd been watching the odd proceedings blankly.

"Sit down, Kayo, and give me those pills you took. They're not going to help the pain you're feeling."

"How do you know?" Kayo shot back. "Maybe my ankle's killing me!"

"I know because I've been there." Bobby looked at Kayo steadily, until Kayo looked away.

"I owe you a big apology for playing fast and loose with your feelings. You showed such—such promise that I encouraged you more than I should have. It was unfair to you, and unfair to the rest of the Savages. My only excuse is that it's my first year teaching and I've made some mistakes. Some real doozies." Bobby thought back over the past few months, amazed at all that had happened.

"You're just saying that because you lost against Adena today and want me back on the team," Kayo retorted. "All you care about is winning!"

"That's not true," said Bobby earnestly. "I care about the physical, emotional, and moral development of every girl in Metamora's athletic program! Besides, we won today."

"You did? Because of Angle, I suppose. She only apologized to me because she's got that grudge against the Holy Virgins. I bet she wasn't sorry at all. I've tried, really tried to be nice to her, and she just looks at me—looks and says nothing!"

"We won because of teamwork, Kayo. And Angle apologized because she felt bad for you."

Conflicting emotions warred with each other on Kayo's mobile young face. Bobby watched her closely. The teen was like an irresolute child, peering into the adult world, uncertain whether to advance or retreat. What to say? How to give her the gentle push that would take her over the threshold to maturity?

"Grow up, Kayo!" said the coach abruptly. "You're not the only person at Metamora with problems! On the hockey team alone you've got kleptomania, incipient alcoholism, and the troubles of a broken home! Not to mention that your Headmistress is on the verge of insanity and your school is on the verge of collapse!"

Kayo's chin snapped up at this unexpected assault.

Bobby continued on doggedly. "You're Head Prefect and team captain, and you can do something about these things if you choose, instead of hiding behind heartache and pain pills."

"Next you'll be saying I don't have any school spirit!"

"No, never," Bobby protested. "Oh, Kayo, I'm only being tough on you because I believe in your potential!"

"Oh, fine," Kayo said after a moment's silent struggle. "I'll play against the Holy Virgins. I suppose you want your letter sweater back. I feel so humiliated!"

Bobby felt a little better. Kayo was going to be okay. Maybe her captain's pride was more injured than her heart.

"Kayo, next year you'll be going to college and you'll meet scads of wonderful girls, and I bet you'll humiliate lots of them," she assured the tempting teen. "Say, how about if we trade—you return my letter sweater, and I'll give you my lucky stick? It's time I passed it on."

"Really?" Kayo's eyes widened in delight.

"It's a deal." Bobby got up and straddled the window sill. "Now I've got to go, I've left Enid hanging too long. Don't tell anyone you saw us." Bobby swung out the window and swarmed up the ivy to join Enid, who was clinging to the side of the building.

"I'm stuck," said the Math Mistress in a strangled whisper. Bobby helped her move her hands and place her feet until at last they'd reached Miss Craybill's bedroom window.

"If it's closed, I'll murder you," said Enid between clenched teeth.

"Relax," Bobby reassured the terrified teacher. "Miss Craybill is a fresh-air fiend." The window was, in fact, open an inch, and Bobby was able to push it up easily. She boosted Enid over the sill and clambered in after her.

The Headmistress's chamber had changed slightly since Bobby's last visit. The photos were gone and the deranged woman dozed fitfully under the smooth counterpane. A pair of budgies flitted about in a cage that hung from a stand by the bed. The intruders seemed to have agitated the birds, and they flew from one side of the cage to the other, chirping frantically.

Miss Craybill opened her eyes. "Bobby—and Enid. To what do I owe the pleasure?" She struggled to sit up. "I'm afraid I'm not myself. Refer all questions to Miss Otis for the duration." Her eyelids sagged closed.

"Miss Craybill!" Bobby shook the sedated school mistress until her eyes opened. "We found a letter from Miss Froelich we think you should see." Enid helped her prop Miss Craybill up, and Bobby looked around for some sort of stimulant. There was nothing. Then the coach remembered the pint of whiskey, a gift from Adena's field hockey coach, still in her jacket pocket.

"Do you think this'll hurt her?" she asked Enid as she poured a jigger into an empty mug on the side table. Enid shrugged, and Bobby tipped the contents into Miss Craybill's mouth, pinching her nose closed. The Headmistress coughed and sputtered. "Not the demon rum!" Her eyes flew open in horror and she pushed the mug away.

Since the Headmistress's abhorrence of alcohol seemed to have stimulated her into a semi-alert state, Bobby held the letter in front of her. "Read this, Miss Craybill, read this!"

The old woman began to read, without comprehension it seemed. Slowly she sat up straight, and taking the letter in her own hands she read it again. "Why, that scamp!" The words burst forth. "She never canceled!"

It was marvelous to see the pink return to Miss Craybill's pallid cheeks and the sparkle to her dim blue eyes. "Where did you find this?" she demanded. Quickly Enid explained how she'd been casually flipping through the mathematical reference book in the library.

"And it's been there all this time," marveled the Head-mistress. "Like a needle in a haystack. She must have for-gotten about that letter. How like her. She was always leaving a trail of scraps, like Hansel and Gretel. Shopping lists as bookmarks, problem sets mixed in with textbook catalogs . . ." She drifted into a reverie and a tear glim-mered at the corner of her eye. "And she never got to see the blue-crowned trogon," mourned Miss Craybill.

"But the point is, it's not your fault," interrupted Bobby, determined not to let the Headmistress sink again into destructive self-pity. "You've got to get over this guilt complex, this—this—" She threw her hands up help-lessly. "You tell her, Enid!"

"You're used to running the school, the teachers, the student body like the fief of your own little fiefdom." Enid's voice was like maple syrup dripping down a stack of pan-cakes. "You've been doing it for so long that you forget that all of us are individuals, autonomous beings. Miss Froelich was wholly in control of her own destiny—"

The door swung open and the nurse burst into the room. She was not the one Bobby had seen before, but a brawny young woman, with muscles that rippled under her white uniform. "I thought I heard voices," she said, advancing on the uninvited visitors menacingly.

"Hush, Nurse, you're interrupting." Miss Craybill spoke with her old authority. She threw the covers aside. "Make yourself useful and give me my dressing gown," she com-manded.

"And so you see," Enid continued as the bewildered nurse searched for the garment, "you have nothing more to do with her death than I do with the death of a Chi-nese peasant on the other side of the world."

The nurse handed Miss Craybill her quilted dressing

gown. "Would you like some beef tea?" she asked uncertainly.

"Beef tea? I could eat a whole side of beef," Miss Craybill cried, wrapping herself in the dressing gown. "But first I think I'll take a bath. I'm feeling terribly frowsty."

Bobby didn't want to return to the morbid topic, but she had to ask. "Miss Craybill, what was it Miss Froelich said before she died?"

Miss Craybill furrowed her brow. "It makes no sense now. Did I mishear her? I thought she said something like, 'You've gambled with our lives'—or was it 'their lives'? Something lives. What could she have meant?"

Chapter Thirty

Cocoa in the Common Room

Bobby and Enid took the stairs for their descent, circumnavigating the special sub-prefect, who was engrossed in a comic book.

"Maybe what she said was 'I've been rambling all my life,'" suggested Bobby. "Or 'scrambling with chives'? No wait, I've got it! 'You've scrambled their drives'— Miss Froelich was trying to warn Mona about nutrition and the students' energy level!"

"I think you're right about one thing," Enid said decisively. "Miss Froelich was addressing Mona, not Miss Craybill. But she wasn't talking about nutrition— she was talking about betting!"

"You mean Mona Gilvang is a gambler?" Bobby tried to picture the wholesome housekeeper dealing cards to a table of men smoking cigars and listening to horse races.

"I think so," declared Enid. "But let's ask her."

As they retraced their steps to Dorset, Bobby asked, "Miss Froelich said 'gambling with *lives.*' What does that part mean?"

Enid didn't reply. She just walked faster.

The common room in Dorset was still crowded with Savages eagerly chattering to their classmates, reliving the triumphs of the Adena game. Edie and Misako were toasting marshmallows at the fireplace, while Linda and Joyce argued about the finer points of obstruction. In the back corner of the room, Angle and Kayo were sitting together, evidently deep in a serious conversation.

"Have you seen Mona?" Bobby asked Hoppy. She and Netta were observing the whole scene, as avid as birdwatchers before a nest of ivory-billed woodpeckers. Netta looked up at Bobby's question, but Hoppy only waved them impatiently toward the kitchen.

In the shining, industrial kitchen Mona was humming a little tune as she ladled cocoa from a bubbling vat into the empty mugs crowded together on a tray.

"Bobby, congratulations!" Mona called out. "Hello, Enid! Aren't you girls thick as thieves these days! I wonder, would you mind giving me a hand—just add a squirt of whipped cream to these mugs I've already filled, and then we can take the trays in."

Obediently, Bobby shook the bottle of whipped cream and began squirting a gob of the stuff into each mug. "I don't want to pry," Bobby began, somewhat embarrassed. "But do you have a gambling habit you haven't mentioned?"

"Gambling? What will these girls think up next!" Mona laughed gaily. "I'm happy to say that gambling is *not* one of my vices. Careful, Bobby, not *quite* so much whipped cream," she cautioned the Games Mistress, who was absentmindedly making towering mountains of the foamy treat.

"You can't laugh this off," declared Enid, who stood to one side with her arms folded. "We know what Miss Froelich said—we know that her last words, 'You've gambled with their lives,' were intended for *you*, not Miss Craybill. These are serious charges, Mona!"

Before Mona could reply, a sudden intake of breath made them turn. Netta Bean had slipped into the room. Looking straight at the housekeeper, she asked sadly, "Oh, Ramona, what have you done now? You told me you'd reformed!"

"Ramona? You know her?" Bobby wondered if the mismatched pair had met at the Knock Knock Lounge.

Enid was struck by Netta's revelation as well. "Reformed?" she asked tersely.

"We were girlfriends once." Netta answered Bobby first, her tone mournful. "Until she turned to blackmail, dope dealing, who knows what else." She looked at the harried housekeeper. "I can't believe I ever loved you! I can't believe I trusted you last week when you told me you were through with crime!"

"Keep your shirt on, Netta," Mona began in a placating tone. "You always exaggerate that business in Bay City. I'm not doing anything wrong. I take a little flutter on the high school sporting events from some of the locals. It's a fine old American tradition!"

"You're a bookie, not a bettor," Enid realized.

"The high school sporting events!" Horror filled Bobby and she set down her can of whipped cream. "You mean you take bets against the Savages?"

"Calm down, Coach." Mona was on the defensive now. "What's the harm? These bluffs are crawling with fervent field hockey fans, eager to place a wager on the home team, as well as wealthy housewives bored with bridge, ex-hockey players, and not a few parents who like the added interest in the games."

"Ramona," moaned Netta. "How can you? You trained as a teacher once. You're gambling with lives!"

"You're the one who's behind these 'accidents'!" Angrily, Bobby advanced on the housekeeper. "You're the one who rubbed the Pioneers' shin guards with poison ivy! Who slipped the Ants' star center a mixed drink instead of a milkshake!"

"I swear, Bobby, it wasn't me!" Some of the housekeeper's insouciance slipped away. "Believe me, I have a hard enough time calculating the odds of an honest game!"

"What I can't understand is the cold-blooded cruelty that let you stand by and do nothing while poor Miss Craybill went half crazy, blaming herself for her friend's supposed suicide," put in Enid hotly. "That's much worse than any illegal betting."

Mona threw out her hands. "She jumped to conclusions! Was I supposed to incriminate myself to argue her out of her guilty conscience? I told her over and over again that it was an accident."

"But was it an accident?" Bobby heard herself asking the question almost without her own volition.

The sudden stillness in the big kitchen was broken only by the simmering of cocoa, which took on an ominous sound, like the bubbling of quicksand as some helpless animal is trapped and sucked under.

"What are you talking about?" Mona said finally. "She had her binoculars. She was observing nuthatches. *She was observing nuthatches!*"

The kitchen door swung open, and music and noise filled the tense kitchen as Linda poked her head in. "Mrs. Mona, Mrs. Mona, is there any more cocoa? And Misako broke a chair, demonstrating the Twist Push-Pass Feint."

"I did not break it." Misako appeared behind Linda. "Beryl broke it when she fell on it."

Mona seized the tray of cocoa. "We'll have to finish our chat another time," she told the three teachers. "These girls will tear the common room to shreds in their high spirits!" She exited through the door the fourth formers held open for her. As it swung closed behind her, the words "Girls will be girls!" floated back.

"We *must* report her to the Midwest Regional Secondary School Girls' Field Hockey League, there's just no way around it," Bobby said for the tenth time.

She and Netta and Enid were sitting in her office in the gym.

"I should have said something when I recognized her last week," Netta mourned for the twelfth time. "Why did I believe her? Why do I still fall for her line? Oh, I wish Lois were here, instead of at that collating conference!"

Enid sighed. "We're repeating ourselves and not getting anywhere. Bobby, I know you want action—"

"This whole hockey season has been tainted! Do you realize that?" raged the young coach. "And how many other high school sports has this terrible vice infected?"

"I know, I know," Enid tried to soothe the infuriated Games Mistress. "As a matter of fact, the Problem Solvers were using Metamora's sports stats in a probability exercise, and I noticed an odd predictability to the field hockey games. The underdog won, every single time! However," she added hastily as Bobby opened her mouth, "you also want Metamora to survive, don't you? We have to deal with this discreetly. Remember, the Old Girls are coming this weekend."

Bobby closed her mouth. She knew Enid was right. Then she opened it again. "But we have to make sure Friday's game is clean," she declared. "I don't want the Holy Virgins getting the plague or finding ground glass in their shoes on my turf! If we win against them, I want it to be fair and square!"

"Mona said she had nothing to do with that," objected Netta.

"Netta, I can't believe after everything you've told us you're still defending your ex!" retorted Bobby. "She masquerades as the widow Gilvang, and instead it turns out this Mr. Gilvang is alive and living in New York—"

"She married him to help him emigrate from Sweden," muttered Netta. "The quota for Scandinavians was full."

"Just a second, Bobby, I'm with Netta," interjected Enid. "Let's look at bookmaking mathematically. Your bettor puts down eleven to earn ten, you set your line to balance the action, and if you don't get middled too often you'll earn, no matter who wins. A heavy bettor is the likeliest culprit, not Mona the bookie."

Netta wasn't paying attention anymore. "What was that noise?" she asked nervously.

They all listened intently. Then Bobby and Enid heard it too—a faint creaking that seemed to be coming from the big gymnasium she'd thought was empty. Switching off her desk lamp, she eased open the door and peered out. She could see nothing except the faint outlines of the vaulting horse and balance beam. Night had fallen. It was dinnertime by now, and everyone should be in Dorset, tucking into their Yorkshire puddings. But someone was out there. Who? What did they want?

Enid's shoulder was pressed against Bobby's. "Do you see anything?" she whispered.

"No," Bobby whispered back. She went behind her desk and took her lucky stick down from its place of honor.

"You think Mona's out there, don't you?" whispered Netta frantically. "You think she killed your Math Mistress somehow, just because she had this—this secret! Mona wouldn't deliberately hurt anyone! Anyway, it's impossible."

"I'm not betting my life on that," Bobby told her. She eased open her office door.

"I'm coming too!" Enid grabbed on to Bobby's shirt-tail, which had come untucked during her climb through the ivy.

Bobby didn't want to alert the intruder with an argument. Biting her lip, she moved into the gymnasium, with the headstrong Math Mistress hanging on behind.

The gymnasium was like a big, dark pool. Bobby's mind was filled with the sinister possibilities of gym equipment—the free-weight that could crush a skull, the jump rope that could wrap around a throat. Had she locked away the bows and arrows after archery? The big room was a veritable warehouse of weaponry!

She heard something, like the scrape of a foot. It sounded like it was coming from the corner, behind the big exercise ball. She made her way slowly around the vaulting horse. The intruder was breathing heavily, as if she were nervous.

Was Mona capable of murder? All Bobby knew was there'd been a startled look in her eye when Bobby had tossed the possibility of foul play like a cold codfish into the middle of the kitchen. The housekeeper's hands had been shaking when she carried the cocoa to the common room. Sure, Mona had been with Miss Craybill when she found the body, but what about a booby trap? An invisible wire stretched tautly, a few granite blocks removed and then replaced. Bobby could picture the handy housekeeper busily recementing the blocks while funeral preparations were made.

Bobby was between the intruder and the door now. Her hand felt for the light switch, and she raised her stick in the air. The next moment the gymnasium was flooded with illumination.

"Why, girls! What are you doing?" Bobby lowered her hockey stick as Angle and Kayo scrambled up off the pile of gym mats in the corner. "I mean, here, what are you doing here?" The gym teacher amended her first question hastily, as it was quite clear what the hot-blooded teens had been up to. She felt Enid release her shirttail. "Why aren't you at dinner?"

"We wanted someplace quiet to finish our conversation," Angle began. "It was so noisy in the Common Room."

"And we were looking for you," added Kayo. "We have some ideas for strategy against the Holy Virgins."

"The Twist Push-Pass Feint will throw them for a loop, and then me and Kayo will mop the floor with them! We've got moves they've never seen!" Angle radiated enthusiasm. Where was the embittered loner of only a week ago?

"Girls, I think it's just great you've put your heads together for the team this way," beamed Bobby as the flushed pair smoothed down their skirts and retucked their shirts. "And I want to hear your ideas, certainly. However," she sobered up, "the gymnasium is *not* the place for your private, er, conversations. Scoot yourselves along to dinner now."

"Okay, Coach Bobby!" the pair chorused.

"Just a second." Bobby held out her stick to Kayo. "This is yours now."

"Thanks, Coach!" Kayo's eyes forgave Bobby for all her blunders.

"I never would have thought it." Enid was staring after the two girls. "They have nothing in common. They disliked each other so!"

"Never mind that," said Bobby brusquely, trying to hide her relief at Kayo's quick recovery. "Now that they've learned to work as a team, the Martyrs haven't a chance against us!"

"Oh, you—you field hockey coach!" Enid burst out angrily.

Chapter Thirty-two

Milk Run

Quietly, Bobby closed the door of Cornwall behind her and breathed deeply the frosty air of early morning.

She jogged across the quadrangle, past the banner that hung over the entrance to Dorset and read "Welcome Old Girls." They would begin arriving today.

Bobby's feet in their worn gym shoes thudded down the path to the gymnasium. Last night after dinner, Serena and Alice had regaled her with stories of Old Girls' Weekends past. "The Old Girls are worse than the young ones," the big German Mistress declared. "Don't plan on accomplishing anything in class tomorrow."

"What do you mean?" Bobby had asked. "They're not going to be in classes, are they?"

"It's the tradition," Alice explained. "They call it Old Girl Observation, but the Old Girls like to get into the spirit of things and participate fully in all classroom activities."

"Bryce has learned to make sure the biology class is *not* doing dissection when the Old Girls visit," Serena added darkly.

Bobby had had a hard time absorbing the latest Metamorian lore from the veteran teachers. She kept glancing at Enid, on the other side of the room, grading papers with her usual single-minded focus. Would she ever stop resenting Bobby's profession?

Bobby jogged around the track, picking up her pace now that she was warmed up. Still her thoughts flew faster than her feet.

After the false alarm in the gymnasium the other night, she, Netta, and Enid had managed to come to an agreement—they'd wait until after the Old Girls' Weekend to take action. In the meantime, they'd keep a close watch on Metamora's housekeeper. Netta had returned to Bay City, but had promised to come back Saturday to help. The idealistic teacher clung to the belief that Mona could be reformed. "There's no such thing as a bad girl!" she declared.

Did Enid agree? After her outburst, the Math Mistress had been tight-lipped. Bobby pulled to a panting stop and swung one leg up on the fence, stretching her hamstrings. What was behind Enid's sudden coolness? Bobby had thought they were drawing closer, working as a real team, but after Enid's outburst last night, it was clear the Games Mistress had fallen from her favor. Did she distrust Bobby's steadiness? Did she suspect the complication with Kayo, or resent her affair with the Art Mistress?

Bobby changed legs and repeated her stretch. Thank heavens she'd never responded to any of Mona's overtures!

That's it! Bobby jerked upright, hamstring health forgotten. Now she knew what had bothered her about Mona's professed passion for Dot Driscoll—if the housekeeper was so gone on the Kerwins' aunt, why was she constantly fingering Bobby's biceps and inviting the gym teacher over for cocoa?

Bobby turned and jogged up the rise to the quadrangle,

her mind working furiously. Dot and Mona weren't in love with each other—they were bound together by a love of betting. *I'm going to brace that bookie right now,* Bobby decided, loping across the quadrangle.

Her hand was on Devon's doorknob when Bobby heard an engine sputter to life, breaking the morning stillness. The gym teacher turned instantly around Devon and ducked between Dorset and Manchester, running toward the paved road that circled the quadrangle.

The paneled station wagon was just rounding the turn from the parking lot. Bobby leapt to the middle of the road, waving her arms. "Stop!" she shouted, but the car only picked up speed. Jumping back, she caught a glimpse of Mona's set face behind the wheel as the vehicle swerved at the last minute, narrowly missing the Games Mistress. Bobby dashed back through the quadrangle, running as fast as she'd ever run, down the hill, toward Route 32. Bursting from the foot path to the drive, she saw the car jerk to a halt at the closed gate. Mona jumped out of the wagon and ran to tug at the heavy wrought iron with all her strength.

Bobby put on a superhuman spurt of speed. She reached the car as Mona succeeded in swinging open one side of the gate. Gulping air into her burning lungs, Bobby leaned in the window and turned off the engine. She shoved the keys in her pocket as Mona turned back to the station wagon.

"Bobby—what are you doing?" Mona attempted a laugh. "We're out of milk, and I need to get twenty gallons before breakfast!"

"You almost killed me!" Bobby shouted. She glanced at the backseat of the station wagon, piled high with luggage. "Milk! Think up a better one, Mona!"

Mona wilted. "I'm not a killer, Bobby, whatever you might think! I'm just a little jittery from too much coffee.

I've been up all night packing." She stepped close to the sweating phys ed instructor, close enough for Bobby to smell the lily-of-the-valley scent that clung to the attractive housekeeper. "Give me those keys and let me go, Bobby," she begged. "Believe me, it will be better for Metamora!"

"You're not going anywhere until you tell me what you and Dot were really up to," Bobby ordered the desperate housekeeper. "And don't try to tell me you were trysting in the replica cabin!"

"I'll come clean," Mona promised. "Dot was my banker, my silent partner. Her actuarial experience was useful when it came to calculating the odds. Math was never my strong suit," admitted Mona. "I made the mistake of asking Miss Froelich for advice on setting the line for last spring's archery tournament, and that must have awakened her suspicions."

"Yes—Miss Froelich!" Bobby pounced. "What happened to Miss Froelich?"

"All I know is what Dot told me!" Mona cried. "And she swore it was an accident. We used to meet up in the tower to settle accounts—we switched to the replica cabin after Miss Froelich's fall. When we settled up after the softball season ended last May, we never suspected Miss Froelich was on the other side of the turret, looking at nuthatches. Dot told me afterward that Miss Froelich startled her, jumping out and spouting accusations. She said Miss Froelich tried to grab the envelope of money as evidence. Dot pulled back, and the next thing she knew, Miss Froelich was over the parapet."

Mona closed her eyes and shuddered, like a third former having a bad dream.

"This year has been a nightmare," she told the Games Mistress. "The sabotage, the uncertainty. I told Dot I wanted out, but she threatened me with exposure. All I want is a second chance—or call it a third chance—anyway, another chance to try to find my place in the world—legit, of course!"

Bobby thought hard. With Mona gone, no scandal would taint Metamora. And was Mona really a career criminal—or just a girl who'd never had proper vocational counseling?

"You'll stay away from sports betting?" Bobby said sternly.

"I swear on my mother's grave," Mona said solemnly. "All those numbers and bookkeeping—I'm sick of it!"

Bobby held out the keys. She suspected she was being soft, but Mona had been so helpful all semester. And she did make a mean cup of cocoa. "Get out of here, before I regret this," she said gruffly.

Mona snatched the keys and wrapped Bobby in a brief embrace that left the gym teacher gasping. She slid into the driver's seat and slammed the door. Releasing the clutch, she began rolling toward the open gate and freedom even before she started the engine, as if afraid Bobby might change her mind.

Once through the gate, the car stopped with a jerk. Mona rolled the window down and stuck her head out. "Watch out for Dot. I'll bet she's the one who's been sabotaging the top teen teams this season—I hear she takes her share of the book and bets big money on the long shots with a bookie over in Beaverton. She'll be looking to recoup the loss you handed her the other day at Adena, when you missed the point spread she needed."

The car spurted into motion again, swinging right toward Adena. Bobby lifted her hand in farewell.

"Be good," she murmured.

Chapter Thirty-three

Old Girls

"You let the only witness go?" Enid practically spat the question at Bobby.

The two teachers were walking to Dorset for breakfast, dodging the gathering groups of Old Girls, middle-aged, well-dressed women for the most part, wearing crimson and white carnations pinned to their lapels. "Buzzy—Buzzy!" shouted one to a friend on the other side of the quad. "Let's go to Gussie's class after breakfast and see if we remember any Xenophon!"

"These Old Girls are a raucous bunch, aren't they?" Bobby tried to distract Enid.

It didn't work. "How are we going to prove Dot Driscoll's guilt?" she demanded.

"We'll get Dot somehow," pleaded Bobby. "Honestly, Enid, I thought this would be the best way to spare Metamora more scandal!"

"You weren't thinking at all—you acted on your emotions!" Enid snapped. "You've always been attracted to Mona and so you let her go!" With that she stalked away.

Bobby watched Enid go. The Math Mistress's opinion of her as a brainless womanizer seemed as unshakeable as the rock of Gibraltar. The worst of it was, Enid had a point about Dot. How were they going to prove the gambler's guilt?

Miss Craybill was standing on the steps of Dorset, flanked by Miss Otis and Gussie Gunderson, greeting the Old Girls, smiling, chatting, shaking hands. Bobby knew none of the alumnae would suspect that the Headmistress had been almost catatonic only the day before. "Why, Harriet Hurd! Little Hattie Hurd, still late for breakfast," Miss Craybill jokingly chided a plump woman whose curly blond hair was showing some gray.

"It's just jet lag, Miss Craybill," the Old Girl laughed. "I came straight from Laos."

At least Bobby could take pleasure in Miss Craybill's stunning recovery. When the Headmistress rose to make the announcements at breakfast, there was a spontaneous burst of applause from the student body, which had drifted through the past weeks like a rudderless ship. The Old Girls joined in with enthusiastic affection for Miss Craybill, never suspecting the true cause.

"Welcome, Old Girls!" Miss Craybill smiled and waited until the whoops and cheers, the bursts of "Hail to thee, Metamora" had died down. "I know you're going to have a wonderful three days greeting old friends and teachers, reflecting on all Metamora taught you and thinking, perhaps, of how you might repay your alma mater." Laughter rolled through the dining hall at Miss Craybill's sly wink.

"She seems in wonderful form, doesn't she?" Hoppy whispered to Bobby as the two teachers sat with the rest of the junior faculty at a table in the back of the room. Bobby nodded. She was too choked up to speak. *Gosh, I love this place,* she thought.

"I'd like to tell you about a most generous gesture from Vivian Mercer-Morrow, class of thirty-nine. She is founding a scholarship in honor of our late Math Mistress,

Nerissa Froelich," Miss Craybill paused and Bobby tensed, but after a barely perceptible moment the Headmistress continued, her voice steady, "whom many of you loved and learned from. We thank Vivian for her generosity—"

"Thank the Business Machine Corporation stock split and my tax advisor," called a narrow-faced woman as she stubbed out a cigarette. A ripple of amusement went around the room.

". . . and any contributions to the scholarship fund will be deeply appreciated." Miss Craybill finished with a smile. "And now, on to the day's activities . . ."

Alice Bjorklund spoke for all the teachers. "I think she's finally starting to accept Nerissa's demise."

"Thank heavens," said Bryce.

"*Sie hat mir herz gebrochen . . .*" murmured Serena.

"I will withdraw my application from Les Hautes Écoles," remarked Madame Melville. "Annette would like to graduate with her friends, I think."

"Madame, you weren't really thinking of leaving, were you?" Hoppy asked reproachfully.

"Did not you secretly think of a, how you say it, an escape plan?"

"Time heals everything," said Ken sententiously. "The Hopi Indians of Arizona—"

"Shhh," said several teachers simultaneously.

". . . and after the game, tea will be served in Dorset Common Room. Tonight's Old Girl Follies will be performed in the chapel at eight P.M. Ginger Knowles, forty-two, and Leona Durst, forty-three want me to remind all the performers in the Music Hall sketch that they must bring their own tomatoes." Miss Craybill paused dubiously and then concluded, "I look forward to seeing you there." She sat down amidst the clatter and bustle as the waitresses began to serve corned beef hash and waffles.

"Who'll be making tea?" Laura asked plaintively. "I

mean with Mona away. Did you all hear Mona's been called away?"

Bobby kept her eyes on her hash, not daring to look at Enid.

"Kayo offered the Prefecture's services," Alice volunteered. "And Mona arranged for some additional assistance from Adena, after she got the phone call."

"The perfect *hausfrau*," sighed Serena, pouring more cream into her coffee. "Her mother's on her deathbed, and she thinks of our stomachs."

Bobby risked a quick glance at Enid. The Math Mistress was eating her waffles with a preoccupied air, perhaps thinking only of her future inventing new computational devices at Business Machines Corporation.

Then Bobby froze. Over Enid's shoulder the gym teacher spied a familiar well-coifed fashion plate. The Kerwins' aunt Dot was at a tableful of fellow alumnae.

Bobby's heart began to pound. Of course Dot would attend the Old Girls' Weekend. Wasn't she a dedicated alumna? A wave of panic swept over the Games Mistress. How could she prevent the dastardly dowager from doing further damage?

"Enid." She cornered the Math Mistress as soon as breakfast was over. "Dot Driscoll's here! What are we going to do? The Holy Martyrs will arrive right after last period—we've got to stop her sabotage!"

"We'll enlist the other teachers," Enid said immediately. "I'll convince them to keep an eye on her. Maybe I can start by asking her to come to my calculus class." Businesslike, she turned to search for Dot in the throng of departing Metamorians.

"Gosh, Enid, I guess you were right and I was wrong," Bobby burst out impulsively. "But you're not going to write me off for a little mistake, are you? I really think it's more than physical with us! I think we've got the stuff for a long season!'"

Enid winced, and Bobby immediately regretted the sporty expression. "Look, Bobby." The Math Mistress chose her words carefully. "When we got together the night of the Harvest Moon Mixer, I wasn't looking for anything more than a tawdry affair. Then I saw the shocked look in Kayo's eyes, and—well, it was like being on the other side of the looking glass. I haven't thought of Miss Schack or that swim captain once since then. I even toyed with the idea that our fling could turn into something more."

"Well then—" Bobby began eagerly.

"And it's not really your woman-chasing ways—"

"Enid, the only woman I've thought of for the past few weeks is you!" Bobby told her earnestly.

"But this obsession with the game, the game above all else!" Enid's voice cracked with emotion.

"It's just a metaphor," Bobby tried to excuse herself. "You know the old saying, life is like a field hockey match, you have to learn to play your position, develop your ball-handling skills . . ." The gym teacher could tell she'd fouled again by the look in Enid's eye.

"It's a terrible metaphor!" cried Enid. "It reduces life's complexity to the level of a sandbox! Do you even understand what you're saying? It's just a rationalization for emphasizing sports to the exclusion of all else!"

"That's not true," Bobby groped for the words to convince Enid that field hockey need not divide them.

"I see Dot. We don't have time to think about our feelings now," and Enid hurried after the perfidious Old Girl.

Maybe we don't have time to think of them, but we can't stop ourselves from feeling them, Bobby thought sadly, watching Enid link arms with Dot and walk toward Essex.

She tried to put the Math Mistress out of her mind, at least until after Dot was dealt with. At lunch, Bobby button-holed Hoppy, whose class Dot had attended, to check up on the unscrupulous blonde. "Has she done anything funny?" the gym teacher asked anxiously.

Hoppy said that Dot had behaved beautifully in Home Ec for Independent Living. "She was the fastest in class, rewriting a recipe for six so it works for one," Hoppy reported. "I didn't see any signs of that tendency Enid talked about."

"Oh, that tendency, what was it again?" Bobby asked, wondering what ruse Enid had used to put the teachers on guard. Hoppy leaned forward over her coleslaw.

"She has a thing for young girls, especially athletic types. You should keep a weather eye out. I understand she's planning to join your modern dance class this afternoon."

Sure enough, when the girls, old and young, filed into the gymnasium for the last period of the day, Dot was among them. She and a group of friends laughed inordinately as they emerged from the locker room, wearing their ancient gym tunics. Bobby felt a wave of fury at this harpy housewife who had dared to tamper with the good clean fun of field hockey. She moved to the record player and put on Bernstein's *Age of Anxiety*. The discordant moaning of the clarinets sobered everyone up.

"Today, we're going to learn how to fall," Bobby announced. "How to fall without hurting ourselves."

One of Dot's cohorts raised her hand. "Must we learn how to fall to the accompaniment of this sort of music?" she implored.

"This *is* modern dance," said Bobby severely. Actually, she had turned the fifth form dance class into a vehicle for teaching various martial arts techniques. As long as she played discordant music in the classical style, she believed, no one would be able to tell the difference.

However, today would be the real test of her teaching skill. She would use her lesson plan to trap Dot Driscoll into an admission of guilt!

"Falling without getting hurt is a valuable skill." Bobby let her eyes rove over the group of women and girls. "Whether you're seven or sixty-two." Would Dot recognize that reference to Miss Froelich's age? "Start from a position of perfect posture: firm feet, tucked tummies, straight spines, shy shoulders, chin above chest. Now bend your knees. Deeply bend your knees. Lower . . . lower. Try to get as low as you can. You want to be so low that your tailbone almost touches the floor. Curve your spine. Pretend you're a snail . . . then sit, and roll back. Good!"

"Ow," said one Old Girl as her head snapped back on the mat.

"Tuck your chin," cautioned Bobby. "Let's try that again."

She walked up and down the rows of students offering helpful comments as the rhythmic thud of falling bodies sounded over the screech of violins. At the back of the class, where the Old Girls had clustered, Bobby noticed that Mamie McArdle, the well-known Bay City columnist, was taking the lesson seriously. Her earnest round face was bedewed with perspiration as she struggled back to a standing position. "This takes it out of you," she panted. "If I did this every day I could really reduce!"

"You're doing fine," Bobby praised her. She turned to Dot. "You've had some experience with falling, haven't you, Dot?"

"Why, no." Dot seemed flattered. "Do you really think I'm doing well?"

Bobby moved away, wondering if she was being too

subtle. She glanced over her shoulder at Dot's handsome, laughing face. Had she made a mistake, trusting Mona's version of events?

"Now, I need a volunteer. Mrs. Driscoll, how about you?" Dot came forward with a smile.

"The ability to fall is essential when you are attacked," Bobby told the class as the music built to a crescendo. She took hold of Dot's tunic, jerking her off balance and kicking her feet out from beneath her. Surprised, Dot still curled gracefully and rolled to the floor.

"Very good." Bobby couldn't help praising the startled woman. She lowered her voice as she helped her up and said, "If you haven't fallen before, you must have *watched* someone fall."

"Not that I can think of," Dot assured her.

"Pair up!" Bobby clapped her hands. "I want you to take turns throwing and falling." She demonstrated again with agile Shirley Sarvis, and the class followed their example to the best of their ability. Dot had paired up with Mamie, and Bobby approached them, determined to take another run at the impervious assassin. "Will you be visiting Kent Tower this trip?" she asked. But Mamie had knocked Aunt Dot to the ground and, forgetting to curl, the suburban housewife landed flat on her back and was gasping for air.

"Oh, the tower!" said Mamie reminiscently. "Do the girls still sneak up there and throw pebbles down at their friends in the quadrangle? It would be fun to see it again, but oh, those stairs!" She gave a mock shudder. "No, I'm staying on solid ground. I'm afraid your class has quite worn me out, Coach Bobby—may I call you Coach Bobby? The girls tell me that's what everyone calls you."

The bell rang, signaling the end of the class. Bobby felt furious with herself. She'd failed. Dot's sangfroid had foiled her.

The columnist followed Bobby as she went over to the phonograph to stop the record.

"I'd love to have a real powwow with you. You used to be quite the field hockey star, didn't you? Tell me—confidentially and just between us two—do you ever feel bitter, knowing your career is over and all that's left is teaching young girls who will soon outstrip you?"

"No, I don't, not at all," protested Bobby. She said it automatically, and yet as soon as the words were out of her mouth, she realized they were true.

"You had a bad fall, didn't you?" Mamie pursued. "I noticed you seemed a little, well, *focused* on falling. Do you find your accident has unbalanced"—Mamie chortled a little at her joke—"your curriculum?"

"Really, Miss McArdle, I can't discuss this with you now," said Bobby. Dot had vanished with the rest of the class. "I need to start getting ready for the field hockey game this afternoon."

"The big game, of course!" Mamie patted Bobby's hand. "I'll be in the stands, cheering for the team."

Bobby followed her out the door and saw her hurry to join Dot and her other friends farther up the path. As she watched, Ole joined the Old Girls. Bobby breathed a sigh of relief. Ole wouldn't let Dot harm the Holy Martyrs.

Then she saw Enid running down the path. The Math Mistress flew by Aunt Dot and her chums and hurtled straight at the Games Mistress. Staggering with exertion, she fell breathlessly into Bobby's astonished arms.

"In my math class—talking about odds—one of the Old Girls—said Savages favored—four to two!" Enid gasped out the message.

At first Bobby felt a warm glow of pride. The next instant, realization hit her like a cold wave breaking over her head. If the Savages were favored to win, that made them Dot Driscoll's target!

"And she had free run of the locker room!" Bobby exclaimed, horrified.

Dropping Enid, she dashed back through the gymnasium and into the locker room. The scene in the locker room was typical—girls in various states of undress, open lockers, more girls coming in from the side door. Bobby stood craning her neck, trying to look everywhere at once.

Then she spotted Mimi Nakagawa, shaking her head as Linda, a cupcake in one hand, held out a plateful of the delicious-looking morsels, frosted in strawberry, chocolate, and vanilla. "Go ahead," urged the fourth former. "My aunt made them!"

"American desserts too sweet," the Japanese girl responded. As Bobby pushed past the disrobing girls, Kayo lifted one from the plate. "Vanilla, my favorite!" She opened her mouth, and Bobby dove through the crowd and knocked the sweet from the surprised girl's hand. "Don't eat that!" she ordered.

"I'm sorry, girls, I can't have you breaking training," Bobby told the startled Savages as she swept the cupcakes into her athletic bag. "Let's save the sugary snacks for our post-game party, all right?"

The firm discipline Bobby had established stood her in good stead. The field hockey players obediently handed over their cupcakes. The only player who had consumed more than a nibble was Penny Gordon, who apologetically gave Bobby the remaining half of her strawberry cupcake.

"It has a funny taste anyway," she said.

Bobby compressed her lips. "Come with me," she told Penny. The halfback followed Bobby through the gymnasium and out the field entrance, where Enid was sitting on the ground, her back against the building, still panting.

"I want you to go with Miss Butler to see Miss Rasphigi in the chem lab," Bobby told Penny, helping Enid to her feet. "I'm afraid you won't be able to play the game today."

Penny's eyes filled with tears. "It was only half a cupcake!"

"I know, I know," said the harried coach. "It's not that—I'll explain later." She handed Enid the bag with the cupcakes. "See if you can get Miss Rasphigi to analyze these," she told Enid in an undertone. "Maybe we can get Aunt Dot on attempted poisoning, if nothing else." She looked at the stalwart teacher, her eyes aglow with admiration. "You saved the Savages, Enid!"

Enid flushed and brushed off the praise. "It took teamwork," she replied.

Bobby's heart caught in her throat. "Enid—did you say teamwork?"

Enid tried to frown. "It's just an expression. Come on Penny, let's get going."

Bobby looked after the sobbing fourth former and the girl of her dreams for a moment. Maybe she'd win at this game of love yet!

Before she sent the Savages out on the field to warm up, she assembled them one last time. Her heart swelled as she looked over her team, unified in their determination to beat the Holy Martyrs. Mimi Nakagawa stood between Linda and Sue. Angle and Kayo were in the back row, between Edie and Annette.

"Girls, before you go out there, before you win or lose, I want to tell you how proud you've made me." Bobby choked up a little and had to blow her nose before continuing. "When you started out at the beginning of the season, many of you were completely ignorant of field hockey techniques. Many of you had never even held a hockey stick. You were unsure of yourselves, and unsure of each other. Today, you're not only playing for the trophy, which is a heck of an accomplishment, but what's more important, you've learned to play together. You've become a real team. And that's what it's all about, isn't it? Now remember: do not accept food or drink from *anyone* but me. Go get 'em!"

The girls burst into cheers and ran enthusiastically onto the field, just as the Holy Martyrs descended from their bus, looking as brawny and tough as ever.

The bleachers were beginning to fill with students, Old Girls, and faculty, all eager for a good seat at this climactic game. Hoppy's Young Integrationists were sitting together, holding a vertical banner that said something in Japanese. Peggy Cotler was in the front row, with her reporter's notebook ready. Ole waved to Bobby from a spot midway up. Bryce, wearing a tie striped in Metamora's crimson and white, was next to him, trying to light a cigarette in the chill breeze, Serena, Alice—even Madame Melville was there, smoking one of her foul-smelling cigarettes.

Then she saw Dot, a few rows above, sandwiched in between Mamie McArdle and another Old Girl. It riled the Games Mistress to the core to see the Savages' would-be saboteur playing the part of the faithful fan.

At least she's where I can see her, Bobby reminded herself. As the referee blew the whistle to clear the field, Miss Craybill settled herself in the bottom row, between Miss Otis and Vivian Mercer-Mayer. "What an attractive Games Mistress!" Bobby heard the high-society heiress exclaim.

A stillness settled over the bleachers as the rival teams took up their positions. It was as if the whole school instinctively felt that this game was about more than just field hockey. Winning it would be a kind of vindication of all that Metamora stood for—curiosity and a passion for learning, gay camaraderie and loyal sisterhood, tolerance, courage, honesty—and all those indefinable things which made it so special. Victory, in some strange way, would wipe out the ugly falsehoods about Miss Froelich's death that threatened to besmirch Metamora's noble character.

Kayo was poised, tense and still, at the bully. A shrill whistle set her into motion, and so rapidly did she and her opponent tap sticks and ground the regulation three times that the clacking of sticks was like the rat-a-tat of a machine gun. Then Kayo had the ball, pulling it to herself and sending it back to Angle on her right in one fluid motion. It all happened so fast that Bobby could hear the murmurs in the stands, "What happened? Where's the ball?" The players were all in motion now, a pair of hefty Holy Martyr halfbacks closing on Angle as she dribbled up field.

"Don't power through," muttered Bobby. "Pass, Angle, pass!"

As if she could hear her coach, Angle feinted and passed back to Kayo. Kayo kept the ball only a few seconds before sending it to Annette, who with her usual subtle skill had evaded her guard. Annette dribbled the ball up and shot. It was a difficult shot; the angle was too oblique to be certain. It looked like it would clear the far post and be out. The Holy Martyr goalie thought so too; she waited an instant too long before diving for the ball, just as it sneaked inside the far post and bounced into the side net.

A deafening cheer rose from the bleachers. "Yeaaaaah, Metamora! Yeaaaaah, Annette!"

The Holy Martyrs were angered. Their center beat the ground with her stick in frustration. Their anger made them careless. They racked up more fouls than goals in the first half. Even without the penalty hits, which Bobby's endless drilling made a sure thing, the combination of Angle, Kayo, and Annette was unbeatable.

At halftime the players trooped off the field, sweaty and happy. "What did you say to that right wing that made her drop her stick?" Sue Howard asked Linda.

Linda replied, "Oh, she tried that old ghost business on me. So I just asked her a few questions about her sexual adjustment." She added seriously, "I've decided I'm going to be a field researcher for Dr. Kinsey, and I need practice collecting histories."

Bobby felt a wave of gratitude for Sandy Milston and her library.

"Lemonade, anyone?" Turning, Bobby saw Aunt Dot carrying a big thermos and a package of paper cups.

"Lotta," Bobby called, spotting the fourth former in the stands. "Get these players some ice water." With the alacrity of a punished dog being called to his master's side, Lotta leaped recklessly down the crowded bleachers and flew to do Bobby's bidding. Bobby grabbed Dot's elbow and hustled her around the corner of the gymnasium to relative privacy.

"Too much sugar?" inquired Dot. "I can get them something else. Iced tea? I want to help—"

"I'm sure you do!" Bobby's anger spilled over. "You must be hot and tired from rushing around wrangling refreshments. Have a glass of lemonade yourself, why don't you?" She grabbed a paper cup and filled it from the thermos.

"I'm not thirsty." Dot was taken aback.

"Have a sip!" Bobby urged.

"No, really, I—"

"Drink it!"

Dot shrank away as Bobby tried to force the glass of lemonade to her lips. "I said no!" She struck the cup from Bobby's hand, and the lemonade spattered the dead grass.

The mask was off. Anger, fear, and greed danced across Dot's face like a trio of demented ballerinas.

"I know what you're doing," Bobby told Dot. "And I

know what you've done. But this—this perversion of good, clean fun ends here, if I have to tie you to the vaulting horse!"

Dot turned away. "You're insane. I don't know what you're talking about."

Bobby grabbed her arm. "Don't you? Mona told me everything. Maybe I can't prove you killed Miss Froelich, but I've got plenty of evidence that you tried to poison a bunch of teenagers!"

Dot turned white. "Mona's a pathological liar!" She forced the words out from between her bloodless lips. "You can't believe a word she says."

The whistle blew, signaling the end to halftime. Bobby turned and left the defeated Dot, who was standing as if frozen.

"Bobby!" It was Enid, panting from the unfamiliar exertion again.

"Enid!" Unconsciously Bobby grasped Enid with both hands. "Exercise agrees with you."

"Oh Bobby, you're indefatigable," Enid couldn't repress a smile. "I had to take Penny to the infirmary. She threw up in Miss Raspighi's lab. Miss Rasphigi says the tests she has to run may take a while. How's the game going?"

The players were taking their positions for the bully. The Holy Martyrs had replaced the brawny center with a wiry redhead.

"Pretty good," Bobby told the Math Mistress.

A groan rose from the stands as the redhead flipped the ball over Kayo's stick. Already the swift Holy Martyr forwards were running parallel to her as she dribbled and dodged up the field.

"What was Miss Craybill doing just now?"

Sue Howard tackled the redhead, forcing her to pass. Joyce just managed to intercept.

"Miss Craybill? What are you talking about?"

"She was standing around the corner from you, while you were talking to Dot," said Enid. "She looked so queer—like the night we interrupted the séance."

The freckled girl with the squint had tackled Joyce, stealing the ball while Joyce fell backwards. "Foul!" cried Lotta shrilly.

"I didn't even know she was there," Bobby said. "She— oh my gosh, she must have heard me accuse Dot of murdering Miss Froelich!"

She turned and looked to see where Dot had gone. The two-faced blonde was climbing the path to the quadrangle. As Bobby watched, she saw Miss Craybill walking briskly after her.

A shout from the stands made her whip around. Evidently the Martyrs had shot on goal. Edie blocked the ball, but a Holy Martyr scooped up the rebound.

"Bobby, I think Miss Craybill's gone haywire again," Enid was saying, "What are we going to do?"

A shrill whistle and a roar from the crowd. Shirley had the ball, not ten yards from Metamora's goal. As Bobby watched, she managed to pass to Annette on the sidelines.

"Maybe . . ." Bobby shot a look at the path. Miss Craybill had caught up to Dot and the two women were conversing. "Do you think maybe the Headmistress just wants to talk to her?" Bobby suggested weakly, her eyes pulled back to the ball.

"Oh, forget it!" exploded Enid. "Go back to your *game*. I can prevent murder without you. I don't know why I even bothered . . ." Her words trailed off as she ran along the edge of the field to the path.

Bobby took a few hurried steps after her, and then stopped and looked back. Angle had the ball now. Bobby looked toward Enid. The Math Mistress was jogging with evident fatigue up the path, after Miss Craybill and Dot. Angle was dribbling up the field. Bobby felt like she was in some horrible nightmare, unable to move either after Enid or back to the game. Angle passed to Kayo. Bobby's thoughts darted around like minnows in shallow water. Miss Craybill was surely out for revenge—Kayo was passing back to Angle—Dot would be desperate—the Holy Martyr halfbacks were tackling—Enid would be caught between a crazed Headmistress and a killer—

"I would hypothesize that she used an over-the-counter emetic." Miss Rasphigi had come up behind Bobby and stood next to her now, watching the game with her usual cold disinterest. "This looks like a very tiring activity."

The spell that held Bobby transfixed was broken. "Miss Rasphigi, I have to step away. Fill in for me, will you?" She was moving as she spoke. The Holy Martyrs' goalie stopped Angle's shot and Metamora's cheering section booed. Bobby was halfway to the path, when she called, "Remind them to use the Twist Push-Pass Feint!"

And then she turned and ran.

Chapter Thirty-five

Winners and Losers

When she reached the quad, it was empty. Bobby looked both ways, and a flicker of movement caught her eye—the door to Kent slowly closing. Had Miss Craybill taken Aunt Dot to her office? On what pretext had she lured the murderous gambler to the deserted building?

Inside Kent the empty hallway stretched dimly before her. The turnout for the game had really been terrific, Bobby thought with a stab of pride. Everyone was there. Well, not quite everyone. She heard a retching noise from the infirmary. Poor Penny. From farther down the corridor came the faint sound of footsteps.

She hurried in the direction of the sound and stopped at an intersecting corridor, looking in all directions. Nothing. With fevered haste, she began opening and closing doors. The faculty lounge—empty; a broom closet, likewise. The third door revealed the stone spiral staircase that led to the tower. Bobby stopped in dismay.

The sound of heels on stone echoed down the hollow cylinder of the tower, and Bobby could even hear the faint sound of voices.

Bobby's tennis shoes made no noise as she climbed the

steps. She craned her ears. By some trick of acoustics, fragments of conversation reached her clearly only to fade away into an indistinct mumble. "Plaque in her honor," she heard Miss Craybill say before her voice melted into meaningless sounds. There was a silvery peal of laughter—whose?—then Aunt Dot's voice, ". . . happy to contribute, as you know . . ." Where was Enid?

Perhaps all Miss Craybill was after was a hefty donation from a wealthy alumna, Bobby tried to tell herself. Perhaps that was all the revenge the Headmistress wanted. Yet if that were true, surely Dot could write a check on the ground as easily as at the top of the tower!

A creak and a clatter told her that Miss Craybill and Aunt Dot had reached the top and were opening the door. Their voices faded away completely, and now Bobby heard more footsteps, muffled ones, doggedly plodding, not like the sound of Dot's pumps or Miss Craybill's old-fashioned lace-ups. Enid's penny loafers, perhaps?

"Enid!" Bobby called softly.

There was no response. Bobby ran up the remaining stairs, two steps at a time. The open door was a square of bright light above her now. She heard the sounds of a scuffle, a shrill scream; then Enid's voice, "No!"

Her eyes were too dazzled by the sudden brightness to see anything as she hurled herself through the door and onto the circular platform. Then her vision cleared and she took in the scene: three women locked in a deadly struggle. Dot was astride the crenelated battlement, clinging to Enid desperately as Miss Craybill pried at her leg, trying to heave it over the side. Even as Bobby realized what was happening, Miss Craybill succeeded, and both of Dot's legs swung into the void. The imperiled woman gave a muffled shriek, and Enid stumbled as the sudden jolt of dead weight jerked her off balance.

Bobby leapt forward. She was hardly aware of shoving

Miss Craybill to one side as she leaned over the battlement and grabbed at Aunt Dot. She didn't care for Dot's life. To Bobby, the woman was only a weight that would pull Enid over the wall to her doom if she wasn't relieved of it. The field hockey coach tugged at Aunt Dot's heather tweed, heard the fabric rip, but managed to get a grip around the woman's waist, and then her leg. "Pull!" she gasped to Enid. She felt Miss Craybill's fists beating on her back, and she elbowed the Headmistress in the stomach. With a final heave, she and Enid dragged Aunt Dot back over the wall to safety.

"You do care!" Enid panted as Aunt Dot, scraped and bruised, skirt torn and missing a shoe, fell into a gasping heap behind them. "I mean more to you than the game, don't I?"

"Of course you do!" said Bobby. "I've never felt this way about a girl before!" She looked at the face that had become so dear to her. Enid's glasses had been knocked off in the struggle, and her eyes were like warm brown pools of maple syrup.

"Nerissa must be avenged!" Miss Craybill moaned. "This woman must pay for her crime!"

"I'm afraid she's had another breakdown," Bobby said regretfully, looking at Metamora's Headmistress. "Love is the devil, isn't it?"

"It was an accident!" whimpered Aunt Dot. "An accident, I tell you!"

Bobby and Enid looked at each other. Would the whole truth of what had happened on top of the tower last June ever be known? "Accident or no accident, you've behaved shamefully," Enid told the bruised gambler. "Betting against the Savages! You really owe your school a little loyalty!"

"I'll donate any amount you say," babbled the cowed woman, looking fearfully at Miss Craybill. "But I'm into

Fast Eddie for eight thousand. The vig alone is killing me. Maybe I should just disappear . . ."

A bird landed on the stone wall and cocked its head at them.

"Look, Miss Craybill, isn't that a nuthatch?" Bobby said encouragingly.

Hope dawned in the Headmistress's eyes. "Ken said the natives believed that the dead come back to you in the form of a bird," Miss Craybill murmured. She stretched out her hands toward the little bird. "Nessie, is that you?" The bird chirped and flew away.

"Bobby—your vertigo—it's gone!" Enid exclaimed.

"Why, yes, I guess it is." Bobby tested herself by peering over the tower wall to the quadrangle below. The round white sundial didn't even blur. In the distance, they heard cheering and applause. Bobby shaded her eyes and could see Louth Athletic field filling with people.

"Sounds like we won!" said Enid.

"Damn," cursed Dot behind them.

Bobby looked down at the Math Mistress. She knew there'd be problems. Enid would take that job with the Business Machines Corporation and their careers would pull them in different directions. They'd probably be arguing in another minute about what to do with Aunt Dot. Enid wouldn't think much of Bobby's half-formed scheme to put her on a train to Vegas. But what did it matter? Bobby loved Enid. She was just plain goofy for this girl.

"Yes, we've won," she said as their lips met. "In more ways than one."

Author's Note

Thanks are owed to several people who helped me as I wrote this book: to Matthew Nolan, for his assistance with Ancient Greek; to Susan Sutton, for field hockey fact-checking; and to John Scognamiglio, a patient editor.

I am deeply grateful to two early readers, Ann Goulder and Shari Kizirian, for their criticism and comments. Thank you, Ann, for spotting a nuthatch, and thank you, Shari, for caring so deeply about the five points of perfect posture.

Julie Ann Yuen provided many things as the book progressed: random lines, payday advances, meals on trays, and even cups of cocoa—I appreciate them all more than I can say.